Praise for *Rogue Island*

"Writing with genuine authority, a dose of cynical humor, and a squinting eye on the world, Bruce DeSilva delivers a newspaper story that ranks with the best of them."
—Michael Connelly, bestselling author of the Harry Bosch novels

"DeSilva accomplishes something remarkable: He takes everything we love about the classic hard-boiled detective novel and turns it into a story that's fresh and contemporary, yet timeless. By turns gripping, funny, and touching, it's a tale filled with characters so vivid they jump off the page."
—Joseph Finder, *New York Times* bestselling author of *Paranoia*

"Not since Dennis Lehane's *A Drink Before the War* have I read a first novel as compelling and sure-handed as *Rogue Island*. Investigative reporter Liam Mulligan has the gritty, tough-talking charm, old-school street smarts, and sexy chivalry of a Marlowe or Spade."
—James W. Hall, Edgar Award–winning author of *Hell's Bay*

"The tight description, deft pacing, and coming-alive-off-the-page characters will have me standing in line for the next one."
—Tim Dorsey, *New York Times* bestselling author of the Serge Storms mysteries

"Imagine Don Winslow peppered with Peter Dexter and you'd have the flavor and pace of this novel. The writing has a balanced poise that is perfectly suited to the narrative. There are no tidy solutions, and the ending leaves a fierce chill lingering. A terrific slow-motion burn of a novel."
—Ken Bruen, critically acclaimed Irish master of noir

"When it comes to fresh noir-on-wry, readers could not ask for more—except for the author to hurry up with Mulligan's next adventure in detection."   —Otto Penzler, dean of America's crime novel editors and owner of New York City's famous The Mysterious Bookshop

"A stunning debut. Authentic, hilarious, and compelling. I've read hundreds of crime books, but this one bleeds the truth."
    —Ace Atkins, critically acclaimed author of *Devil's Garden* and *Infamous*

"A rollicking debut crime thriller . . . Adopting a crisp, fast-paced style that echoes the work of Jimmy Breslin, Mike Barnicle, and Mike Royko—renowned real-life journalists upon whom Mulligan is loosely modeled—DeSilva colorfully evokes the drama of crime reporting in a gritty, urban atmosphere where rules are made to be broken."   —Associated Press

"DeSilva creates an entire authentic realm that bristles with intrigue, revenge, and paybacks, along with folks who bellow, 'Shut up, daboatayuz' (the both of you), and 'Jeet yet?' (Did you eat yet?). Ya gotta love 'em."   —*The Providence Journal*

"With charisma, grit, and the knowledge that all will be right in the world as long as the Red Sox win the pennant, DeSilva leads us through the world of the local newspaper reporter. In this tough, barred-knuckles fight the good guy is triumphant this time . . . until the next big story, and boy I'll be waiting to read that one, too."   —*Suspense Magazine*

"If you 'know a guy'—and if you've been a resident of the fine state of Rhode Island and Providence Plantations for more than a day, you probably do 'know a guy'—you'll be wise to buy a copy of a new novel by Bruce DeSilva, *Rogue Island*."

—WJAR-TV, Providence, Rhode Island

"This tremendously entertaining crime novel is definitely one of the best of the year." —*Booklist* (starred review)

"DeSilva's impressive first novel . . . combines wit with a fondness for mystery traditions in Mulligan's dogged pursuit of truth. DeSilva has created wonderfully quirky characters, a tangled plot, and a likable, sarcastic protagonist."

—*Library Journal* (starred review)

"A blistering debut . . . Mulligan is the perfect guide to a town in which the only ways to get things done are to be connected to the right people or to grease the right palms."

—*Kirkus Reviews*

"DeSilva's portrait of the city is at once jaundiced and adoring, and in his hands Providence becomes an appealingly noir backdrop." —*Kirkus Reviews*, (fall debut fiction special insert)

"Smart-ass Mulligan is a masterpiece of irreverence and street savvy, and DeSilva does a fine job of evoking the seamy side of his beat through the strippers, barkeeps, bookies, and hoodlums who are his confidantes and companions. They all contribute to the well-wrought noirish atmosphere that supports this crime novel's dark denouement. A twist in the tale will keep readers turning the pages until the bitter end."

—*Publishers Weekly* (Fall 2010 "Fresh Fiction" Top 10 selection)

ROGUE ISLAND

Bruce DeSilva

A Tom Doherty Associates Book

NEW YORK

ROGUE ISLAND

Copyright © 2010 by Bruce DeSilva

A Forge Book
Published by Tom Doherty Associates, LLC
175 Fifth Avenue
New York, NY 10010

www.tor-forge.com

Forge® is a registered trademark of Tom Doherty Associates, LLC.

ISBN 978-0-7653-2981-3

Printed in the United States of America

D 10 9 8 7 6 5 4

In the fall of 1994, I received a note from a reader praising a "nice little story" I'd written. "In fact," the note said, "it could serve as the outline for a novel. Have you considered this?"

The note was from Evan Hunter, who wrote the brilliant 87th Precinct police procedurals under the pen name Ed McBain.

I sealed the note in plastic, taped it to my home computer, and started writing.

I was twenty thousand words into the novel when my home and work life both turned upside down. Years flew by. Each time I bought a new computer, I taped Hunter's note to it, but my busy new life allowed no time for novel writing.

Then, a couple of years ago, I met Otto Penzler, the dean of New York City crime-novel editors, and happened to mention that long-ago note from Hunter.

"Evan never had a good thing to say about anything anyone else wrote," Penzler said. "He really wrote you that note?"

"He did. I still have it."

"Well, then you've got to finish that novel," he said.

And so, at long last, I did. This one is for you, Evan. I wish you were still around to read it.

evan hunter

box 339

324 main avenue

norwalk, connecticut 06851

September 27, 1994

Dear Bruce:

MALICE is a nice little
story. In fact, it could
serve as the outline for a
novel. Have you considered
this?

best,

This is entirely a work of fiction. Although a few real people (hello, Buddy Cianci) are mentioned, none of them but baseball player Manny Ramirez have speaking parts, and he is permitted only a single word of dialogue. All the other characters who speak are made up. Some of them are named after old friends but bear scant resemblance to them. For example, the real Paul Mauro is a young New York City police captain, not a wizened old Providence priest. Rhode Island history and geography are accurately portrayed for the most part, but I have played around a little with time and space. For example, Hopes, like most newspaper bars, is long gone, but I enjoyed resurrecting it for this story. Good Time Charlie's closed years ago. And there never was a Nelson Aldrich Junior High School in Providence's Mount Hope neighborhood.

1

A plow had buried the hydrant under five feet of snow, and it took the crew of Engine Company No. 6 nearly fifteen minutes to find it and dig it out. The first fireman up the ladder to the second-floor bedroom window laid a hand on the aluminum siding and singed his palm through his glove.

The five-year-old twins had tried to hide from the flames by crawling under a bed. The fireman who carried the little boy down the ladder wept. The body was black and smoking. The fireman who descended with the little girl had already wrapped her in a sheet. The EMTs slid the children into the back of an ambulance and fishtailed down the rutted street with lights flashing, as if there were still a reason to hurry. The sixteen-year-old babysitter looked catatonic as she watched the taillights disappear in the dark.

Battalion Chief Rosella Morelli knocked the icicles off the brim of her fire hat. Then she whacked her gloved fist against the side of the gleaming red pumper.

"You counting?" I asked.

"Makes nine major house fires in Mount Hope in three months," she said. "And five dead."

The neighborhood of Mount Hope, wedged between an old barge canal and the swanky East Side, had been nailed together before the First World War to house the city's swelling class of immigrant mill workers. Even then, decades before the mills closed and the jobs moved to South Carolina on their way to Mexico and Indonesia, it hadn't been much to look at. Now lead paint flaked from the sagging porches of tinderbox triple-deckers. Flimsy cottages, many built without garages or driveways in an age of streetcars and shoe leather, smelled of dry rot in summer and wet rot in winter. Corroding Kenmores and Frigidaires crouched in the weeds that sprouted after the city dynamited the old Nelson Aldrich Junior High, where Mr. McCready first introduced me to Ray Bradbury and John Steinbeck.

The neighborhood's straight, narrow streets, many named for varieties of trees that refused to grow there anymore, crisscrossed a gentle slope that offered occasional glimpses of downtown office towers and the marble dome of the statehouse. Real estate agents, fingers crossed behind their backs, called them "vistas."

Mount Hope may not have been Providence's best neighborhood, but it wasn't its worst, either. A quarter of the twenty-six hundred families proudly owned their own homes. A community crime watch had cut down on the burglaries. Only 16 percent of the toddlers had lead poisoning from all that peeling paint, darn right healthy compared to the predominantly black and Asian neighborhood of South Providence, where the figure topped 40 percent. And five dead meant business was picking up at Lugo's Mortuary, the neighborhood's biggest legal business now that Deegan's Auto Body had morphed into a chop shop and Marfeo's Used Cars had given way to a heroin dealership.

The battalion chief watched her crew aim a jet of water through the twins' bedroom window. "I'm getting real tired of notifying next of kin," she said.

"Thank God you haven't lost any of your men."

She turned from the smoldering building and hit me with a withering glare, the same one she used to shame me when she caught me cheating at Chutes and Ladders when we were both six years old.

"You're saying I should count my blessings?" she said.

"Just stay safe, Rosie."

The glare softened a little. "Yeah, you too," she said, although in my job the worst that was likely to happen was a paper cut.

Two hours later, I sat at the counter in my favorite Providence diner, sipping coffee from a heavy ceramic mug. The coffee was so good that I hated cutting it with so much milk. My ulcer growled that the milk wasn't helping anyway.

The mug was smeared with ink from a fresh copy of the city edition. A pit bull, Rhode Island's unofficial state dog, had mauled three toddlers on Atwells Avenue. The latest federal crime statistics had Providence edging out Boston and Los Angeles as the per-capita stolen-car capital of the world. Ruggerio "the Blind Pig" Bruccola, the local mob boss who pretended he was in the vending machine business, was suing the newspaper for printing that he was a mob boss pretending to be in the vending machine business. The state police were investigating game rigging at the state lottery commission. There was so much bad news that a perfectly good bad-news story, the fatal Mount Hope fire, had been forced below the fold on page one. I didn't read that one because I'd written it. I didn't read the others because they made my gut churn.

Charlie wiped beef-bloody hands on an apron that might have been white once and topped off my cup. "The hell you been, Mulligan? You smell like a fuckin' ashtray."

He didn't expect an answer, and I didn't offer one. He turned back to his work, tearing open two packs of buns. He balanced a dozen of them from wrist to shoulder along his sweat-slicked left arm, slapped in twelve Ball Park franks, and added mustard and sauerkraut. A snack for the overnighters at Narragansett Electric.

I took a sip and flipped to the sports page for the spring training news from Fort Myers.

2

From the outside, the drab government building looked like randomly stacked cardboard boxes. Inside, the halls were grimy and shit green. The johns, when they weren't padlocked to save civil servants from drowning, were fragrant and toxic. The elevators rattled and wheezed like a geezer chasing a taxi. I played it safe and climbed the gritty steel stairs to the third floor, then navigated four narrow hallways before I spied the sign "Chief Arson Investigator, City of Providence" painted in black on the opaque glass window of a battered oak door. I shoved it open without knocking and stepped inside.

"Get the fuck out of my office," Ernie Polecki said.

"Good to see you too," I said, and slumped into a wobbly wooden chair across from his army-green steel desk.

Polecki lit a cheap black stogie with a disposable lighter, leaned back in his oak office chair, and thunked his weary wingtips on a green blotter scarred with tobacco burns. The chair groaned under the weight he'd packed on since the wife left and Kentucky Fried wasn't just for breakfast anymore. His assistant, a bum named Roselli, who got the job because he was first cousin to the mayor, sat stiffly on a gray metal chair under a cracked window skimmed over with ice on the inside.

"So it's arson again," I said.

"Either that or somebody thought it was a good idea to burn

trash in the basement," Polecki said. "With all the junk they had piled up down there, that dump was begging for a fire anyway."

"Could have told you this on the phone, Mulligan," Roselli said.

"Yeah," Polecki said.

"But I couldn't have looked this over by phone," I said, and stretched for the case file on the desk.

Polecki raised his right hand and slammed it down so hard that the desk bonged like a cracked bell, then looked startled when he saw that the file wasn't under his fat knuckles. It wasn't anywhere else on the desk either. He glared at me. I shrugged. Then we both looked at Roselli, back in his seat now and clutching the file to his bony chest. He'd moved so fast I almost missed it.

"Investigative file," Roselli said. "Not open to reporters or assholes, and you're both."

"Sure," I said, "but how about to a First Amendment watchdog from the Fourth Estate?"

"Not to one of them either," Polecki said.

"Any connection to the other fires?"

"None," Polecki said.

"Ain't nothin'," Roselli said.

"Any pattern to who owned the buildings?" I asked. "Were any of them overinsured? Did the fires start the same way?"

Polecki took his feet off the desk and leaned forward, the shift in weight making his chair scream for its life. Patches of red flared across his cheeks, maybe from anger, maybe from exertion.

"Trying to tell me my business, Mulligan?"

"We know what we're doing," Roselli said.

No, you don't, I thought, but I kept that to myself.

Polecki's stogie had gone out. He relit it, blew the exhaust at me, and grinned like he'd accomplished something. Then he took a few more puffs and flicked hot ash into his red dollar-store wastebasket.

"So Mount Hope is just having a run of bad luck?" I asked.

"Luck of the Irish," Polecki said.

"Worst kind," Roselli said.

"If you had the luck of the Irish, you'd be sorry and wish you were dead," I said.

"Huh?" Polecki said.

Jesus. Doesn't anybody remember John Lennon anymore?

A wisp of smoke rose from the wastebasket, where the cigar ash smoldered in a greasy fried-chicken bucket.

"Look, asshole," Polecki said, "I told you before, we got no comment on ongoing investigations."

"Which this is," Roselli said. "Why don't you go cover a traffic accident? Better yet, have one."

As much as I enjoyed Roselli's sense of humor, I decided not to stick around for another punch line. The wastebasket was smoking like Polecki's stogie now and not smelling much better, so it seemed like an excellent time to go. I pulled the fire alarm in the hallway on my way out. Who knew the damned thing would actually work?

3

Veronica Tang, the courthouse reporter, rolled her eyes and snickered like a cartoon mouse. Except for a few Disney characters, I don't think I'd ever heard anyone snicker like that before.

"What happened after you pulled the alarm?"

"Don't know. I didn't stick around for the show."

Veronica snickered again. I liked it when she did that. Then she tossed her hair and playfully punched me in the shoulder. I liked that too.

It was happy hour at Hopes, the local press hangout. Reporters and editors from the paper and producers and on-air "talent" from the city's TV stations were just beginning to trickle in.

"So why was Polecki being so uncooperative?" Veronica asked.

"Because he's an asshole."

She stared at me until I added, "Okay, we've got some history."

Fifteen years ago, the police academy had overlooked Polecki's youthful b&e conviction and admitted him as a favor to his father-in-law, the chairman of the Fourth Ward Democratic Committee. As a patrolman, he crashed a couple of patrol cars in high-speed chases. But hey, it was only two. He aced the sergeant's exam by paying the going rate of five hundred dollars for the answers, then rose through the ranks the Rhode Island way, slipping envelopes to the mayor's bagman. Two grand for his lieutenant bars, five grand to make captain. A Providence success story. I'd written about some of it, but it was too much to go into now, so all I said was:

"Three years ago, when he headed the tactical squad, I wrote a piece about his propensity for playing fungo with black kids' heads. A couple of Baptist preachers got hot about it and threatened to bring Al Sharpton to town for a protest march. Made the chief so jumpy that he transferred Polecki to the arson squad, a job that doesn't include a nightstick as standard equipment."

Veronica lifted her stemmed glass and took another sip. "You're lucky he didn't shoot you when you walked through the door," she said. "So what's your next step?"

"No idea," I said. "If I could just find a fresh angle on this thing, maybe I could get out of doing that sappy Lassie-come-home story."

Her eyes widened.

"You mean you haven't finished it yet?"

"Can't finish what I haven't started."

"Jesus, Mulligan. Lomax gave it to you last Monday, for Chrissake."

"Um," I said.

Veronica's brown eyes danced in amusement, but she shook her head disapprovingly, the neon bar lights doing the samba in her hair. Hair as black as the night sky when I was a kid. I hadn't found the nerve to ask her if she colored it.

She fished a handful of quarters out of her purse and swayed down the narrow aisle between the battered Formica tables and the pockmarked thirty-foot mahogany bar. I watched her progress in the mirror that ran the length of the room and saw that her little black skirt wasn't traveling in a straight line. She'd sipped a little too much chardonnay. I craved Bushmills, the best Irish whiskey that fit my wallet, but my ulcer kept asking the barkeep for club soda.

Journalists have been drinking themselves to death in this place ever since a reporter named Dykas sank his meager savings into it forty years ago. He named it Hopes because all of his were riding on it. It didn't look like much now and probably never did. Rickety chrome bar stools, a splintered floor, a stock high on octane and low on finesse. I'd been drinking here since I was eighteen, and the only renovation I'd noticed was the addition of a condom dispenser in the men's room.

But Hopes had the best jukebox in town: Son Seals, Koko Taylor, Buddy Guy, Ruth Brown, Bobby "Blue" Bland, Bonnie Raitt, John Lee Hooker, Big Mama Thornton, Jimmy Thackery and the Drivers. Veronica punched up something heart-wrenching by Etta James and steered her skirt back in my direction.

"The perfect song for a woman who's thinking of taking up with a married man," she said as she settled back in her seat. I hated being reminded I was still officially hitched to Dorcas, but I reached across the table and took Veronica's hand as Etta set the mood.

Veronica was gorgeous and I wasn't. She was Princeton and I was Providence College. She was twenty-seven and I was on a collision course with forty. Her father was a Taiwanese immigrant who'd taught mathematics at MIT, gambled his life savings on Cisco and Intel stocks, and walked away with over a million before the dot-com bubble burst. My dad had been a Providence milkman and died broke. With only five years in the business, Veronica already worked her beat like a pro, while I filched confidential files and pulled fire alarms in government buildings. Maybe Veronica had lousy taste in men. Or maybe I was just an overachiever.

4

Ed Lomax hunched in his fake leather throne at the
city desk, his huge hairless head swiveling like the turret of a Sher-
man tank. When he made city editor twelve years ago I thought he
hated my stuff, the way he always grimaced and shook his head in
apparent disgust as he read. Took me a month to figure out that he
moved his head instead of his eyes as he tracked each line of type
across the computer screen.

Lomax considered it his sacred duty to root out curse words in
our copy. Such words, he believed, have no place in a family newspaper. Or, as he put it whenever a wayward "hell" or "damn" pro-
voked him to speech, "I don't want any of that goddamned fucking
shit in my goddamned fucking paper."

He didn't speak often, preferring to communicate with his staff
in terse orders dispensed through the newsroom's secure internal
computer-messaging system. Every morning we'd arrive for work,
log on, see the message function blinking, and find our assignments.
They would look something like this:

WEINER WAR.

Or this:

OVERFLOW FOLLOW.

Or this:

BRASS KNUCKLES CAPER.

If you hadn't watched the local TV news, read everything on our paper's Web site, devoured our seven zoned print editions, studied the AP state wire, and scanned the five small competing Rhode Island dailies, you'd have to walk up to his desk and ask him what he was talking about. And he would give you that look. The one that meant you ought to consider opportunities in retailing.

I logged on and found this waiting for me:

DOG STORY. TODAY. NO MORE EXCUSES.

I messaged Lomax back and got an immediate reply:

CAN WE TALK ABOUT THIS?
NO.

I stood and caught his eye sixty feet across the newsroom. I smiled. He didn't. I shrugged on my brown leather bomber jacket and headed for Secretariat, my eight-year-old Ford Bronco parked at a fifteen-minute meter in front of the newspaper building. It had been sleeting, and the yellow parking ticket tucked under my wiper blade was sopping. I peeled it off the glass and slapped it on the windshield of the publisher's BMW, parked unticketed at an expired meter. It was a trick I'd picked up from the hero of a Loren D. Estleman detective novel, and I'd been using it for years now. The publisher just tossed the tickets at his secretary to be paid with company money. The secretary noticed the tickets were mine right off—but she's my cousin.

The dog story was waiting for me in the Silver Lake section of the city, just a few miles west of downtown. I decided to go east instead, sloshing on foot across Kennedy Plaza toward an old red-brick office building on the other side of the Providence River.

By the time I got there, my Reeboks were full of slush. I wasted ten minutes watching a secretary flash her thighs and waiting for feeling to return to my toes before I was waved through to the fire insurance investigator's cluttered inner office. Autographed photos of Providence College basketball greats lined the cream-colored walls. Billy Donovan, Marvin Barnes, Ernie DiGregorio, Kevin Stacom, Joey Hassett, John Thompson, Jimmy Walker, Lenny Wilkins, Ray Flynn, and my old teammate, Brady Coyle. No Mulligan. Benchwarmers didn't rate.

I'd met Bruce McCracken back in the days when he was a skinny kid trying to find himself, and I was a skinnier kid with dreams of being the next Edward R. Murrow. We'd taken a couple of journalism classes together at the little Dominican college before he decided the First Amendment was for suckers. Lately he'd become a gym rat, and he proved it with a crushing handshake. New muscles strained the seams of his blue Sears blazer.

"What do you think we're dealing with?" I asked, wiggling my numb fingers.

"Well, it's more than just a run of bad luck," he said.

"I gather you talked to Polecki."

"And his ventriloquist dummy. I swear, when Roselli talks I can see Polecki's mouth move. I can't decide if they're totally incompetent or if they just enjoy being assholes."

"The choices are not mutually exclusive," I said.

McCracken grinned. Even his teeth had muscles.

"We wrote policies on three of the Mount Hope houses," he said. "The claims total more than seven hundred grand, so naturally we're interested. Polecki gave me copies of his files on all nine fires. He's happy to have me do his work for him. Can't say I mind if you do mine for me."

He shoved a stack of manila folders to the edge of his desk.

"Just don't take them from the office. And no, you can't make copies."

I flipped through the nine files and set aside two cases that were not labeled "arson" or "suspicious origin." Then I settled down with the rest. Method of entry varied, but not by much. Sometimes the torch had gone in through the bulkhead, snapping off the padlock with a bolt cutter. More often he'd just kicked in a cellar window. Each fire had started in the basement, which is where I'd whip out the Zippo if I wanted to burn a house down. Even I knew fire spreads upward. Each fire had at least three points of origin, proof that they were not accidental.

In two of the cases, scrapings Polecki and Roselli had sent to the state police crime lab showed no signs of an accelerant. The lab techs had worked with the two goofballs before, so they went to the scenes themselves to collect more scrapings, this time from spots below the heaviest charring. Gas chromatology tests on the new samples showed both fires were started with generous splashes of gasoline, same as the others.

But those seven burned tenement houses were owned by five different real estate companies. They were insured by three different insurance companies. None seemed to be insured for more than its market value. I scribbled all the company names in my notepad, but I couldn't see anything in it.

"What do you make of it?" I asked.

"What do *you* make of it?"

"Doesn't have the look of an insurance scam."

"Probably not," McCracken said, "although you can't rule it out entirely. In Providence, half of all fires are started by someone rubbing his mortgage and his insurance policy together."

He waited for a laugh, but I had heard the line before.

"Well," he said, "we've got seven arsons, all within a half mile of each other, all set the same way, all strictly amateur. A pro would use a timing device and be in Newport knocking back boilermakers at the White Horse Tavern before anybody smelled smoke."

"A firebug, then?"

"Maybe. What's 'Chief Lesbo' telling you?"

"I told you before. Rosie likes guys."

"Something you know from experience?"

You could say that. In first grade, I pushed her on the swings.

In junior high, she bent down to cry on my shoulder when some boy she liked called her "Stilts." In high school, I took her to the prom. And the summer before college we made love, but we'd been pals for so long that it was like sleeping with my sister. Every straight man I knew would think me a fool, but Rosie and I never twisted the sheets again.

"Know where that rumor comes from?" I said. "Male recruits in her class at the Providence Fire Academy started it after she dusted them in every fitness test. She put up with it as long as she could, but when a fellow firefighter called her a dyke in the firehouse a few years back, she kissed him on the lips and then dropped him with a right cross. Six weeks later a beam fell on the jerk, and she threw him over her shoulder and lugged him out of a burning building. Today she's the Providence Fire Department's first woman battalion chief. Nobody calls her names anymore."

"So," McCracken said, "does that mean I've got a shot?"

"Sure. All you've got to do is grow another six inches and stop being an asshole."

"For her, I'd get lifts. But she's your friend, so I figure she must be okay with assholes."

"When I said you needed to grow six inches, I wasn't talking about your height."

McCracken's eyes narrowed. Then he grinned and fired a carefully placed left jab that whizzed past my right ear.

We called the testosterone contest a draw and got back to business.

"Look," McCracken said. "You always think arson-for-hire first because pyromania is rare. Some psychiatrists aren't sure it even exists. But it's the only thing that fits the facts here. My guess is we're dealing with a psycho who sets houses on fire and gets a hard-on watching them burn. Most likely someone who lives in the neighborhood."

"You asked Polecki for his pictures of the spectators at the fires?"

"Of course."

"And of course there aren't any."

"Oh, but there are!" he said. "Not for the first six arsons. It took that long for Polecki and Roselli to figure out what they should be doing. But there are forty shots from the seventh. Want to see them? Twenty-eight bad exposures and twelve artsy close-ups of Roselli's left thumb."

5

Next morning, my eyes were among two dozen pairs trained on Veronica. It was hard to know what the women were thinking. The men, not so much.

She stood in the middle of the newsroom, an unlit Virginia Slim dangling from plum-tinged lips. She had taken to chewing on the filters since the publisher's no-smoking edict. Now that I was fond enough of Veronica to care about her health, I had to concede the ban was a good thing, even though it kicked me to the curb for my daily Cuban.

Still, it rankled. The ban was another of those incremental changes that had turned our traditional newsroom into an urban-renewal project gone bad. Gone were the overflowing ashtrays, the banks of dented metal desks, the ink-stained tile floor, and the harsh fluorescent lights that forced copy editors to wear green eyeshades. The clacking typewriters had disappeared during my first year on the job, and I still missed their staccato beat. Now we had recessed lighting, a maroon carpet, and computers humming on fake butcher-block desks. The desks were walled off with four-foot-high dividers so you had to stand up to ask your neighbor how to spell *delicatessen*, then strain to hear him say "Look it up, asshole." Turning the newsroom into an insurance office had cost a lot of money, but it hadn't made the daily paper any better.

It took somebody like Veronica to do that. This morning, her story on the federal labor-racketeering grand jury, with direct quotes from the clever perjury of Giuseppe "the Cheeseman" Arena, was stripped across page one. Even the managing editor had ventured out of his office to join in the attaboys. If he hadn't blown so much on carpeting and room dividers, maybe he could have given her a raise.

This made the third time this year that Veronica had gotten big hunks of secret grand-jury testimony into a story. Each time, the U.S. attorney demanded to know how she had done it. Each time, she politely told him to stuff it. When I asked her how she was managing it, she just Mona Lisa smiled. The smile made me forget what I'd asked.

I forced myself to stop leering, logged on, and found a message from Lomax:

SEE ME.

As I sauntered to his desk, he shot me that opportunities-in-retailing look.

"Listen, boss . . ."

"No, you listen. The dog story wasn't in the paper yesterday. It wasn't in the paper today. It had better be in the paper tomorrow."

"Why not give it to Hardcastle? He's got a touch with the fluff."

"I gave it to you, Mulligan. I know you think you've got better things to do, but let me explain something to you. Circulation has been falling sixty papers a month for the past five years. The most common reason people give for dropping the paper is that they don't have time to read. Know what the second most common reason is?"

"CNN? *The Colbert Report?* Matt Drudge? Yahoo!?"

"No, but you can bet those are some of the reasons they don't have time for the paper anymore. The second reason is they think we print too much bad news."

"I know how they feel," I said, but Lomax was still talking, running over my words like a snowplow flattening a paperboy.

"We need good-news stories like a gangbanger needs bullets.

It's hard to find good news. It's not every day that a scientist finds a cure for cancer or a Good Samaritan opens fire at a Democratic fund-raiser. So when good news smacks you in the face, you've got to write it. And the dog story is a genuine, honest-to-God good-news story."

"But . . ."

"No buts. I'm not crazy about fluff, either, but we've got to give readers what they want if we're going to be able to keep giving them what they need. The Internet and the twenty-four-hour cable news channels are killing us, and we've got to do everything we can to fight back. Folks want to read about something besides organized crime, political corruption, and burned-up babies. You're overspecialized, Mulligan. I'm trying to help you out here."

"People are dying, boss."

"And you think you can stop it? You've got an inflated opinion of yourself. Investigating fires is the arson squad's job. After they solve this thing, you can write about it."

"Let me tell you about the arson squad," I said, and gave Lomax a quick rundown on the Polecki-Roselli vaudeville act.

"Jesus Christ!" he said. "Why the hell don't you write *that* story?"

"Yeah. Okay. How about for Sunday?"

"First the dog story. Today, Mulligan. Don't make me talk to you about this again."

He dropped his hands to his keyboard, a signal that our talk was over. I'd never heard Lomax put so many words together. Maybe nobody had. I figured I better do as I was told.

Maybe the star of the dog story would turn out to be a Portuguese water dog, I thought as I headed for the Bronco. Dorcas had custody of ours, a six-year-old psycho named Rewrite. I missed that dog. I would have paid the pooch a visit, but that would have meant running into Dorcas. I'd rather run headfirst into a train.

Dorcas didn't like the dog, but she kept him for the same reason she wouldn't let me have my turntable, my blues LPs, my collection of *Dime Detective* and *The Black Mask* pulp magazines, and the hundreds of tattered Richard S. Prather, Carter Brown, Jim Thompson, John D. MacDonald, Brett Halliday, and Mickey Spillane paperbacks I'd been picking up at flea markets since I was a kid. Anything to punish me.

Dorcas had seemed to be a perfectly decent human being until she woke up married to me. Once the rice was tossed and she figured she'd hooked me for life, she grew a pretty impressive set of horns. Suddenly, I spent too many hours at work. I didn't make enough money. I never touched her. I groped her nonstop. I didn't love her. I smothered her with love. She accused me of bedding every female from Westerly to Woonsocket, and those I hadn't conquered were on my list: the dental hygienist, the supermarket bagger, her friends, her sisters, the Channel 10 weather girl, the mayor's daughter, the models in the Victoria's Secret catalog. I had boinked or was planning to boink them all.

After a year of it, I dragged her to a marriage counselor, who wasted several sessions listening to her tales of my rampant infidelity. When he finally caught on and suggested she might have jealousy issues, she branded him an idiot and refused to go anymore. The last six months of our marriage settled into a familiar pattern: Dorcas would say I thought she was an unattractive shrew and must be cheating on her, and I would tell her she was wrong.

Until she wasn't wrong anymore.

I had just turned onto Pocasset Avenue when the police scanner crackled. Someone had pulled a fire alarm in Mount Hope. I slowed, ignoring the honking behind me on the two-lane street, and waited for the first engine on the scene to broadcast the code. "Code Yellow" would mean false alarm. "Code Red" would mean no dog story this morning.

It came in four minutes, by the digital clock on the dash.

6

I made an illegal U—turn in front of a boarded—up Del's Lemonade stand and headed back at forty, a reckless speed on a frigid day that had turned yesterday's slush into icy ruts. I held the wheel tight as Secretariat, his suspension beaten to mush by too many Rhode Island pothole seasons, bounced hard enough to loosen my fillings. At the intersection of Dyer and Farmington, I blasted my horn at a stooped old man painting a snowbank yellow with his dachshund.

Turning onto Doyle Avenue in Mount Hope, I pulled over to let an ambulance race past, its siren screaming. Bitter tendrils of smoke stung my nostrils, even with the windows up. Ahead, a dozen red emergency lights flashed. I pulled to the curb, climbed out, flashed my press pass, and talked my way past the police line.

Firemen had knocked down most of the flames, but smoke still seeped from the rafters of the ruined triple-decker. The dirty, crusted snow in the front yard was peppered with evidence of lives lived. A melted plastic kitchen chair, a smoldering yellow blanket, a Tickle Me Elmo streaked with soot. On the top floor, a fluttering lace curtain caught on a jagged piece of glass, all that was left of a window.

Smoke from house fires used to smell like burning wood, but that was a long time ago. Now, house fires stink of burning vinyl,

polyester fabrics, chipboard, wood glues, electric appliances, hazard-
ous cleaning products, and polyurethane foam that generates poi-
sonous gases, including hydrogen cyanide. This fire smelled like an
exploding petrochemical plant.

The world turned eerily silent as I stared at the scarred frame of
the collapsing building, mesmerized by what the fire had done. But
as soon as I pulled my gaze away, sound flooded in—the insistent
wail of sirens, the hoarse shouts of the firemen, Rosie screeching
orders into a walkie-talkie. The usual assortment of gawkers leered
at the destruction, hoping the flames might come back for an encore.
Everyone was talking at once, dishing out useless advice to the firemen and the cops in a version of the English language spoken only
in little RowDIElin.

"Y doan dey spray moah wahduh awn duh ruf?" (Why don't
they spray more water on the roof?)

"Dey orda." (They ought to.)

"Ats wut I bin sayin." (That's what I've been saying.)

"Shut up, daboatayuz." (Shut up, the both of you.)

"Jeet yet?" (Did you eat yet?)

"Gnaw." (No.)

"We kin take my cah tuh Caserduz if I kin fine my kahkis."
(We can take my car to Casserta's if I can find my car keys.)

"Wicked pissa!" (Good idea!)

I spotted Roselli by the police lines, snapping pictures of his
gloved thumb with a digital camera. He saw me and threw me the
finger. I flashed him a thumbs-up.

An old woman, unkempt silver hair a halo around her face, saw
my notepad and dug her fingers into my arm. "I banged on all the
doors," she said, her eyes bright with panic. "I think everybody
got out. If somebody's still in there, God help 'em."

I pumped her for a few more details, thanked her, and started
to turn away.

"You're Louisa's boy, aren't you?"

"That I am."

"She'd have been so proud, seeing your name in the paper on all them stories."

"Thanks. I'd like to think so."

I turned and skidded across a patch of ice to the battalion chief's car.

"I don't have time for you right now," Rosie said, her gray eyes locked on the smoking building as she cinched her air-pack strap tight. Flanked by five firemen hefting axes, she strode toward the blackened front entry. At six foot five, an inch taller than when she was ripping down rebounds for a Final Four team at Rutgers, she towered over all five of them.

I glanced at a fireman who slumped against the chief's car as a paramedic cut the insulated gloves from his frostbitten fingers. His cheeks were blistered scarlet, and his breath rasped in short bursts. The perils of firefighting in subzero temperatures: You freeze while you burn.

"The chief's going in after DePrisco," the fireman volunteered. "The poor bastard was inside with a hose when the first floor collapsed into the cellar."

"Tony DePrisco?"

"Yeah."

"Aw, shit." Now the fire had a face. Tony had gone through Hope High School with Rosie and me. Ten years ago, I was an usher at his wedding. He was a family man and I wasn't, so we hadn't seen all that much of each other the last few years, but last week at Hopes he'd shown me pictures of his three little kids. The girl was still in diapers. What was her name? Michelle? Mikaila?

I stood in the cold with the gawkers, pretending a professional detachment I didn't feel. Together we gulped the acrid, frigid air and waited to see what Rosie would be carrying when she came back out.

When the chief finally strode from the building into the light, cradling something blackened and broken in her arms, sound seemed to stop again. I squeezed my eyes shut, but that didn't prevent me from seeing the toothless grin of a baby girl waiting for her daddy to come home.

I dashed off a quick news brief for our online edition, but it was late afternoon by the time I filed the full story for the paper. My computer flashed with a message from Lomax. It didn't say "Good job." It said:

DOG STORY.

He glared as I shrugged on my jacket and walked to the elevator. As soon as the door slid shut, I tugged off the jacket and punched the button for the second floor, which housed the cafeteria, mailroom, and photo lab.

"Everything or just what we published?" said Gloria Costa, the photo lab tech.

"Everything," I said. "Especially crowd shots."

Gloria pecked at her keyboard, and a menu of Mount Hope fire photos filled the screen of her Apple monitor. We stood close, our shoulders touching as we bent toward the screen. Her skin smelled of something spicy and sweet. She was a little pudgy, but subtract twenty pounds, give her a makeup lesson, squeeze her into something by Emilio Pucci, and you've got a young Sharon Stone. Add twenty pounds, dump her into a shapeless shift, and you've got my almost-ex.

It took us nearly an hour to examine every frame and pick out about seventy crowd shots—at least a few from each of the fires.

"You want prints?"

"Soon as you can, Gloria. There'll be crowd shots from today's fire too. This morning I asked the picture desk to make sure we shoot spectators at Mount Hope fires till further notice."

"Prints could take a few days, baby. We're understaffed here."

"Have them by Monday and you can drink on my tab at Hopes for a week."

7

"Can't you turn off that damn police radio?"

"No."

"Why not?"

"You know why not."

"Who has a police radio in his bedroom anyway?" Veronica said.

"I do."

She smirked and shook her head, then rolled on top of me. We kissed, all open mouths and heat. But it was a heat with no flame. What I pulled down, she pulled up. What I tried to unsnap, she twisted away. We were consenting adults, but she wouldn't consent. I had more luck in middle school.

It was the first time I had brought Veronica to my place, three rooms on the second floor of a crumbling tenement building on America Street in Providence's Italian neighborhood of Federal Hill. Three rooms was an extravagance because I was living in just one of them, unless you counted the time I spent in the kitchen opening and closing the refrigerator.

I'd tidied up the place in anticipation of Veronica's arrival, even dragged a damp paper towel through the dust. I would have tried distracting her from the decor with music, but Dorcas still had my LPs, and my only CD player was in Secretariat's dash.

All the floors were covered in the same linoleum made to look like red brick. Real brick wouldn't have had all those scuffs. The beige walls were bare except for a few plaster cracks and my only piece of art, a shadow box holding a Colt .45. It had been my grandfather's gun when he wore Providence PD blue. He carried it until the day someone laid a pipe across the back of his skull on Atwells Avenue, jerked it from his holster, shot him dead with it, and dropped it on the body.

Veronica asked about the gun, so I had to tell the story again. As she listened, she rested her hand on my shoulder.

"Every once in a while I take it down and clean it," I said. "Makes me feel close to him."

It was late Saturday afternoon, and through the walls we could hear my neighbor, Angela Anselmo, screeching out the window at her little darlings, the eight-year-old budding concert violinist and the thirteen-year-old fledgling smash-and-grab virtuoso. She had already started supper, the garlic aroma from her kitchen slipping easily through the inch-wide crack at the bottom of my front door. We were lying on my tag-sale bed and Salvation Army mattress because there was no place else to sit. I was still pissed about the LPs and the mystery novels, but for the first time, I was glad Dorcas had all the furniture. Veronica's lips flirted with the side of my face.

"How mad do you think Lomax will be?" I said.

"Pretty mad."

"Maybe I should do the dog story this weekend."

"No working this weekend. Just us. You promised."

"Unless there's a fire in Mount Hope," I said.

"Unless there's a fire," she said.

"I hope the fire-scene pictures tell me something."

"What are you hoping to find?"

"The same face in the crowd at several fires."

"A firebug?"

"Maybe. They like to hang around and admire their work."

"Mulligan?"

"Um?"

"Could we talk about something else?"

Again with the lips.

"Sure. Why don't you tell me how you managed to get that grand-jury testimony?"

"Forget it, buster."

"What, then?"

"Ask me something else."

"Do you color your hair?"

"What?"

"Do you color your hair?"

"No. Okay, my turn. How's that divorce coming along?"

"I had a pleasant conversation about that with Dorcas just this morning."

"And?"

"Unless I agree to lifetime alimony, she'll tell the judge I beat her."

"She's been saying that for two years, Liam."

"I asked you not to call me that."

"I like it."

"I don't."

"It's a fine name, baby."

But it was my grandfather's name. Every time I hear it, I see a chalk outline on a bloodstained sidewalk. I didn't want to go into it, so I just shook my head.

"L. S. A. Mulligan. Maybe I could call you by one of your middle names."

"Seamus or Aloysius?"

"Oh. . . . Ever have any nicknames?"

"My teammates on the Providence College basketball team used to call me 'Stew.'"

"Why?"

"Mulligan Stew?"

"I'm sorry."

"Thank you."

"It seems odd calling you Mulligan when your hands are on my butt."

"It's the only name I answer to."

"Like Madonna?"

"Like Seal."

"I think I'm going to call you Liam."

"I wish you wouldn't."

"Pleeeeeease," she said, stringing out the syllable and rubbing all that woman against the front of my jeans. The rubbing didn't work. It just made me forget what she was asking. I rolled her over, pinning her beneath me and nipping at the space between her neck and the swell of her breasts. My hands fumbled with the top button on her blouse.

"Liam?"

I ignored her, my fingers working on the second button.

"Mulligan?"

"Mmm?"

"I want you to get an AIDS test first."

8

Efrain and Graciela Rueda had arrived in Provi—
dence seven years ago from the little town of La Ceiba in south-
eastern Mexico. He went to work as a day laborer. She made beds at
the Holiday Inn. Two years later, the twins were born. Graciela wanted
to name them Carlos, which means "free man," and Leticia, which
means "joy," but Efrain insisted on Scott and Melissa. He wanted
them to be American through and through. Their children were
their life. Now they didn't have enough money to bury them.

Their fellow parishioners at the Church of the Holy Name of
Jesus raised enough for two little wooden coffins. The Providence
firefighters' local donated the headstone. In a paroxysm of gener-
osity, Lugo's Mortuary supplied the hearse at half price.

On Monday morning, the crowns of the tallest headstones in the
North Burial Ground poked above the crusted snow cover. Rosie
and I stood with a little knot of mourners huddled at a pit hacked
into the frozen turf. Mike Austin, the firefighter who had brought
Scott's body down the ladder, helped carry him to his grave. Brian
Bazinet, who had descended with Melissa, helped carry her.

I cocked my head to catch the priest's ancient words of comfort
and glory, but they were swallowed by Graciela's keening and the
white noise of hundreds of Bridgestones, Dunlops, and Goodyears
swishing by on the interstate thirty yards to the west. Off to the east,
the gravedigger watched from his backhoe, its engine muttering.

After the mourners slogged to their battered Toyotas and Chevrolets, Rosie and I picked up clumps of frozen earth and dropped them into the grave. They landed on the little coffins with hollow thuds. Then we stood aside and watched the gravedigger finish the job. I tried to find calm in the steady rhythm of his work, but in my mind I could still hear Graciela's anguished wail and the low rumble of her husband as he tried to comfort her.

Journalism professors preach that you should never get emotionally involved in your stories, that to remain objective you must cultivate a professional detachment. They are so full of shit. If you don't care, your stories will be so bloodless that readers won't care either.

I said a prayer in case He was listening. But where was He when the snowplow was burying the hydrant? Where was He when the twins were screaming for help?

Rosie and I crunched through the snow to the Bronco, then turned and looked back at the patch of brown earth in a blinding field of white. We didn't speak. What was there to say?

Somebody had to pay for this, and Polecki and Roselli weren't up to the job.

Twenty minutes later, I walked into the newsroom and found a thick manila envelope on my desk. On the front were the words "You owe me—Gloria." She'd stuffed the envelope with eight-by-tens.

I thought about logging on, but I didn't want to deal with the latest Lomax message just yet. I dumped the envelope out on the desk, studied the prints, and found a lot of familiar faces. Old Mrs. Doaks, who had babysat the Mulligan kids when we were little, stood at the police lines and craned her neck. Three of the Tillinghast boys, apprentices in their older brother's truck-hijacking start-up venture, scowled at the flames and looked like they wanted to hurt somebody. Jack Centofanti, a retired fireman who missed the action so much that he spent his afternoons hanging around the firehouse, lent a hand by directing traffic. That face took me back. When I was a kid, Jack and his tackle box appeared at our front door at 4:00 A.M. every time the fish were biting at Shad Factory Pond across the river in East Providence. He'd been a steady loser at the low-stakes poker-and-beer nights that had filled our parlor with bawdy stories and good fellowship every Saturday night. Jack had been my father's best friend. When he spoke at Pop's funeral, he made a Mount Hope milkman sound like a hero for raising a girl who didn't wind up pregnant and two boys who managed to stay out of jail.

I kept flipping through the same pictures over and over. Each time I saw a face at more than one fire, I circled it in red grease pencil. Best I could tell, fourteen faces showed up at two or more fires. At first I was surprised there were so many, but when I thought about it, I was surprised there weren't more. After all, the fires were all in the same neighborhood, all but the last one breaking out at night when most people were home.

Jack's face showed up at a record seven fires, and I'd bet a year's pay that he'd directed traffic or handed out hot coffee at all of them. Another face showed up at six. It belonged to an Asian male, late twenties, wearing a black leather jacket. In two pictures, he was carrying a flashlight, and in one, his eyes were lifted to the roof of a burning building. On his face was a look of rapture.

I knew exactly how he felt. I was a cub reporter when the old Capron Knitting Mill in Pawtucket burned down, and even though that was a long time ago, sometimes, when I closed my eyes, I could still see it: firemen silhouetted against orange fireballs soaring hundreds of feet against the blackest of skies. It was so horrifyingly beautiful that for several long minutes, I forgot why I was there.

Suddenly I remembered that two of the Mount Hope fires hadn't been labeled suspicious origin. I flipped back through the pictures, tossing out those from a fire that had started from careless smoking and another caused by a faulty kerosene heater. When I was done, I still had a dozen faces to check out. I recognized three of them, but I'd need help identifying the others, including Mr. Rapture.

The name made me think of Veronica, and my loins tingled a

little. I picked up the phone and punched in the number for my doctor. Unless it was an emergency, his receptionist said, the first available appointment would be seven weeks from Tuesday.

"It is an emergency," I said.

"What is the nature of the emergency?"

"It is of a delicate nature."

"I'm very discreet," she said.

"My girl won't screw me until I have an AIDS test," I said, and she hung up.

I called the Rhode Island Department of Health's VD clinic and learned they could draw my blood today, but the lab was so backed up that it would take five weeks to get the results.

After I hung up, I logged on to my computer and found the message I expected from Lomax:

WHERE'S THE GODDAMNED DOG STORY?

I shot back a reply:

I'M WORKING ON IT.

But first I needed to see my bookie.

9

Dominic Zerilli had lived for seventy—four years, and every morning for the last forty-two of them, he would get up at 6:00 A.M., put on a blue suit, a white dress shirt, and a silk necktie, and walk four blocks to his little corner market on Doyle Avenue in Mount Hope.

Once inside, he would wish a cheery good morning to the skanky high school dropout manning the register. Then he would climb four steps to a little elevated room with a window that looked out over the grocery aisles. He would remove his suit jacket, put it on a wooden hanger, and hang it on a clothes rod he had rigged in back. Then he would do the same thing with his pants. He would sit there all day in his shirt, tie, and boxer shorts, chain-smoking unfiltered Luckies and taking sports and numbers bets through the window and over three telephones that were checked for bugs every week. He would write the bets down on slips of flash paper and deposit them in a gray metal washtub next to his chair. Whenever the cops came to bust him, which only happened when the Rhode Island Lottery Commission got worked up about lost revenue, he would remove the cigarette from his lips and toss it into the washtub.

Whoosh!

The officially sanctioned gangsters at the lottery commission, who pushed worthless scratch tickets and chump numbers games, resented Zerilli because he gave the suckers a legitimate chance to win. The Mafia always gives better odds than the state.

Just about everybody in Mount Hope dropped by Zerilli's store from time to time, either to lay down a bet or to replenish dwindling supplies of malt liquor, soft-porn magazines, and illegal tax-stamp-free cigarettes. They called him "Whoosh," and it was said he knew them all by name. I bought my first pack of Topps baseball cards from Whoosh when I was seven years old, and he started taking my bets on the Sox and Patriots when I turned sixteen. Now, thanks to the snow-induced parking ban, I found a spot for Secretariat right out front.

"Pictures?" Zerilli said. "You want me to look at fuckin' pictures?"

"That's right."

"Ah, shit. I thought you was gonna ask me about the DiMaggios."

We were sitting in Zerilli's inner sanctum, only one of us wearing pants, the photographs fanned out on his keyhole desk. We had already gone through our ritual: him presenting me with a new box of illegal Cubans and asking me to swear on my mother that I wouldn't write about anything I saw in there; me swearing, opening the box, getting a cigar going, and not mentioning there was nothing to write about because everybody already knew what went on in there. Except for the part about the pants.

I said, "What's the DiMaggios?"

And he said, "Watch where you flick them fuckin' ashes."

"A new way to bet baseball or something?"

"Nah! Ain't no new way to bet nothin'. S'all been done."

"So?"

"So last week I started in thinkin'. Do I sit around waitin' for some asshole to torch my store, or do I do somethin' about it? Cops been tellin' me not to worry, said they put on an extra patrol. Big fuckin' deal. Prowl car makes a few extra passes through the neighborhood, like that's gonna do any fuckin' good. Last Thursday night I got two dozen of the guys together. Guys what come in the store regular, live in the neighborhood. You ain't heard about this?

You must be slippin'. I figured you woulda heard about this. I broke 'em up into two-man teams, give each of 'em four-hour shifts, overlapping, you know, so they's always at least four guys on the streets. Some of the guys ain't workin', so we can cover the whole day no problem. They're all good guys, mostly micks and wops, coupla spics."

"The DiMaggios?" I said.

"Yeah, well, they needed somethin' to carry, you know, in case they run into trouble. Don't need no more fuckin' guns on the street. Got enough headache, pukes strollin' in here with UZIs they buy in schoolyards, scarin' the help half to death. So I got the guys twenty-four brand-new Louisville Sluggers. Woulda set me back a few hundred bucks if Carmine Grasso hadn't had 'em sittin' around, you know, from the time he . . . ah . . . acquired a truckload of sporting goods. Charged me two bucks apiece. Ended up buyin' eighty of 'em. Gonna stick the rest out front the store this spring, sell 'em to the kids. If spring ever comes—this fuckin' snow—Jesus!"

"And since they're carrying bats," I said, "why not name them after the best wop baseball player who ever lived."

"Fuckin' A! The two spics are callin' themselves the 'A-Rods' just to piss me off, but they're okay, those guys. Good they got some pride."

When we finally got to the pictures, Zerilli's reputation for knowing everyone in the neighborhood turned out to be a mite exaggerated. Of the nine faces, he put names to six.

"Lemme keep these awhile, show 'em to the DiMaggios," he said. "Maybe get some more names to go with the faces."

"Fine," I said.

"We got a meeting here at nine tonight, 'fore the night shift hits the streets. Probably do it then."

"Maybe I'll drop by," I said, "bring a photographer, do a little story on the DiMaggios, if it's okay."

"Get some pictures of the guys holdin' the bats," he said. "Scare the piss outta the asshole settin' the fires. Maybe convince him to pick on some other neighborhood."

I'd been neglecting my cigar, and it had gone out. As I fished in my pockets for my Zippo, Zerilli handed me his Colibri, the Trifecta model with three compact flames, designed to fit perfectly in your palm.

"Keep it," he said.

"I can't do that, Whoosh. You know what these things cost?"

"Grasso gets 'em for me cheap, as many as I can move," Zerilli said, "long as I keep my mouth shut about where they come from. 'Sides, you take the Cubans, and you know damn well what they cost."

"I see your point," I said. I stuck the lighter in my shirt pocket and got up to go.

"Aaay, just a fuckin' minute," he said. "Did you say 'best wop baseball player'? Is that what you fuckin' said? Fuck you! Best baseball player that ever lived, period, you fuckin' harp."

When I got back to the office, I logged on to check my messages and found this from Lomax:

THE DOG PEOPLE SAY THEY'RE CALLING CHANNEL 10 IF YOU DON'T TALK TO THEM TONIGHT. IF THAT HAPPENS, I WOULDN'T WANT TO BE YOU.

10

The dog people turned out to be Ralph and Gladys Fleming. They lived in one of those one-story boxes thrown together on concrete slabs in the seventies under a program designed to give folks with modest incomes a chance to get into the housing market.

The police radio had honked like a goose all the way to Silver Lake. Holdup in progress at the Cumberland Farms on Elmwood Avenue. Trash fire on Gano Street. Domestic dispute on Chalkstone Avenue. Some chatter about proceeding to locations and apprehending suspects. But no fire alarm in Mount Hope.

Fourteen inches of snow had fallen overnight, and the Providence Highway Department had done its customary crackerjack job of snow removal. The Flemings' street was a glacier. Ralph and Gladys must have been watching me negotiate their unshoveled walk, because as soon as I raised my hand to knock, the door swung open. I was about to introduce myself when something big and hairy forced its way between Ralph and Gladys and slammed into my groin. I toppled off the porch and crash-landed in the snow.

"Sassy, no!" Gladys piped, a bit tardily I thought.

Ignoring her, Sassy pinned me to the snow and sandpapered my face with her tongue. One of us seemed pretty happy.

Ralph helped me up, Gladys asked me six times if I was all right, four hands brushed snow from my clothes, apologies and "bad dog" were spoken in multiples of ten, and we were all seated cozily now on Gladys's floral seat covers. I in a rocking chair with a cup of coffee steaming beside me on a rock-maple end table. Ralph and Gladys on the sofa. Sassy at my feet, nibbling a Beggin' Strip. She looked like a cross between a German shepherd and a Humvee.

We quickly established that Ralph and Gladys were both fifty-six, had two grown daughters, and had moved here from the state of Oregon nine months before to work nights in a tool-and-die factory. They liked Oregon all right, but the move became necessary when the Sierra Club, the Environmental Protection Agency, and a couple of spotted owls conspired to abolish Ralph's job at a sawmill near the Willamette National Forest.

"Funny thing," Ralph said. "When I went to the bank to open an account, the clerk looked at me strange and asked me why in heaven's name I had moved to Rhode Island. Same thing happened when I went to the registry to get a Rhode Island driver's license."

"And the cable man," Gladys said. "Don't forget the cable man."

They both looked at me now like I was supposed to explain it. The littlest state's inferiority complex is as big as the chip on its shoulder. I imagined Ralph and Gladys would figure it out for themselves if they stuck around long enough.

"Well," Ralph said after a moment, "I sure did hate to leave Sassy behind in Oregon. Didn't seem there was much choice, though. No way to know where we'd be staying once we got here."

"Turns out we could have brought her," Gladys said—a bit huffily, I thought.

"So we had to leave her," Ralph continued. "Neighbors name of Stinson, John and Edna their Christian names, were kind enough to take her in."

"Couldn't even call to ask about her when we got out here," Gladys said, " 'cause the Stinsons got no phone."

"Weekend 'fore last," Ralph said, "on Sunday, wasn't it, Glady?"

"Saturday," Gladys said.

"Well, Saturday then. We got up the usual time. 'Round eight, I'd say it was. I was reading the paper while Glady made breakfast. Eggs, wasn't it, Glady?"

"Don't I make 'em for you every morning?"

"Suddenly there was this scratching at the door. I believe we both heard it, didn't we, Glady?"

"I heard it first, Ralph; you know I did. I heard it and I said, 'What's that scratching, Ralph?' and you said, 'What scratching?' and then you heard it, too."

"So I put the paper down, and I got up from the table and went to the door, right, Glady?"

I wondered if Ralph had ever done anything without asking "Glady" if he'd actually done it.

"When I opened it," Ralph said, "Sassy bounded in and skittered round on the kitchen floor, then leaped up on me and nearly knocked me down. Slobbered all over my face and then turned round and started in on Glady."

"I was so glad to see her that I let her," Gladys said. And then she blushed. "Had to pinch myself to be sure I wasn't dreaming."

"How do you suppose she got here?" I asked.

"Walked, most likely," Ralph said.

"Well," Gladys said, "she could have run some, too."

Or hitched a ride with a long-haul trucker or flown first-class on American Airlines, I thought, but figured I better keep my mouth shut.

"Once all the face licking was over and she'd settled down some, I gave her water and leftovers," Ralph said. "Sassy gobbled it down like there was no tomorrow."

"Poor thing was starving to death," Gladys said. "I told Ralph, I said, 'You get out to the store right now and bring back some dog food.'"

"When I got back," Ralph said, "she wolfed down three cans of Alpo fast as I could open them up and dish them out, didn't she, Glady?"

"I told him, 'Three cans is enough,'" Gladys said. "I told him,

'Ralph, you're gonna make that dog sick, you don't stop feeding her.'"

"Would of ate more if I'd let her," Ralph said.

"No call to make her sick," Gladys said.

"Perhaps you'd like to stay for lunch, Mr. Mulligan?" Ralph said.

"Thank you, but no, I've got to get back."

"Be no trouble at all," Gladys said. "Got some olive-loaf sandwiches all made up."

"No. Thank you."

"So the next day," Ralph said, picking up the story, "we got to talking about how amazing it was. The way Sassy tracked us all the way across the country like that, just like them dogs in the movies. Glady said we ought to call the TV, but I figured we should give it some thought."

"*Amazing Animals* would have paid a pretty penny," Gladys said, a bit wistfully, I thought.

"Maybe so," Ralph said, "but seems to me nobody'll believe our story 'less they read it in the paper."

"I thought Channel 10," I said.

"What was that?" Ralph said.

"I thought you were thinking of calling Channel 10."

"Well, sure," Ralph said. "That's the channel *Amazing Animals* is on, ain't that right, Glady?"

"No it ain't, Ralph. It's on one of them cable channels."

On the way out, I gave a wide birth to Sassy. I wasn't all that eager to write about Ralph, Gladys, and their amazing animal, so I decided to stop at the health department on the way back to the paper, even though it wasn't really on the way back.

11

I made it to the clinic forty minutes before closing and spent half an hour guessing what everyone else in the waiting room was there for.

The pimply redhead with the gnawed fingernails? She had unprotected sex with her lout of a boyfriend and was afraid she might be pregnant again. The bald guy with the bulbous honker? He wanted to be sure the city council president, who'd picked him up on karaoke night at the Dark Lady, hadn't passed him AIDS along with the bar nuts. The middle-aged guy in the mirror across the room, the one with the tousled hair, the Dustin Pedroia T-shirt, and the hangdog expression? He hated needles but would have gone under the knife without anesthesia if it meant that the woman with the cartoon-mouse snicker would finally let him. . . .

The clerk was calling my name.

The phlebotomist spiked me three times before she struck a vein. The clerk reaffirmed that the lab was backed up.

"Be seven weeks before the results come back," she said.

"This morning, on the phone, they said five."

"Seven," she said. "Look at this stack of blood test orders, most of 'em for HIV, which you say no way you got anyway. So what's your rush?"

When a Rhode Islander needs something he can't flat out steal, there are two ways to get it. Need a plumber's license but can't pass the state test? Want those fifty parking tickets fixed? Or maybe you'd just like a rush job on an HIV test. Chances are, in a state this small, you know somebody who can help. Maybe your uncle's on the state plumbing board. Maybe you went to school with a police captain. Maybe the health department clerk is married to your cousin. No? Then you have the option of offering a small gratuity.

Graft, Rhode Island's leading service industry, is widely misunderstood by citizens of states you can't stroll across on your lunch break. Those of us who live here know that it comes in two varieties, good and bad, just like cholesterol. The bad kind enriches politicians and their greedy friends at taxpayers' expense. The good kind supplements the wages of underpaid government workers, puts braces on their kids' teeth, builds college funds. Good graft is fat free. It's biodegradable. It dissolves red tape. Without the lubricant of graft and personal connections, not much would get done in Rhode Island, and nothing at all would happen on time.

Graft has been part of our heritage since the first colonial governor swapped favors with Captain Kidd. Call me old-fashioned. I took a twenty out of my wallet and slid it across the counter.

"Four weeks," she said. "Have a nice day."

By the time I got back to the office, Lomax had gone home for dinner. The night city editor, Judy Abbruzzi, occupied his chair.

"The dog story photos are great," she said. "Couple of hicks smiling their asses off, big ugly dog slobbering all over them. Even you can't screw this up enough to keep it off page one."

"It's not ready," I said.

"You still got an hour to write," she said.

"After I make a call."

The police chief in Prineville, Oregon, had a peculiar notion about what it means to be a public servant. She was courteous, helpful, and never asked for a bribe. "Yeah, we got a John and Edna Stinson," she said. "Got themselves a cabin out by the Deschutes River, about forty miles from town."

"Any way I can get in touch with them tonight?"

"This an emergency?"

"No, nothing like that."

"Well, then, I don't see how. They don't have a telephone, and we're short a man today so I can't take a run out there for you."

"Can I get a message to them?"

"They come into town about twice a month to stock up on groceries and pick up their mail. I suppose I can stick a note in their mailbox for you. It's against federal law, of course. Mailboxes are supposed to be just for mail, you see. But I can always tell the postmaster it's police business."

I thanked her, gave her my home, work, and cell numbers, and asked that John or Edna call collect.

"You know John and Edna well?" I asked.

"Pretty much," she said.

"Do you happen to know if they have a dog?"

"Had a big hairy mutt for a while, but I heard something happened to it. Now what *was* the story with that dog? Got distemper, maybe? No, that was the Harrisons' spaniel. I think what I heard was that it just run off."

After I hung up, I turned to my computer and pounded out a snappy lead about Ralph, Gladys, and Sassy.

12

I got to the meeting just as the photographer was leaving. Twenty-four men in identical red baseball caps were milling about the grocery isles. I knew several of them from high school, several more from the police blotter, and a couple from both.

"It's on me," Zerilli was saying as I walked in. "One bag of chips and one can of soda apiece. Aaay, Vinnie! One bag, one bag. Let you eat all the stock, might as well burn the fuckin' place down myself."

The caps were decorated with crossed bats and the words "The DiMaggios" in black letters.

"Are the caps fuckin' great, or what?" Zerilli said to me. "Got 'em made up special. Your photographer, who's got great knockers, by the way, she loved those fuckin' caps. Couldn't stop talkin' about 'em, honest to God. Posed the guys out front the market, all lined up with their bats. Guys in the front row down on one knee like a team picture, for Chrisssake."

"So why are you doing this?" I asked several of the DiMaggios as the group got ready to head out. Tony Arcaro, who had one of those no-show highway department jobs, muttered a few words about "giving something back to the community." Eddie Jackson, a police-blotter regular for rearranging his wife's dental work, said he was "protecting my loved ones." Martin Tillinghast, a ragged jailhouse tattoo seared into his forearm, said he wanted to "take a stand against crime." I scrawled their bullshit in my notepad.

"Got names to go with all but one of the faces," Zerilli said once we were alone, the store eerily quiet now without the sound of seven hundred teeth crushing potato chips. "Only one nobody knows is the chink," he said, pointing to the photo of Mr. Rapture. "One guy says he thinks he's seen him around, but he ain't sure."

Zerilli turned the pictures over, showing me where he had scrawled the names along with addresses done in Providence fashion: no street numbers, just landmarks, such as "peeling yellow house on Larch between Ivy and Camp, blue Dodge Ram on blocks in the yard."

When I finished with Zerilli it was only quarter to ten. I climbed in the Bronco and drove four blocks to Larch Street.

"Mrs. DeLucca?"

"Yes? Who is it?"

"My name is Mulligan. I'm a reporter for the paper."

"We already take the paper."

I thought I recognized the voice, but I couldn't quite place it. It was a voice that belonged somewhere else.

"No, no. I'm a reporter."

"Yes? What do you want?"

"Is Joseph home?"

"He reads the same paper I get. He don't need his own paper."

I was standing on a crumbling concrete stoop, staring at a solid door with three dead bolts.

"Mrs. DeLucca, this might be easier if you would let me in."

"Whaddayou, nuts? How I know you are who you say you are and not somebody else, maybe somebody come to rape me, huh? How I supposed to know that? Open the door? Fuhgeddaboudit."

"Ma? Who you talking to?"

"Nobody, Joseph. Go back to sleep."

Heavy footsteps.

"Now you done it, you woke up Joseph. Hope you're happy now."

The dead bolts clicked and the door swung open, revealing an ancient speck of a woman in a starched blue duster that matched her bouffant.

Now I remembered. For about a month, Carmella DeLucca had been a waitress at the diner, snarling at customers and shuffling so slowly between the counter and the booths that even kindhearted Charlie finally couldn't put up with it. When he let her go, nobody took her place.

She stood in the doorway now on swollen feet stuffed into bunny rabbit slippers. If Dorcas could see me now, she'd accuse me of sleeping with her.

Behind Mrs. DeLucca loomed her bouncing baby boy. At six foot three and about forty years of age, he looked a lot like me, if you overlooked the fifty extra pounds straining the elastic of yellowed boxers. I didn't want to think about it. He had forgotten his shirt, although I suppose that mat of hair counted for something.

"Why you botherin' Ma?"

Be careful with this one, Mulligan, I thought. One of those extra pounds might be muscle.

"I'm a reporter working on a story about the fires."

"What's that got to do with Ma?"

"Actually, I wanted to talk to you."

"You the guy been writin' all them stories?"

"Uh-huh."

"Don't you know that just encourages him, writin' all them stories and puttin' 'em in the paper like that? That's just what he wants, see all that stuff in the paper. Bet he's cuttin' all those stories out, makin' himself a fuckin' scrapbook. Sorry, Ma."

"Who is?" I said.

"Who is what?"

"Who is making himself a scrapbook?"

"How the hell do I know? What, you some kinda smart-ass?"

"You happen to see any of the fires yourself?"

"Why you askin' that for?"

"I'm just talking to people who've seen some of the fires, asking about what they saw."

"Yeah, I seen three of 'em. No, four. Last one was when the fireman got barbecued. Watched them pull his body out the house. Stunk somethin' awful. It was really cool."

I flashed on Tony at his wedding reception, his arm around the girl everybody wanted. As my eyes slid over the landscape that was Joseph DeLucca, I managed to keep my clenched fist where it was. He probably couldn't spell *asshole,* so maybe he couldn't help being one.

"How did you happen to be there?" I asked.

"I was watchin' *The Brady Bunch,* just like every Friday afternoon since I ain't been workin'. Marcia was complaining 'bout her new braces, and just then sirens started goin' off. She thought the braces made her look ugly, so I told her, 'Yeah, they do, you whiny little bitch.' When my show ended, I walked over there, see what was up."

"I see. Mrs. DeLucca, is that how you remember it? The two of you were watching *The Brady Bunch*?"

"Ma was at the Duds 'n' Suds. Why you care where Ma was at?"

"So you were home alone, then?"

"What the fuck you gettin' at? Sorry, Ma. You accusin' me of something? Get the fuck outta here, 'fore I shove my size-twelve up your ass."

Mark Twain said, "Everyone is a moon, and has a dark side which he never shows to anybody." I wondered what Joseph DeLucca's looked like. If I'd had a half hour to spare, I'd have walked around him to see for myself.

According to Secretariat's dashboard clock, there was time to try another of the names Zerilli had provided. Darned if I could see what good it would do. What had I been thinking? That one of the guys in the pictures was the firebug and that as soon as I showed up he'd pour his confession into my notebook?

I drove home over rutted streets, cursing myself for thinking it would be easy. I unlocked my door and stared for a long minute at my rumpled bed. After gulping a Maalox nightcap, I peeled the Band-Aid and cotton ball off the spot where the needle had gone in and crawled under a blanket that still smelled of Veronica.

13

Breakfast at the diner was coffee cut with lots of milk, eggs over easy, and the city edition. Bruccola, the aging mob boss, had been admitted to Miriam Hospital with congestive heart failure. Providence College's star forward, a lock to make McCracken's office wall, had been sentenced to twenty hours of community service for breaking his English tutor's arm with a lug wrench. Our sports columnist trumpeted the good news that, thank God, the player would not have to miss any Big East Tournament games. And our mayor had once again outwitted a political enemy.

Seems that last week, the mayor's probable opponent in next fall's election had legally changed her name from Angelina V. Rico to Angelina V. aRico so she would be listed first alphabetically on the ballot. But yesterday, Mayor Rocco D. Carozza legally changed his name to Rocco D. aaaaCarozza. It was a strong front page, even without the dog story. I couldn't find Sassy anywhere else in the paper, either.

A couple of stools away, a city councilman was checking the news on his laptop. The paper was too cheap to buy me one, but I didn't much care. I preferred holding a real newspaper in my hands.

"Hey, Charlie."

"Yeah?"

"I ran into Carmella DeLucca last night, and she was as charming as ever."

Charlie turned from the grill, rested both hands on the counter, and bent toward me. "I took her on 'cause she needed the dough, but she couldn't keep up with all the work around here."

I grinned and looked down the counter at the diner's only other customer, waiting for Charlie to burn his pancakes. Charlie followed my gaze.

"Fuck you, Mulligan."

In the newsroom, I logged on and found a message from Lomax on my computer:

YOUR DOG STORY SUCKED. ABBRUZZI GAVE IT TO HARD-CASTLE TO REWRITE. HOPE YOU WEREN'T EXPECTING A RAISE THIS YEAR.

Hardcastle, a rawboned Arkansas transplant who wrote occasional features and a twice-weekly metro column, was hunched in his cubicle, drumming at his keyboard with his big red hands. I ambled over and said, "What gives?"

"Mulligan, you never could write, but your Sassy story was dog shit," he said, blessing the word with an extra syllable—*shee-it*. "You take a homey little yarn about some nice folks and their amazing animal, and you write it up like you just caught the governor with his hand on your wallet. 'Fleming claimed.' 'Alleged to have walked.' 'Could not be confirmed.' What the hell was you thinking? Story like this, gotta stroke it like it's your dick, have a little fun with it."

"Well," I said, "it couldn't be confirmed."

"The hick sheriff told you the Stinsons live in town, that they had a mutt, that it run off. Sounds like confirmation to me. What the hell was you waiting for? Paw prints? Doggie DNA?"

"Have it your way, Hardcastle. Just make sure my byline isn't on it."

"Don't skip your nap over that, Mulligan. You blew your shot. Got so many page-one stories you can afford to piss 'em away?"

I saw it clearly now. My story was dog shit, and I pissed it away because I didn't stroke it like it was my dick. Why bother with journalism school when Hardcastle Academy is tuition free?

Back at my desk, the message function was blinking with another rocket from Lomax:

PRESS RELEASES.

As I read it, a copy boy deposited a beer keg–sized plastic box beside my desk. It was white with "U.S. Mail" stenciled in blue letters on the side. Inside was the day's incoming from every press agent and political candidate with a hope of hoodwinking us into putting something worthless in the paper. Usually an intern sorted through them, but today I was being punished.

I picked up the one on top. In it, Marco Del Torro promised that if reelected to the city council he would do something about the long lines for the restrooms at the civic center. Just what he would do he didn't say.

The phone rang as I was dumping the contents of the box into my big green wastebasket. I accepted the collect call, asked a question, listened for a few minutes, hung up, and scanned the newsroom. I spotted Hardcastle schmoozing at the copydesk. He slapped his thigh and squealed as several deskmen joined in the laughter.

"Hardcastle," I called out as I walked over. "Got something you need to know."

"Hey, here's our boy now," he said. "I was just recounting your Pulitzer-worthy work on the Sassy story, but how 'bout you tell it in your own words?"

I turned my back on him, walked back to my desk, checked my computer messages, and found another from Lomax:

AND WHAT'S WITH THE JACKET AND TIE TODAY? DID SOMEBODY DIE OR SOMETHING?

. . .

That afternoon, Rosie sat beside me in a church pew and wept into my shoulder.

Firefighters from six states had come to Tony DePrisco's funeral at the Church of the Holy Name of Jesus on Camp Street, just two blocks from the cellar where he'd burned to death.

A few rows in front of us, I saw the bent figure of Tony's wife Jessica, her sleeping daughter Mikaila curled in her lap. A dazed little boy sat stone still on either side of her—Tony Jr. and Jake.

Father Paul Mauro, a wizened little man who had presided at Tony's confirmation more than twenty-five years ago, stood in front of the closed casket and spoke of heroism, integrity, sacrifice, and salvation. I had to smile a little. The Tony I knew was a goof-off who'd passed math and English by copying from my exam papers, and whose lone contribution to our school's athletic prowess was kidnapping other schools' mascots. Somehow he'd managed to snag the senior-prom queen and then squeak through the fire academy after washing out twice. In nearly twenty years as a fireman, he'd never won a commendation. He would have wondered who Father Mauro was talking about.

A hand closed around mine and squeezed hard enough to make me cringe. *Rosie,* I thought to myself, *we really need to stop meeting like this.*

Late that afternoon, I finished knocking out the feature on the DiMaggios for the next day's paper, describing the hats and bats and laying the bullshit quotes on thick. By then it was too late to catch the end of the Sox spring-training game, even if I'd been in the mood, so I decided to get a head start on the weekend piece about Polecki and Roselli. I double-checked the stats on their abysmal record for closing cases and called McCracken at home for a not-for-attribution quote about how insurance investigators all over New England were calling them "Dumb and Dumber."

The Farrelly Brothers' lowbrow comedy was a local favorite because Dumb and Dumber hailed from Providence, the movie starting with an establishing shot of Hope Street. Another reason to be proud.

Me? Call me Dumbest. By midnight I was cruising Mount Hope on the off chance that I might spot something. It was no way to investigate anything, but I couldn't sit around doing nothing, and I was out of ideas.

14

On Larch Street, a big—screen TV glowed blue behind the thin white curtains of a two-story bungalow where I covered a mob hit ten years back, the widow and her teenage daughter living comfortably there now on their monthly Mafia pension. On Hopedale Road, the lights were all out in the second-floor tenement where Sean and Louisa Mulligan had managed to raise two boys and a girl on a milkman's salary. On Doyle Avenue, an idle front-end loader with "Dio Construction" in green letters on its flank sat among the ruins of a burned-out triple-decker.

Neighborhood trash pickup was Thursday morning, and by the look·of the mess in the snow, most folks had already dragged their trash barrels and Hefty bags to the curb. At the corner of Ivy and Forest, Norwegian brown rats, their eyes burning red in my headlights, yanked food scraps from holes they had burrowed in the plastic. Down the street from Zerilli's store, a half dozen dogs had toppled a couple of trash barrels and were partying at the curb.

I decided to join them. I unscrewed the lid from my thermos, swigged coffee, and popped in a CD. Tommy Castro rocked the Bronco with electric blues:

All my nasty habits . . . they just won't let me be

I'd been circling for most of an hour when I spied someone crossing the street half a block ahead, silhouetted in the wash of a streetlight that hadn't been shot out yet. The figure walked like a woman and carried something. Too small for a gasoline can. Could have been a large handgun, or maybe a camera with a telephoto lens. Before I could check it out, blue lights flashed in my rearview.

I pulled Secretariat to the curb and listened in on my police scanner as the cops ran my plate. In the mirror, I saw one cop climb out of the cruiser's passenger-side door and position herself at the rear of the Bronco, her gun unholstered and pressed against her right leg. Her partner got out on the driver's side and walked toward me, flashlight in his right hand, left hand resting on the butt of his revolver. I rolled down the window, the cold hitting me like a karate chop, as he shined his light in my face.

"How you doing, Eddie?" Ed Lahey had been in my brother Aidan's posse back in the days when the word wasn't synonymous with *gang*.

"Mulligan? That you? The hell you doing out here middle of the night?"

"Same as you, Eddie. Wasting my time."

"Got that right," he said. "Supposed to cruise the neighborhood all night, stop anyone looks suspicious. Ever see anyone in Mount Hope who *didn't* look suspicious?"

"Just the pedophile priest," I said. "I hear the bishop is transferring him to Woonsocket."

"Not planning on burning anything down tonight, are you, Mulligan?"

"Not right this minute," I said, "but I've got a cigar I'm saving for later."

"No cans of gasoline in back?" His tone was light, but he shined his flashlight into the backseat, then walked back and peered through the window of the empty cargo space.

When he was done, he narrowed his eyes and told me to head for home.

"Okay, maybe I will."

"Uh-huh. Sure you will. Look, you got a cell phone?"

"Yeah."

"Here's my cell number," he said, handing me a card. "Call it if you see anything. And next time you talk to your brother, tell him . . ."

I rolled the window up before he could finish. I had enough problems.

I drove down the block and turned right, looking for the figure I'd seen crossing the street, but of course, she was gone. A few minutes later, cruising up Cypress, I saw a couple of the DiMaggios, bats on their shoulders, smoking cigarettes and stamping their feet in the snow. I slowed, rolled the passenger-side window down, and leaned toward it.

"Hey, Vinnie! Seen anything unusual tonight?"

"Nothing 'cept for Lucinda Miller standing in her window, giving us a good look at her tits."

His colleague snorted. "That ain't so unusual."

I pulled out the three-flame Colibri that Zerilli had given me. I didn't have anything that needed welding, so I used it to fire up a Cuban and smoked as I prowled the empty streets. I didn't see anyone skulking about with a can of gasoline. I didn't see anyone resembling Mr. Rapture. Except for the DiMaggios, I didn't see anyone at all.

The CD cycled around to "Nasty Habits" twice before I shut it off. Around three in the morning, the Bronco's heater coughed and surrendered. The eastern sky was lightening when a newspaper delivery truck pulled up in front of Zerilli's store and heaved out two bundles of city editions. I headed home to catch a couple hours' sleep, see what my dreams could conjure.

I heard the phone ringing through the apartment door, stepped in, and picked up the receiver.

"You!
fucking!
bastard!"

"Hello, Dorcas."

"So, who is she?"

"Who?"

"The bitch you've been out fucking all night."

"What makes you think it was only one?"

"I'm still your wife, you evil bastard!"

"Good morning, Dorcas," I said, and hung up. Just before I set the receiver down, I thought I heard Rewrite bark.

By the time I dragged myself in to work, the editors were meeting behind closed doors, discussing an issue that required their collective experience and judgment: Should the paper start printing the mayor's name as "aaaaCarozza" or stick with the more headline-friendly "Carozza"? Judging by the muffled sounds coming through the wall, the debate was heating up.

I snatched a newspaper off the stack beside the city desk and saw that page one was dominated by a four-column picture of Sassy. She had her paws on Ralph's shoulders, digging at his ear with her tongue while Gladys stood by looking embarrassed. Looking at the page made me feel bad about what I'd done. Not that I gave a damn about Hardcastle, but I cared a whole lot about the paper.

I was just a kid when Dan Rather broke into a Red Sox broadcast with the news that Pope Paul VI had died. "Maybe so," my dad said, "but we won't know for sure till we read tomorrow's paper." In a state where politicians lie like the rest of us breathe, the newspaper is the only institution people trust to tell the truth. I knew right then that I wanted to be a part of it.

That night, I prowled Mount Hope again in the heatless Bronco, giving it up around three in the morning, when hypothermia set in and even Tommy Castro's guitar couldn't heat things up. My apartment was warm only by comparison, the landlord thrifty with his heating oil.

Sleeping alone under a thin blanket, I dreamed of Norwegian brown rats with glowing red eyes and fierce cartoon dogs that wore red baseball caps and wielded Louisville Sluggers. The hair on the backs of their necks stood up as they growled in the dark and swung their bats at a man clutching a gas can in his left hand. He tried to escape the blows by crawling headfirst into an overturned plastic trash barrel, but the dogs clamped their jaws on his ankles and yanked him out. Their snapping teeth tore chunks of flesh from his thighs, and the rats scurried to devour the bloody pieces. A police car, blue lights swirling, roared down the street and screeched to a stop. The cops leaped out, shouted "Good dogs," tossed them Beggin' Strips, and stomped the man with their gleaming black jackboots. His mouth opened in a silent scream.

He had my face.

15

On Saturday, my clock radio roused me just before noon, blaring that we were in for a cold snap, which got me wondering what we'd *been* having.

I dropped Secretariat at the Shell station on Broadway to see what they could do about the heater. The mechanic was a lanky, murmuring dude named Dwayne who had "Butch" embroidered over the pocket of his blue work shirt. Five years after his dad died and left him the station, he was still wearing the old man's clothes.

"Secretariat off his feed again?" he said. "How 'bout I take him out back and shoot him so you can break in a new nag?" Dwayne had been tending to Secretariat for years, and he never tired of the same horse joke.

"I just can't bear to let him go," I said, and told him about the heater.

On the walk back to my place, I called Veronica.

"Mulligan! I was beginning to think you didn't like me anymore."

"No chance of that, cutie. What say I take you out on the town tonight?"

"On the town or *around* the town? We're not cruising Mount Hope sniffing for smoke, are we?"

She was on to me. "Well," I said, "that *is* the part of town I had in mind. I thought maybe you'd like to drive."

"Secretariat in the shop again?"

"Yup."

"Pick you up at seven."

And she did, driving her slate-gray Mitsubishi Eclipse straight to Camille's on Bradford Street, where we shared a bottle of wine and ate mounds of spaghetti. Veronica treated, tapping into the five-hundred-dollar monthly allowance from Daddy that supplemented her meager paycheck. Good thing, or I'd have had to do some business with the loan shark eating with his aged mother at a table by the windows. Then it was off to the Cineplex in East Providence for the new Jackie Chan movie, he and his comic-relief sidekick doing a better job of catching the bad guys than I was.

This wasn't the romantic evening of street prowling and rat watching I'd had in mind, but I was having a pretty good time, especially whenever she leaned over to kiss me. Besides, she had the car keys, so there wasn't much I could do about it.

Afterward, she came up. We sat together on my bed and watched Craig Ferguson on my sixteen-inch Emerson. She sipped Russian River, her favorite kind of chardonnay, straight from the bottle, and I did the same with Maalox. The police radio, turned down low, chirped benignly in the background. Veronica thought Ferguson was the funniest man on television. I didn't watch enough TV to know if she had a point.

"Mulligan?" Veronica said, sleep lurking at the edges of her voice. "Are you seeing anybody else?"

I flashed on Dorcas asking, "How many bitches are you fucking now?" Same Mulligan, different woman, better vocabulary.

"Do Polecki and Roselli count?"

She smiled and shook her head.

"Well, then it's no," I said.

"Hardcastle says you've been stepping out with the blonde in the photo lab."

"Gloria Costa?"

"Yeah, her."

"Not happening," I said. "And Hardcastle is an asshole. You

shouldn't be getting your news from him, and that includes what he writes in his lame column. I've got a bad feeling he makes some of it up."

"Maybe. But I do think Gloria's sweet on you."

"I think you could be right."

The police radio chirped again, making me wonder how I was going to get to Mount Hope if something happened after Veronica went home. I was still thinking about that when she stripped down to her bra and panties and slid under the covers. I didn't put up a fight. I snapped off the light, took off everything but my boxers, and crawled in beside her. It had been a long time since anyone felt that good in my arms. Maybe no one ever had.

"Mulligan?"

"Um?"

"Is that an erection?"

"God, I hope so."

"Well, quit poking me with it."

"You sure? Man my age, no telling when I'll get another one."

She laughed, reached under the sheet, and ran a finger along my length, and for just a moment I thought she was relenting.

"Nice try, funny man" she said, "but it's just not happening until the test results come back."

I was still trying to think of a snappy comeback when she drifted off. I watched her sleep as my hard-on processed the bad news. Was she really paranoid about AIDS or just trying to slow things down? I didn't know, and her deep, even breathing told me this was not the time to ask. The ulcer was grumbling, so I got up for another gulp of Maalox, then slid back into bed, buried my face in her hair, and breathed all of her in.

In the morning, I discovered she'd gotten up during the night and turned off the police radio. I decided not to make an issue of it.

Veronica had come prepared, scrubbing her teeth with a yellow toothbrush she pulled from her purse. When she was done, she placed it next to mine in the holder under my bathroom mirror. That seemed promising—and a little scary.

"Anything else you want to store in there? Some Jean Naté? A blow-dryer? I could use some clean towels."

She laughed. We kissed. The toothbrush stayed.

Veronica lived in an efficiency apartment in Fox Point, the modern red-brick building an unsightly intruder in a neighborhood of well-preserved early nineteenth-century shingle-clad colonials. We swung by there so she could dress for church, then drove to St. Joseph's, where I'd been an altar boy as a kid. She tried to coax me inside, but I hadn't been to mass since the sex scandal broke.

I took her car to the diner for one of Charlie's heart-attack cheddar omelets and the Sunday paper. The savior who stood between me and starvation had already scanned the front page.

"Great headline," he chuckled, then bent his sweating bald pate over an acre of sizzling bacon.

The head over my story read, ARSON SQUAD IS DUMB AND DUMBER. The managing editor had gotten unexpectedly playful with the layout, juxtaposing photos of Polecki and Roselli with head shots of Jim Carrey and Jeff Daniels, who'd played the title roles in the movie. I scanned the paper for other fire news, but there wasn't any. Then I called fire headquarters on my cell and confirmed Mount Hope had been quiet overnight.

I picked Veronica up just as St. Joseph's was emptying the faithful into a day that couldn't decide between drizzle and sleet. As the worshippers spilled into the street, I recognized three "made men," four state legislators, and a judge. Tomorrow they'd be back to labor racketeering, truck hijacking, and bribe taking.

At her apartment, Veronica changed into a man's faded blue oxford shirt and a snug pair of low-rise Levis while I watched and admired the view. I wondered if the shirt had a previous owner of the male persuasion, but once again I kept my mouth shut. By the time we got to O'Malley's Billiards on Hope Street, the shirt had begun to smell like the woman who was wearing it.

My plan was to teach Veronica how to shoot eight ball. I lost three games out of five. Must have been distracted by the low in those low-rise jeans.

Late that afternoon we lay on my bed and caught an ESPN report out of the Red Sox spring camp in Fort Myers. Jonathan Papelbon, one of the stars of the 2007 World Series, was thumping his chest and saying there was no reason the team couldn't repeat. "He's a major-league blowhard," I said, "but I think he's going to have another big year."

And she said, "Why do you care so much about a stupid baseball team?"

Back when you could sit in the center-field bleachers for ten bucks, I spent a lot of weekend afternoons at Fenway with my dad. "Just one World Series championship in my lifetime, that's all I ask," he used to say. His heart quit pumping the winter after Mookie Wilson's grounder skidded between Bill Buckner's legs.

How do you explain it to the uninitiated? How do you explain why you draped a Curt Schilling jersey over the shoulders of your dad's gravestone after that glorious night in 2004? How do you explain why you sat by his grave with a portable radio last fall so you could listen to the clinching game together?

"I've gotta have something to care about, Veronica," is all I said. I was just realizing she might take that wrong when the phone rang. I grabbed it on the second ring.

"You!
fucking!
bastard!"

"Can't talk now, Dorcas," I said, and hung up.

Later, Veronica and I discussed whether she'd stay the night again. I'd need her car if there was a fire, she said, but I suspected she really liked the way it felt. I liked the way it felt, too, and expected to like it a whole lot more once we had the test results. We agreed it would be just an occasional thing. The toothbrush could stay, and she could have her own key, but feminine products were out of the question.

That night, before we slipped under the covers, I moved the police radio to my side of the bed. About four in the morning, it woke me. Something was burning in Mount Hope. I found her car keys and tried to dress without disturbing Veronica, but she stirred, heard the radio chatter, got up, and pulled on those jeans.

16

Police had Catalpa Road blocked off, so we parked and walked in through a flurry of embers.

Rosie's crew had given up on saving the four-story rooming house and was soaking down the triple-deckers next door and across the street to stop them from catching. A window exploded, showering a five-man pumper crew with shards of glass.

At least no one's going to die tonight, I thought. The wood-frame building had been empty since September, when it was condemned by the city housing department. The winos and welfare mothers who had been living there protested that they had nowhere to go, but the building inspector explained it was for their own good. Some of them were still sleeping in junk cars and cardboard boxes.

My next thought was the kind that always made me feel dirty at times like this: *Just a flophouse and no bodies? This might not make page one.*

The fire was putting on a show. Flames jitterbugged in the windows. Hungry red tongues lapped at the eaves. Majestic fireballs rose from the roof. I don't know how long I stood there, mesmerized, until the wind shifted and a cloud of smoke sent me sprinting for air. When I could breathe again, I looked around for Veronica. Two minutes later, I found her scribbling notes in the lee of a fire truck. Gloria was there, too, methodically snapping away with her Nikon digital camera.

"I worked late in the photo lab," Gloria said as she adjusted her focus, "and was on my way home when I smelled the smoke."

Cracks loud as gunshots made me jump, and the roof collapsed into kindling. When the rubble cooled, this one wouldn't need a wrecking crew—just a front-end loader and a dump truck to haul the ashes.

At dawn, Veronica scooted back to the paper to write while I hung around to feed her notes in case anything newsworthy happened in the mop-up. Firemen were curling their hoses now, except for a couple who were still drenching the wreckage, making sure. That's when I caught a faint whiff of something new in the air.

I found Rosie by a pumper truck.

"You smell that?" I said.

She sniffed and said, "Oh, shit!"

Odors are particulate. When you smell an orange or savor the aroma of my cigar, molecules that were once part of those objects are entering your body through your nasal passages. So what do you suppose is cruising through your bronchia when you smell the candied stench of death? The thought, more than the smell, made me retch. Sometimes it's better not to know how things work.

Rosie spoke a few words into her radio, and within the hour two cadaver dogs were on the scene, yipping as soon as their paws hit the ground. I already had a pretty good idea what they'd find.

I paced, chatted with some of the exhausted firefighters, looked at my watch a lot. It took an hour to dig the victims out of the wreckage. There were two of them, most of the clothes burned from their bodies. Firefighters laid them on the sidewalk where Polecki and Roselli squatted to look them over. Then firefighters covered the corpses with a tarp to await the medical examiner.

"If they had ID, it got burned up," Roselli told Rosie as I sidled over to eavesdrop. "Most likely they got sick of sleeping on the street and snuck back in for a little warmth."

"Then they came to the right place," Polecki said, his laugh making his belly jiggle.

Rosie's hands clenched into fists. "I ought to kick your ass," she said, "but it wouldn't be a fair fight."

Two hours later, I was looking over Veronica's rough draft when Gloria came by to show us her photos. Firemen ducking for cover in a hail of glass and sparks. An ice-encrusted Rosie, silhouetted against a row of flaming windows, muscling a hose. A wide shot of firemen and equipment looking small in the foreground of a building engulfed in flame. A cadaver dog straining at his leash, snout speckled with ash.

"Wow," I said.

"When they hired me, they promised I'd be in the lab no more than a year before I got my chance," Gloria said. "It's been four years now. When I called it in from the scene, know what the night desk told me? Said to sit tight while they woke up a real photographer. I told them I had it covered, but they called Porter in anyway. I just looked at his stuff. Mine's better. The photo desk says they're gonna use one of his and four of mine. And I get page one."

"The one of Rosie reminds me of Stanley Forman's work," I said, "back when he was winning Pulitzers for the *Boston Herald*."

"Thanks," Gloria said, and she touched my arm. "By the way, I thought you'd like to have this one."

It was a picture of me staring wide-eyed at the flames. I looked like I was in a trance. As I stared at it, I felt the heat stinging my skin again as sparks danced in the dark. Behind me in the photo, I could make out a string of gawkers. I held the print close for a better look. I couldn't be sure, but one of them might have been Mr. Rapture.

17

First thing Monday morning, my computer flashed
with a message from Lomax:

MAYOR PRESS CONFERENCE, CITY HALL AT NOON.

So what? I wasn't the city-hall reporter. But asking Lomax why
he wanted something always carried the risk of public humiliation.
I wandered down the street to see what was up.

City hall, a Beaux-Arts atrocity at the southern end of Kennedy
Plaza, looked as if a madman had sculpted it from a mound of
seagull shit. I walked up the guano-slicked stone steps and into the
foyer, then turned right and entered the mayor's office, with its crys-
tal chandelier and floor-to-ceiling windows with a panoramic view
of a Peter Pan bus stop. Carozza stood behind his desk, the same
mahogany antique Buddy Cianci had fancied before they packed
him off to a federal penitentiary for getting caught doing business
as usual.

TV cables snaked across the red-and-blue oriental carpet. Camera crews and on-air reporters from Channels 10, 12, and 6 had
arrived early and hogged the best spots up front. Channels 4 and 7
in Boston were there, too, along with an AP reporter and a woman
I recognized as a stringer for *The New York Times*. Mount Hope
was getting to be a big story.

The occasion had flipped the mayor's "on" switch. Everything about him, from his spritzed silver pompadour to his crisp Louis-Boston suit, was camera ready. Police Chief Angelo Ricci, stiff under the best of circumstances, stood beside him in full-dress uniform complete with medals, visored hat tucked under his left arm.

They exchanged a few words and turned to face the cameras. The chief had a Louisville Slugger over his right shoulder. I started to get a bad feeling.

"We ready?" Carozza asked. He paused as TV lights switched on. "All right, let's get started. We're going to begin with an announcement from Chief Ricci."

"At 11:57 last night," the chief began, "two Providence police officers on patrol in Mount Hope observed two male subjects armed with baseball bats committing an assault upon another male subject at the southeast corner of Knowles and Cypress streets. The officers exited their vehicle, drew their weapons, and apprehended the suspects, who did not offer resistance. The suspects were then transported to police headquarters for questioning. There, detectives advised them of their rights, which they agreed to waive.

"The suspects identified themselves as Eddie Jackson, twenty-nine, of 46 Ivy Street, and Martin Tillinghast, thirty-seven, of 89 Forest Street. Both have criminal records, Mr. Jackson for assault and battery on his wife, and Mr. Tillinghast for truck hijacking and assault with a deadly weapon. They further identified themselves as members of a recently organized Mount Hope vigilante group calling itself the DiMaggios. The suspects stated that they were proceeding west on Cypress when they observed the victim walking toward them carrying an object. They subsequently determined that this object was a metal two-gallon gasoline can. The patrol officers did, in fact, recover such a can at the scene. They also recovered two baseball bats, including this one," he said, holding it up for the cameras.

I was pretty sure now that I knew where this was going. I pulled a roll of Tums out of my pocket, peeled off a couple, and chewed.

"The victim was identified as Giovanni M. Pannone, fifty-one, of 144 Ivy Street," the chief said. "He was taken by ambulance to Rhode Island Hospital, where he was admitted with a compound fracture of the right wrist, a concussion, and multiple contusions of the head, arms, and shoulders. At the hospital, Mr. Pannone told detectives that he had purchased gasoline for his snowblower at the Gulf station on North Main and was returning home on foot when he was accosted by the suspects.

"In their statements," the chief went on, "the suspects expressed the belief that they had apprehended the individual responsible for the recent series of arsons in the Mount Hope neighborhood. Subsequent investigation by Providence police detectives determined that Mr. Pannone is employed as a guard on the overnight shift at the Adult Correctional Institution in Cranston and can account for his whereabouts when each of the fires was set. For most of them, he was at work. Mr. Jackson and Mr. Tillinghast have each been charged with one count of assault and battery and are being held pending arraignment. An investigation is ongoing to determine whether conspiracy charges can be brought against the organizer and other members of the so-called DiMaggios. That's all I have."

The chief bowed slightly and took a step backward. The blow-dry boys started shouting questions, but Carozza quieted them by holding up both hands and going "Shhhhhhh" into the microphones.

"I have something to add," he said. "You didn't think I'd be able to keep quiet in a room full of TV cameras, did you?" He paused for the laugh, frowned when it didn't come, and moved on.

"What occurred last night is disturbing, very disturbing. I can't have people prowling my city with baseball bats, taking the law into their own hands. Patrolling the streets is a job for the police, not for citizens with no training in law enforcement. You'd think that's something we could all agree on, but our city's only newspaper apparently takes a different view."

My stomach was a vat of acid. The Tums weren't working.

"Last Thursday, the newspaper published this story by L. S. A. Mulligan," he said, holding up the front page with my feature on the DiMaggios circled in red marker. "For those of you who didn't get around to reading it, I can tell you all you need to know. It's disgraceful. It glorifies these vigilantes and the individual who organized them. An individual, by the way, named Dominic L. Zerilli, who has a record of bookmaking arrests and is known to police as an associate of organized crime.

"Mulligan," he said, pointing a manicured finger at me, "I've had problems with you before, but this is a new low."

With that, Logan Bedford, the asshole from Channel 10, prodded his cameraman to swing the lens my way. I thought of putting my hand in front of my face, but that would have looked too much like a perp walk. I thought of throwing the finger, but Logan would have made it look like I was flipping off the mayor. So I just smiled like a toothpaste model for the camera.

"On Sunday," the mayor went on, "this newspaper published a page-one story by this same reporter criticizing the city's arson squad. It was an outrageous story, full of half-truths and misleading statistics contrived to besmirch the reputations of devoted public servants. I want to make it clear that Chief Ricci and I have full confidence in our arson squad chief, Ernest M. Polecki, who is doing a remarkable job under trying circumstances, and I want to assure the people of this city that we will track down whoever is responsible for the rash of fires in Mount Hope and prosecute him or her to the full extent of the law."

He paused so the print reporters could catch up with their scribbling.

"Okay," he said. "Who's got a question?"

"Mr. Mayor," Bedford shouted, his hand in the air.

"Yes, Logan?"

"Could you please tell us how you'd like your new name pronounced on the air?"

"It's Carozza," the mayor replied. "The four As are silent."

"Way to go, Mulligan," Hardcastle crowed as I stepped off the elevator. "What's next? A puff piece on serial rapists?"

In the newsroom, they'd watched the whole thing live on Channel 10. When I sat down, Lomax wandered over, pushed an empty Casserta Pizzeria box out of the way, and perched on the corner of my desk.

"Don't worry about it," he said. "If you hadn't included those quotes from the cops, the ones telling people to stay home and leave the patrolling to them, we might have had a problem. But you did, so we don't. Just keep writing about what people are doing, whether the mayor likes what they are doing or not."

"Thanks, boss. I will."

"So," he said, "how about a nice little feature on cadaver dogs?"

As he walked off, I decided to proceed on the assumption that he was kidding.

18

Her long legs encased in gray wool slacks, Mc—
Cracken's secretary wasn't flashing any thigh today. Instead, she
wore a frilly white blouse with the top four buttons undone. From
somewhere deep inside, I found the strength not to stare.

"Something tells me they might be real," McCracken said, after
she waved me into his office.

"Good you still got some faith," I said.

"Faith I got, but no hope. Her boyfriend's Vinnie Pazienza."

Vinnie had lost some hand speed after giving up the ring for a
job as a casino greeter, but he could still beat the crap out of your
average middleweight.

"So I hear you've been prowling around Mount Hope at night,"
McCracken said.

"Where'd you hear that?"

"Cop friend of mine."

"Small world," I said.

"No, small state," he said. "Ought to stop wasting your time.
It's not like you're gonna catch the guy in the act."

"I know."

"Terrific story on Polecki and Roselli," he said. "About time
somebody took them on. Maybe it'll do some good."

"I doubt it."

"So do I."

"So is that why you wanted to see me, tell me what a bang-up job I'm doing?"

"Got something for you," he said. "Polecki gave me a look at his preliminary report on the rooming-house fire, and there's something new in it."

"Oh?"

"This time there was a timing device."

"What kind of device?"

"A coffeemaker," he said, and then looked at me like I was supposed to understand.

I stared back at him until he broke the silence.

"You fill the coffeemaker with gasoline, find a live outlet in the basement, and plug it in. Set the programmable timer and be home bopping the wife when the house goes boom."

"Professional job?"

"Maybe," he said. "The pros like them because they're impossible to trace. The rooming-house fire was started with a Proctor Silex Easy Morning Coffeemaker, model 41461. Something you can shoplift in any Target or Walmart."

"But?"

"But anybody who types *arson* into Google can learn to do this in five minutes. Coffeemakers are used for arson so often now that even Dumb and Dumber knew what it meant when they tripped over the melted remains of one in the ashes."

"So our firebug is getting a little more sophisticated," I said.

"That's my guess," McCracken said, "but there are other explanations. Maybe the rooming-house fire isn't related to the others. Or maybe we've been dealing from the start with a pro who wanted the fires to look like the work of an amateur. With the DiMaggios and extra police patrols on the streets, he'd have to be more careful now."

He grinned and sliced the air with an imaginary bat.

"One thing I don't get," I said. "This building was abandoned, scheduled for demolition. Why was the electricity on?"

"Yeah, I checked on that. A salvage crew from Dio Construction's been in there pulling out copper pipe and other stuff. It was turned back on for them."

"How could our arsonist have known about that?"

"Don't know."

"Well," I said, "it's still hard to see it as a professional job. I mean, with most of the torched buildings having different owners, with none of them overinsured, what's the motive?"

"There's that," he said.

"So we really don't know anything."

"Exactly. We don't even know for sure if her breasts are real."

19

The fine dust coating everything in the city hall basement property-records room made my eyes water and my throat itch. I spent two hours with real estate transfer ledgers and property-tax books before I blew my nose and snapped the last one shut.

Records showed that the nine torched buildings had all changed hands in the past eighteen months. But with five different buyers, there was no pattern to it unless you counted the fact that they were all real estate companies I'd never heard of. A little more checking showed that those five companies had snapped up a quarter of the Mount Hope neighborhood in the last year and a half. But a lot of cheap rental property had been changing hands all over the city since the last property-tax increase.

From city hall, it was a short walk to the secretary of state's Corporations Division on River Street. A clerk with a shellacked beehive hairdo snatched my list, made a face, and waddled into a forest of file cabinets. Thirty minutes later she waddled back and slapped the incorporation papers for five realty companies on the counter.

I said, "Thank you." She didn't say you're welcome. State employees in jobs with limited graft potential are seldom happy in their work.

Most states have their incorporation records on computers, but not Rhode Island. Twice, the secretary of state had persuaded the legislature to put money for computers into his budget. Both times, he'd spread the sugar around by ordering them from a local middleman, the brother of the House Appropriations Committee chairman, instead of directly from the manufacturer. Both times, someone leaked the delivery time to an interested party. Both times, the delivery trucks got hijacked. The way I heard it, the Tillinghast brothers pulled the jobs and fenced the computers to Grasso for twenty cents on the dollar.

That's why I was standing at the counter thumbing through paper records again. Along with a few vague remarks under the heading "Purposes of Incorporation," the documents listed each company's address and the names of its officers and directors. The addresses were all Providence post office boxes. I didn't recognize any of the names. Under Rhode Island law, the people behind a corporation could remain anonymous and often did. The names filed with the state could be anyone from the cast of *The Sopranos* to a dozen winos from the Pine Street gutter.

Then I looked again and realized I knew the directors of one of the companies: Barney Gilligan, Joe Start, Jack Farrell, and Charles Radbourn—the catcher, first baseman, second baseman, and best pitcher for the 1882 Providence Grays.

I scrawled it all in my notebook, but I couldn't see anything in it.

When I crossed Westminster Street to fetch Secretariat, it was getting dark, the end of a typical day in the life of L. S. A. Mulligan, investigative reporter: A personal attack from the mayor. A fruitless interview with a source. A tedious records search that produced nothing unless you wanted to count the eye strain and dripping sinuses.

I used to get discouraged by days like this, but over the years I've learned that it seldom comes easy. You spend long working days listening to idiots drone on at public meetings, getting lied to by cops and politicians, chasing down false tips, having doors slammed in your face, and standing in the rain at 4:00 A.M. watching something burn. You get it all down in your notebook, every detail, because you can never be sure what might turn out to be important.

And then you get drunk and spill beer on your notes. Unless you're one of the few who lands a job at *The New York Times* or CNN, the pay is shit, and no one will ever know your name.

Why does anyone do it? Because it's a calling—like the priesthood but without the sex. Because unless somebody does it, Mc-Cracken is right and freedom of the press really is just for suckers. Me? I do it because I stink at everything else. If I couldn't be a reporter, I'd be squatting on the floor at the bus station hawking pencils out of a tin cup.

Sometimes it pays off. A few years ago, a source tipped me to a hot pillow joint in Warwick where the mob occasionally repaid the state police commandant for his frequent acts of kindness. I spent five weeks staking it out, surviving on Big Macs and caffeine, and peeing in a Mason jar. I sang along to my Tommy Castro and Jimmy Thackery CDs so many times that I learned the lyrics by heart. I gained eight pounds, got a bad case of the Red Bull shakes, and was still there holding a camera with a long lens when the commandant rolled up in his Crown Vic. A half hour later, two hookers in halter tops arrived to keep him company.

The best photo showed him standing in the open motel-room door, a half-naked hooker behind him blowing him a good-bye kiss. His hair was mussed, his tie was undone, and he was reaching down to zip his gaping fly. The paper ran it three columns wide at the top of page one, and for a week it was the talk of the town.

If this were Connecticut or Oregon, he might have been in a fix. But this is Rhode Island. He's still on the job.

20

Logan Bedford's insistent tenor blared from the TV over the bar. "Remember Sassy? She's the big loveable mutt who supposedly walked all the way across the country to be reunited with her owners. Well, wait till you hear what really happened. You'll be shocked!"

With that, Channel 10 Action News broke for commercial, and we all returned to drinking and swapping stories about other newspaper screwups. I was on my fourth Killian's. Ulcer be damned; tonight I needed beer.

Logan had called the newspaper for comment, tipping us off to what was coming, so we'd fled the grim visage of the city editor and found a place more suitable for our gallows humor.

We'd been at it for nearly an hour already, Gloria kicking off the game of can-you-top-this by swearing that the small North Carolina paper where she got her start once reported a cat show with the headline NORFOLK PUSSY BEST IN SOUTH.

Abbruzzi had the floor now, spinning a tale about her days with the AP in Richmond, when a reporter trying to get literary with a weather story wrote, "Jack Frost stuck his icy finger into Virginia Tuesday."

Sean Sullivan, a night-side copy editor for forty years, chipped in with a story about the drunk who covered Pawtucket City Hall for us back in the seventies. Not about to let the city fathers cut into his drinking time, he'd skip the council meetings and drop by the newsroom of the rival *Pawtucket Times* later to peek at their story. One day, the *Times*' city-hall reporter banged out a fake lead about three councilmen and the police chief resigning after admitting they'd bought an old motel with city money and turned it into a brothel. Next morning, it was in our paper under the drunk's byline. The big news in the Pawtucket paper was the council debate over whether to hire two more crossing guards.

"Took years, but we eventually lived that one down," Sullivan said, "so maybe we'll eventually live Sassy down too."

Unless you're a member of the tribe, you have no idea how hard journalists take mistakes. Sure, the business occasionally attracts a fraud like Jayson Blair, the reporter who got fired for making stuff up at *The New York Times*. But the lies they tell hurt the rest of us, and so does every honest mistake that makes readers doubt what we print.

"If you write 'Blackstone Street,' which is in the poor part of town, when you mean 'Blackstone Boulevard,' which is in the rich part of town, no one will believe anything in your story," my first city editor, the legendary Albert R. Johnson, once told me. That mistake cost me three nights' sleep.

As we waited for Logan to come back and shock us, it was Veronica's turn to tell a story.

"My first job after college, I had the police beat at a little paper in western Massachusetts. The editor, an old fart named Bud Collins, wouldn't print the word *rape*. Thought it would offend the sensibilities of our delicate readers. He insisted we write *criminal sexual assault* instead. One day, I used *rape* in a quote. I mean, you don't change quotes, right? When my story came out, it had the victim running down the street screaming 'Criminal sexual assault! Criminal sexual assault!'"

We all howled, but the commercial was over now, and the foxlike face of Logan Bedford was smirking again above the bar.

"I'm here with Martin Lippitt in the Silver Lake section of Providence," he said, the camera angle widening to show a thirty-something standing beside Logan. "Martin, please tell us what you know about the amazing dog named Sassy."

"Well, it's like I told you. Her name isn't Sassy. It's Sugar. And there's nothing amazing about her at all."

"Sassy is really Sugar?"

"That's right, Logan. See, I left her with some friends for a couple of weeks to go snowboarding in Vermont, but she managed to get away from them. Didn't wander far though, just a few doors down."

"To the home of Ralph and Gladys Fleming, right?"

"The new people, I guess that's their names. Wouldn't of known where she was, I hadn't glanced at the papers piled up on the porch and seen her picture. That was some surprise, I'll tell you."

Veronica nudged me and started to giggle.

"So, where is Sassy, I mean Sugar, now?" Logan said.

"New people still got her. Won't give her back."

Now Gloria and Abbruzzi were giggling, too.

"They really think it's their dog, don't they?" Logan said.

"Sure do. Miss their own dog so much they convinced themselves it could have walked all the way across the country to find them. Of course, you gotta be a little nuts to believe that."

"And a little nuts to print it," Logan said, gleefully holding up a copy of last week's paper with the big picture of Sassy/Sugar on the front. "So, what are you going to do now, Martin?"

"Cops promised they'd come by tomorrow, get my dog for me."

"And Action News will be there! This is Logan Bedford, reporting live from Silver Lake. Back to you, Beverly."

We were all roaring now, Gloria laughing so hard that tears rolled down her cheeks. This was bad for the paper. It damaged our credibility. It made us look ridiculous. But we were so giddy with drink and wacky newspaper stories that tonight a hockey game would have struck us as hilarious.

We were still giggling five minutes later when Hardcastle slid down from the bar stool where he'd been drinking alone and stomped over to our table. By his expression, it was apparent that at least someone was able to appreciate the gravity of the situation.

"Did you set me up, Mulligan?" he said. Thanks to the evening's diet of boilermakers, his lazy drawl was even lazier. "Did you?"

That made all of us at the table laugh louder. We laughed so hard that a half dozen firemen sitting three tables away joined in, even though they had no idea what they were laughing at.

I could have saved Hardcastle from himself, but I didn't because he was such a jerk. I was going to have to live with that for a long time. That's what I thought. What I said was, "Hardcastle, maybe you should have waited for the doggy DNA."

"Fuck you," he said, provoking more peals of laughter.

"Well," Gloria said as Hardcastle stalked off, "no call for any more newspaper horror stories. We have a winner."

"Not so fast," I said. "My turn."

"No way you can top Sassy," Veronica said.

"It's Sugar," Abbruzzi said, and Gloria laughed so hard that she tipped over her Bud.

"Back in the eighties," I said as a waitress mopped up the spill with a bar rag, "the paper used to crown a Rhode Island Mother of the Year. Winner got a nice write-up in the 'Living' section and a free six-month subscription to the paper. Hundreds of readers would write in to tell us why their mothers were worthy of the honor. The reporter who dreamed up the idea would read each heartfelt letter, choose the best one, interview the letter writer and his mom, and write it up for the Mother's Day paper. In 1989, I think it was, the city editor got a call the day we announced the winner: 'Did you know that four of her sons are in prison?'"

The table erupted again. This time, it was Abbruzzi's Amstel Light that went airborne.

"Nice try," Veronica said, when it quieted down. "But the dog story can't be beat."

"You haven't heard the rest of it," I said. "Guess who wrote the Mother's Day story?"

"Hardcastle?"

"That's right."

"Oh, no, he didn't!"

"Oh, yes, he did."

With that, I got up, gave Veronica a good-bye kiss, and headed for Secretariat.

21

I prowled the Mount Hope neighborhood again that night, looking for Mr. Rapture but harboring no hope of actually finding him. Around midnight, with a Cuban between my lips and Tommy Castro's *No Foolin'* album in the CD player, I swung the Bronco onto Doyle Avenue, and there he was. Mr. Rapture, his hands in the pockets of that black leather jacket from the photographs, was striding purposefully down the sidewalk. I rolled to a stop a few yards ahead of him, got out, climbed over the snowbanked curb, and watched him close the distance between us.

"How ya doing?" I said. "Can I talk to you a minute?"

He studied me for a heartbeat. Then his eyes got big. He spun on his heels and took off. I set out to run him down.

He was ten yards ahead as we raced down the sidewalk past Zerilli's Market, our shoes crunching in the inch of fresh snow covering a month's worth of bad Rhode Island February. I'd been chasing him for less than a minute, and already I was regretting all those cigars and those missed Saturday mornings at the gym. My right thigh was beginning to cramp, there was a stitch in my side, and my heart was a runaway drum.

"Wait!" I called to him. "I just want to talk!"

At the end of the block he cut right and slipped, his arms flying out for balance, his fingers clawing at the frigid air. I was almost on him now, close enough to reach for the collar of his black leather jacket. Then my right shoe landed where he'd slipped, and I went down hard, cracking my left elbow on jagged ice that a snowplow had thrown up from the street.

Pain shot from elbow to shoulder now as I scrambled to my feet and saw him running hard down the middle of the deserted street. I set out once more to chase him down. He ran well for a small man, but my stride was longer. My thigh was cramping badly in the cold, but I fought through it as the distance between us slowly closed.

Fifteen yards.

Ten yards.

Five.

And when I caught him, I was going to do what? Knock him down? Beat him up? Not the sort of interviewing technique I'd learned in Brother Fry's journalism class. And what if he was carrying something? A knife, maybe. Or a gun. If I was right about him, he was already a killer several times over.

I thought about that for an instant, then flashed on the bodies of the twins being loaded into the ambulance. I sucked in a breath, lunged for him, and my feet flew out from under me. I landed hard, face-first, and skidded to a stop. As I raised my face from the ice, he threw me a look over his left shoulder, and I thought I heard him laugh.

Mr. Rapture sprinted to the corner, turned right, slowed to a jog, and was gone.

I was surprised how far we'd run; it was an eight-block limp back to the Bronco. Someone had broken into it and yanked out the CD player. I rummaged in the backseat with my one good arm, found an old T-shirt, and used it to sop up the blood flowing from my nose.

In the morning, my elbow was black and swollen and my nose knew exactly how it felt.

I'd been injured before. I broke my nose three times and my left wrist twice. Errant elbows had opened gashes over both eyes.

I cracked bones in three fingers, and one of them was still crooked. A half-moon surgical scar tattooed my right knee. But the damage was all done on the basketball court. Since when was journalism a contact sport?

I spent two hours reading last year's *Time* magazines in the waiting room of the Rhode Island Hospital emergency department and another hour waiting for an intern to read my X-rays before learning that the only thing broken this time was my pride.

It was early afternoon before I finally got to work, arriving just in time to see a copyboy deposit the day's keg of press releases on Hardcastle's desk. As I walked toward mine, a half dozen people stopped me to ask about my nose.

"Slipped on the ice," I said, which was more or less the truth.

I jerked open my file drawer, drew out the envelope of spectator pictures, and fanned them across my desk. Mr. Rapture stood transfixed in six of them, mocking me. I stared at the pictures for a long time.

I was still at it when Edward Anthony Mason IV walked in. I had to look twice to be sure it was him. He'd gone off to Columbia University Journalism School in a Hugo Boss suit, but now he was back, striding across the newsroom in a wrinkled ankle-length trench coat, a brown felt fedora perched on the back on his head the way Clark Gable wore it in *It Happened One Night.* Yup, it was a Gable getup, all right, complete with cigarette tucked behind the right ear. Maybe he'd seen the movie and thought that was the way real reporters looked.

Mason was old money, the scion of six inbred Yankee families that ran the state for more than two hundred years until the Irish and Italians showed up and took it away from them. Judging by the sour expressions that were always plastered on their faces, they were still mad about it. The families had secured their fortunes by running slaves from the Guinea Coast to the southern colonies and by operating the Blackstone Valley textile mills that spun King Cotton into cloth. But the good times were long gone now, and the newspaper was one of the few institutions left to them.

They'd owned it since the Civil War. For a century it had been an archconservative mouthpiece, spewing nativist propaganda and portraying every human achievement from women's suffrage to Social Security as a slippery slope toward socialism. Somewhere around World War II, the six families mellowed, shedding their crude mill-baron manners and adopting the paternalistic posture of socially superior public benefactors. Since then they had run the paper as a public trust, sacrificing millions in profits to the cause of informing the electorate and educating the masses. They were the sort that would spend an extra million a year on newsprint for the good of the paper and then bridle at buying business cards for reporters. The Newspaper Guild local had been without a contract for the last five years, the families choking at the thought of a 3 percent raise and dental insurance.

Now a new generation was rising, a generation of summer-in-Newport, winter-in-Aspen wastrels who dabbled in the market and squandered their trust funds at the Foxwoods baccarat tables. Young Mason was the only one among them who gave a shit about the paper. It was natural, then, that his elders were grooming him to run it. After wasting twenty grand of daddy's money at Columbia J-School—a hidebound bastion of fuddy-duddies that prepares the young to put out a newspaper that's fifty years out of date—he had returned to begin his apprenticeship for the job that was his by birthright.

All eyes were on the kid as he crossed the newsroom and slipped into the managing editor's office. I turned back to the photographs and stared at them some more. Mr. Rapture had to be stopped, and my nose and elbow were telling me that I wasn't up to the job.

I needed help.

22

"It's Mulligan. I've got something that might inter—est you."

"I've got something for you too. My size-twelve up your ass."

"Second time in a week somebody said that to me."

"Doesn't surprise me any," Polecki said, and slammed down the receiver.

Screw him, I thought. Then I thought about it some more. I thought about the dead twins. I thought about the two scorched corpses pulled from the rooming-house fire. I thought about the DePrisco kids who didn't have a daddy anymore. I thought about Rosie and her crew out there risking their lives night after night. I picked up the phone and called him back.

"You really should see what I've got."

"Why don't you try Roselli? He only wears a size nine."

"Look, I'm offering you some useful information here. You want it or not?"

"How useful?"

"Might make you a hero. Make everybody forget that 'Dumb and Dumber' story."

"Everybody but me, maybe. I plan on holding a grudge."

"Look," I said, "I think I know who's setting the Mount Hope fires. Thought maybe you might want his picture."

He was quiet for a moment, then said, "Seriously?"

"Yup."

"Okay, asshole. Come on over. I'll hold my nose and look at what you got."

"Not there," I said. "Some place we won't be recognized."

"The McDonald's on Fountain Street in fifteen minutes."

"People from the paper get coffee there."

"Central Lunch on Weybosset, then."

"City editor's sister runs the place."

"Okay, Mulligan, how about this. There's a titty bar called Good Time Charlie's near the Sax chicken-and-ribs place on Broad."

"Just up from the YMCA?"

"Yeah. Got any pervert friends that hang out there?"

"I think that'll work," I said, and hung up.

I swung Secretariat around the newspaper building, crossed over the interstate to the Italian tenement district, bounced four blocks south on what passes for roads in Rhode Island, and parked on Broad at the edge of the hood, where sixteen-year-old daytime hookers in hot pants competed for sidewalk space with used condoms and smashed forty-ounce Colt 45 empties.

The joint was dark except for a small floodlit stage where a skinny black girl writhed like a freshly killed snake. The small afternoon crowd sat up close, glassy-eyed and clutching sweating cans of beer. Polecki was already there, squeezed into a dark booth in back. I slid in across from him. A waitress, snapped into a body stocking so transparent I could almost see behind her, materialized to take our orders.

"Hey, Mulligan!" she said. "What's shakin'?"

Polecki looked at me and made a face.

I'd been wondering what had happened to Marie after she quit waiting tables at Hopes. I also used to wonder what she looked like naked. Two mysteries solved already, and it was only two thirty.

We sat silently until Marie returned with my club soda and Polecki's can of Narragansett, a local favorite named in honor of a Rhode Island Indian tribe butchered by our God-fearing colonial ancestors. Marie gave me fifteen back from my twenty and hooked a finger in the red garter on her right thigh. I slid in a dollar, and she winked and went away.

"So," Polecki said. "Which one am I supposed to be?"

"Huh?"

"Am I Dumb or Dumber?"

"Does it matter?"

"Might be the difference between one broken arm or two."

I stared at him over the top of my glass for a long moment.

"Look," I said. "You're never going to invite me to share a box of Kentucky Fried, and I'm never going to invite you to share a box at Fenway Park. But people in the old neighborhood are getting burned to death, and I'm betting that bothers you as much as it does me."

"More," he said.

"So I'm going to show you some photographs," I said. "And then you're going to give them back to me, and we're going to talk about what to do next."

"Okay."

I pulled a manila envelope out of my jacket, drew out the crowd pictures with Mr. Rapture's face circled in red, and fanned them across the table. He picked them up one at a time and studied them in the dim blue bar light. When he was done, I gathered them up, slid them back in the envelope, and stuck it back inside my jacket.

"So, who is he?" he said.

"Don't know. Been calling him Mr. Rapture."

"Because of that look," he said.

"Yeah, because of that look."

"Anything else make you think this is our guy?"

"Found him walking on Doyle last night. When I tried to talk to him, he ran."

"Couldn't catch him, big lanky guy like you?"

"Nearly did, but I slipped and fell."

"That how you got that nose?"

"Yeah."

"Broken?"

"No."

"Too bad."

He flagged Marie down, and we sat quietly as she fetched him another beer. Who says cops can't drink on the job?

"Well," he said, "what you got isn't much. Doesn't prove a damn thing. But it *is* a lead, and we don't have many. What do I have to do to get my hands on those pictures?"

I pulled the envelope back out of my jacket, slid out the best picture of Mr. Rapture, and laid it on the table between us. I kept my hand on it and looked at him hard.

"I'm going to give you just this one," I said, "but there is a condition."

"I'm listening."

"You didn't get it from me, and we never had this conversation."

"Figured it was something like that."

"Deal?"

"Deal."

Polecki drained his beer, picked up the picture, and hauled himself to his feet.

"Hold on a minute. You don't have many? Is that what you said?"

"Huh?"

"Leads, Polecki. You said you don't have many. That means you must have some, right?"

He sat back down and said, "Why should I tell you?"

"I gave you something. Your turn to give me something."

"This ain't *Let's Make a Deal*, asshole."

"Look at it this way. If Mr. Rapture turns out to be the guy, I just cracked the case for you. But until we know, I'm going to keep digging, and some of the people who talk to me aren't ever gonna talk to you."

He stared hard at me for a minute.

"If you learn something you'll call me?"

"Called you today, didn't I?"

He sat silently for a moment, fiddling with the gold wedding band he still wore. Maybe because he still loved her. Maybe because the extra pounds he'd packed on made it impossible to get it off.

"Off the record?" he said.

"Absolutely."

" 'Cause I don't wanna be reading this in the fuckin' paper."

"You won't be."

"Okay, Mulligan. We're lookin' at a retired fireman, an old fart who has nothing better to do than hang around the Mount Hope Firehouse every afternoon and get in everybody's way. Likes to show up at fires and hand out coffee to the crew."

Oh, shit. That sounded like Jack.

"Anything solid makes you thing it's him?"

"Nothing yet, but his alibi sucks. Claims he's home alone every night watching cop shows and FOXNews. 'Stead of being helpful and answering our questions, he got all indignant when we braced him. Roselli's got a hunch this is our guy. Me, I'm not so sure. But he *does* seem the type."

"How's that?"

"Lives alone. Something of a loser. Spent thirty years in the department and never got a promotion. And somebody who used to put out fires would know how to set them."

"You think an ex-*fireman* would do this?"

"You got any idea how many arsonists turn out to be firemen or former firemen?

"How many?"

"I don't know, but it's a lot. Some of 'em do it because they get to be heroes when they put the fires out. Some do it because they love fighting fires with their buddies. Some of them are probably just fuckin' nuts."

"So what's this guy's name?"

"Uh-uh. You're not getting that from me. With what I gave you, you can figure it out for yourself."

Polecki hauled himself to his feet again, Marie calling "Come back and see us" as he headed out. I sat alone for a few minutes, then walked to the door, pushed it open, and studied the street.

It wasn't being seen coming out of Good Time Charlie's that worried me; it was being seen with Polecki. By giving him the picture of Mr. Rapture, I'd strayed way over the line. Reporters don't feed info to cops. Some of us go to jail for contempt rather than answer subpoenas. We have to be loners to do our jobs right. Guys like Zerilli would never talk to us if we smelled like rats.

I'd given Polecki more than a photo. I'd handed the better half of Dumb and Dumber something he could hold over me if he had enough functioning brain cells to recognize it. If he ever told Lomax what I'd done, I'd have to find myself a tin cup and stock up on pencils. But I'd rather be unemployable than have another innocent victim on my conscience.

23

At the Mount Hope firehouse, I asked for Rosie and learned she'd left for the day. In the mess room, a half dozen fire-fighters were sitting on mismatched chairs at a yellow Formica table, watching Lieutenant Ronan McCoun slide a pan of lasagna out of the oven.

"Jack Centofanti around?" All that got me was angry stares.

I looked at McCoun and raised an eyebrow.

"The old goat's not here," he said. "We told him he ain't welcome here no more."

I got back in the Bronco, drove to Camp Street, and parked in front of number 53, a grotesque Victorian that had been built as a single-family home more than a hundred years ago. Now, twelve door-bells pocked the front door jamb. They didn't work, but it didn't matter. I gave the door a push, it groaned open, and I stepped into a hallway littered with cigarette butts and junk mail.

I climbed the stairs, careful not to trip on the loose rubber treads or put any weight on the rickety banister. Jack's place was on the second floor at the end of a dimly lit hallway. The brass numbers on the heavy maple door said 23, with the 3 coming loose and hanging upside down. I raised my hand and knocked.

"It's open."

I turned the knob and found Jack sitting in a stuffed armchair, his bare feet on a matching hassock and a tumbler in his hand.

Beside the chair, a half-empty bottle of Jim Beam rested on a mahogany piecrust table. The room lights were off, and the last light
of a dying day seeped feebly through half-closed Venetian blinds.
The glow from the tabletop TV, tuned to FOXNews with the sound
all the way down, was washing Jack's face blue. I snapped the switch
by the door, the ceiling light came on, and he squinted from the
shock of it, raising his left hand to cover his eyes. Now I could
see that he'd placed the bottle on a crocheted doily to protect the
tabletop.

"Liam? *Madonna*, it's good to see you, boy."

"Good to see you too, Jack." He, Rosie, and my relatives were
the only people allowed to call me Liam.

"Sit. Sit. My place is your place."

As I settled into a matching chair across from him, I noticed
he hadn't shaved in a few days.

"You wanna drink, right?"

"Love one."

He got up and limped into the kitchen, the belt from his terry-
cloth robe dragging on the floor behind him. I heard water run in
the sink. He returned with a wet tumbler in his hand, thrust it at me,
sat back down, and passed the bottle.

"So how ya been?"

"I'm fine, Jack."

"Your beautiful sister? She good?"

"Meg's great. Teaching school in Nashua. Got her own house
in the suburbs. Got married last summer to a nice girl from New
Haven."

"*Merda!*" He stared at me a moment, then snorted. "Well, if
that's your idea of great, then I guess it's okay with me too. What
about Aidan? You two still not talking?"

"I'm talking. He's not."

"Must make it hard to have a conversation."

"It does."

"I never did like Dorcas."

"I know."

"*Pazza stronza.* A real *rompinalle.*"

Crazy bitch. A real ball-breaker. The closest Jack had ever been to Italy was the three-cheese-and-meatball pizza at Casserta's, but he'd mastered the art of cursing in Italian.

"I'll never understand what the two of you saw in her, Liam. I told Aidan when she married you that he was the lucky one."

"Turns out you were right."

"Yeah. You'd think he would have figured that out by now."

"He probably has, but we Mulligans know how to hold a grudge."

Jack laughed. "Man, I could tell you some stories. One time, out at the Shad Factory, I pulled in a dozen beauties. But your papa? He couldn't catch a thing. I busted his balls about it on the drive home, and he got so *incazzato* he wouldn't speak to me for six months. Over a little thing like that."

Jack's tumbler was empty now. I passed him the bottle, and he refilled his glass. Then he carefully put the bottle down on the doily. That's when I noticed the framed photo propped beside it on the table. I got out of my chair and picked it up. Jack and my father, wearing their waders, standing on the shore of Shad Factory Pond holding long strings of fish. I felt a twinge of guilt for not keeping more in touch with my father's best friend.

"He was a stubborn mick, your papa, but I miss him."

"So do I."

He sighed and took a swig from his glass. *"Famiglia. Famiglia."*

Jack never married. The Mulligans were the nearest thing to family he had, once his parents died, and that was a long time ago. I returned the photo to the table and eased back into my chair.

"So what's up with you, Jack?"

"Still got my health, so I can't complain."

"I stopped at the firehouse on my way over. Thought you might be there."

"Nah. I gave enough of my life in that place. I don't hang out there anymore."

I just looked at him for a moment.

"Want to talk about it, Jack?"

"Ah, shit. I guess you heard."

"I did, but I'd like to hear it from you."

"The fellas at the firehouse? Great guys, each and every one. Give ya the shirt off their backs and the pants too if ya needed them. And the girl? That Rosie? I had my doubts when they made her captain. Weren't no women firefighters in my day, that's for damned sure. But she's a real pisser. I don't blame any of them none."

"But?"

"But those two arson cops, Polecki and Roselli? They come waltzing into the firehouse last Monday afternoon, asking me fuckin' questions in front of everybody. Then started in with the fellas. Asked 'em why I was always hangin' around. If they knew where I was when the fires started. If they ever saw me doing anything suspicious. Put it in their heads that I was a suspect. Me. A fireman for thirty years. The fuckers."

"What'd you tell 'em?"

"I told 'em, *'Vaffanculo!'* Next thing you know, they're knockin' on my neighbors' doors asking more questions. Now everybody's lookin' at me funny, and nobody even says hello when I tip my hat."

"Tell me where you were when the fires started, and maybe I can get them off your back."

"I was right here. Alone. Watching my shows just like every night. So unless Bill O'Reilly can see me through the TV, I ain't got no alibi."

"What about the fire in the rooming house? That one was in the afternoon."

"I was at the firehouse. That's what I told those two *cogliones*. But they asked the fellas, and none of 'em could remember if I was there the whole time or maybe ducked out for a while."

"Okay, Jack. Here's what I want you to do. I want you to get out of that chair and go fishing."

"It ain't fishin' season."

"It is somewhere. Alaska, maybe? Florida? Pack up your gear, get on a plane, and don't tell anyone where you're going. Hold on to your airline and hotel receipts, and the next time there's a fire, you'll have your alibi. I'll call your cell and let you know when it's okay to come back."

"Hell, Liam. I ain't got that kinda money."

"It's on me."

"Can't let you do that."

"Sure you can."

"No, Liam. I can't." His voice was stern now, letting me know he meant it.

I sighed, crossed my arms, and thought for a minute. Then I slipped two Cubans out of my pocket and offered him one.

"No thanks," he said, "but you go ahead."

I clipped the tip with my cigar cutter, fired it up, leaned back in the chair, and blew a couple of smoke rings.

"Look, Jack," I said. "They're probably going to question you again. If they do, don't say anything. If they ask you to go with them to the station, ask if you are under arrest. If they say no, don't go with them. If they say yes, ask for a lawyer, and don't say a word until he shows up. You can do that for me, right?"

"Yeah. I can do that."

"And don't tell Polecki and Roselli I told you not to talk, okay?"

"Got it."

"This won't last forever, Jack. One of these days, the arsonist will make a mistake. He'll get caught. And you'll have your life back."

"I hope you're right, boy."

I smoked some more, he drank some more, and we reminisced some more about my father. When the cigar burned down to the ring, I dropped it into the tumbler and got up to leave. Jack rose to see me to the door.

"Wish your dad was around to talk to," he said. "I can't tell you how this feels, the neighbors lookin' at me the way they do."

As I stepped into the hall, he snapped off the light and pulled the door closed. I trudged down the stairs, picturing him alone in the dark, drinking from his tumbler of whiskey.

24

That evening, when the cops came for Sassy/ Sugar, Ralph and Gladys Fleming barricaded themselves inside their little house.

Guns drawn, the cops tried to negotiate with them through a megaphone. When that didn't work, they lugged a battering ram to the front door. As they swung it, they slipped on the icy stoop and toppled onto the crusted snow, giving Logan some great footage for the six o'clock news. The cops scrambled to their feet, picked up the ram, and were about to swing it again when Martin Lippitt, the dog's presumed rightful owner, pointed out that they were being ridiculous. For a while, a dozen cops stood around looking sheepish. Then they jumped into their prowl cars and drove off.

Logan ended his report with the news that Channel 10 had stepped in to settle the dispute. X-rays of the dog's legs and an examination of the pads on its feet could determine conclusively whether Sassy/Sugar had crossed the country or only crossed the street. Tufts University's Cummings School of Veterinary Medicine in Grafton, Massachusetts, would do the examination, Channel 10 would foot the bill, and Lippitt and the Flemings had agreed to abide by the result.

"You know," I said as the TV over the bar broke for commercial, "it's a sad commentary that an idiot like Logan has more sense than the Providence Police Department."

"Wouldn't it be easier for somebody to get in touch with those people out in Oregon and see if they still have the dog?" Veronica said.

Edna Stinson told me a week ago that Sassy had been dismembered by a logging truck, but it was a little late to be bringing that up. So what I said was, "Hardcastle tried, but the Stinsons took off for their annual fishing trip to British Columbia and aren't expected back for a month."

Veronica fished a pack of Virginia Slims from her purse and put one between her lips. I leaned over with the Colibri and gave her a light. She took a puff, then thought better of it and ground the cigarette out in the ashtray.

"Can't smoke at work anymore," she said, "so this is a good time to quit."

I was craving another Cuban, but this seemed like a bad time to fire one up.

Veronica rose from her chair, fed quarters into the jukebox, and punched up some slow songs. When the Garth Brooks cover of Dylan's "To Make You Feel My Love" came on, we got up and danced a little in a cramped space between the tables, our shoes making scraping sounds on the gritty wooden floor. I loved the way her body fit against mine. Then we walked out of Hopes hand in hand into the first clear night in a month.

A bright moon floated over city hall. We stood on the sidewalk and kissed. It was still early, but we agreed we'd both had too many late nights lately. We got into our separate cars and drove to our separate apartments.

25

After bedding Secretariat down for the evening, I climbed the narrow flight of stairs to my place, where Veronica's toothbrush still sat reassuringly in the porcelain fixture.

I tuned the TV to a *Law & Order* rerun and started reading a U.S. government publication titled *21st Century Guide to the U.S. Bureau of Alcohol, Tobacco, and Firearms (ATF): Includes Arson and Explosives, Bomb Threat and Detection, Bomb Task Force, Ballistics Technology to Solve Crimes, Commerce in Firearms, Brady Law, Gang Resistance Education and Training, Special Agent Recruiting, Safety Info, Laws, Regulations, and Manuals, Field Divisions, Laboratories, Forms, ATF Bulletins, Church Arson Task Force (Core Federal Information Series).*

Clint Eastwood owns the movie rights.

I must have dozed off, because the rap on the door startled me. Half asleep, I padded barefoot across the cold linoleum, turned the dead bolt, and found Sharon Stone wiping her white vinyl boots on my straw welcome mat. That was odd. I wasn't expecting anyone from Hollywood. The only person I knew who'd even *been* to Hollywood was a Rhode Island–born comedian named Ruth Buzzi, and she hadn't been heard from since *Laugh-In* was canceled.

"Well?" said Sharon Stone. "Aren't you going to invite me in?"

"Excuse my manners, Gloria," I said as synapses fired and a

handful of brain cells clicked on. "If I knew it was you, I would have put on a shirt."

"Nice pecs," she said as she stepped across the threshold.

Yes, indeed, I thought. She was wearing a white cable-knit sweater that showed the swell of her breasts while concealing that pudgy waist. Two Nikons, one with a wide-angle lens and the other with a telephoto, hung from her neck, the black leather straps digging into her cleavage. She looked around for someplace to hang the green parka that was slung over her right shoulder. Seeing nothing, she let it drop to the floor.

I offered her something to drink, but she declined both Veronica's leftover Russian River and my Maalox. We were sitting now on the edge of my bed, me in an old Pedro Martínez Red Sox jersey I'd shrugged on despite her insistence that I not go to the trouble. Sam Waterston and an anorexic starlet who looked nothing like any assistant district attorney I'd ever seen finished celebrating another triumph of the American criminal-justice system, and the Verizon "Can you hear me now?" guy, who pissed me off every time I looked at him, opened his mouth to sell me phone service. I couldn't reach him with a left hook, so I shut him up with the remote.

"So," she said. "That how you plan to spend the evening? Watching actors pretend to solve crimes? Or do you want to hit the streets again and try to solve a real one?"

"Meaning?"

"Meaning I hear you've been prowling around Mount Hope at night," she said.

"Where'd you hear that?"

"A cop I know."

"Yeah, I blew a few nights cruising around because I couldn't think of anything else to do. But it's a waste of time, Gloria. I'm not doing that anymore."

"It's not a waste of time," she said. "You might get lucky. I already did once."

"How's that?"

"Night of the rooming-house fire, I was the one who pulled the alarm. I shot forty frames before the first fire truck got to the scene."

"I thought you said you ran into it on your way home."

"I lied," she said.

Turned out she'd been haunting the neighborhood after dark almost every night for two weeks, mostly driving, sometimes parking her Ford Focus on the street and getting out to stretch her legs. That figure I'd seen my first night out, the one carrying something that might have been a camera? Chances are it was Gloria.

"So you got lucky once," I said. "It's not likely to happen again."

"A photographer makes her own luck. Those fire pictures? They got me out of the lab. I start as a full-time shooter next week."

"That's great, Gloria. It's long overdue. But I don't much like the idea of you prowling around alone at night."

"So come with me," she said. "That's why I came by, to invite you to keep me company."

"How about we just stay here and watch Craig Ferguson?"

"Come on, Mulligan. It's a clear night with a big old moon. I've got a thermos full of hot coffee and Buddy Guy on the CD player. You can smoke in my car if you want. Or maybe kiss me a little. I think I might like that."

She leaned over and put her lips on mine, trying it out.

"Yes," she said, "I think that might work."

"Worked for me," I said, "but, ah . . ."

"But you're thinking Veronica might not like it."

"Uh-huh."

"You two getting serious?"

"No. I don't know. Maybe."

"Think a night with me might help you figure it out?"

It might at that. It was a perfectly logical and appealing proposition. Still, I had the feeling there might be a flaw in it somewhere. I started dressing for the cold.

I was in the bathroom with the door closed, changing into some warm pants, when the phone rang.

"Mind getting that for me, Gloria?" I said, but I should have known better.

I heard her say "Hello," and then she got very quiet. I zipped up, came out quickly, and took the phone.

"You!

fucking!

bastard!"

"Hello, Dorcas."

"So. Who is she?"

"Just a colleague from the paper."

"Fucking her yet?"

"Not yet."

"Be sure to let me know when you start so I can add another count of adultery to the divorce complaint."

"Good night, Dorcas," I said, and hung up.

"The almost ex?" Gloria said.

"Uh-huh."

"You should have heard what she called me."

"Sorry about that. She's more than a little nuts."

"So I gathered."

"You know, my life's pretty complicated right now, Gloria."

"And I'd just complicate it more?"

"In a good way. But yeah, I'm afraid you would."

"Aw, damn. Well, you know where to find me if you ever get things worked out."

With that, Sharon Stone gave me a parting hug, picked her coat up off the floor, and walked out my door.

26

The managing editor's office, four glass walls in the middle of the newsroom, looked like an aquarium. More than once, I'd been tempted to seal it with a tube of silicone, fill it with water, and add tropical fish.

Through the glass, I could see Marshall Pemberton sitting behind his gleaming oak desk, his red rep tie loosened and the sleeves of his starched white shirt rolled up and ready for business. Lomax was there too, sunk in a maroon leather visitor's chair. I stepped in and collapsed into another just like it.

"You wanted to see me?" I said.

"Mulligan," Pemberton said, "we have selected you for a very important assignment."

"Thanks, but I've already got one."

Pemberton glanced at Lomax, arched an eyebrow, chose to ignore my insolence, and pressed on.

"As you may know, our publisher's son has returned from Columbia, and he is starting work today as a reporter for our online edition. He is a very serious young man with a deep and abiding interest in the newspaper business. He wants to learn from the best, so we have chosen you to be his mentor. He will accompany you on all your reporting assignments until further notice."

"Well," I said, "I am deeply humbled by this honor, but there is one small problem."

"Which is?"

"Which is that I'm hip-deep in the Mount Hope arson investigation, and I don't have the time or patience to wipe his blue-blood nose and change his too-rich-to-stink diapers."

In five seconds, Pemberton's expression raced through a half dozen emotions, from anger to exasperation. He started to say something, thought better of it, and looked to Lomax for help.

"You don't have a vote here, Mulligan," Lomax said.

"Why don't you stick his privileged ass upstairs in the 'Living' section?" I said. "That way, he won't be hanging around the newsroom, getting in my way, and telling you what to put on page one."

"Actually we considered that," Pemberton said. "However, the lad was quite insistent that he begin his career in the newsroom. He was equally insistent that he work with you. Apparently he has been reading your copy and has convinced himself that you are the best we have. I tried to persuade him that this is not the case, but to no avail. Frankly, Mulligan, you are the last person I would have chosen for this. You are something of a dinosaur when it comes to new media, and I'm well aware of your irreverent attitude toward the owners of this newspaper. But the decision is out of my hands."

"Jesus Christ!" I said, but it was out of His hands, too.

"We're all going to be working for the kid someday, Mulligan," Lomax said. "Show him some fucking respect."

I returned to my cubicle to find Edward Anthony Mason IV perched on the corner of my desk, looking now like he'd just stepped off a page of *The Great Gatsby*—narrow cover-girl waist, long legs encased in expensive black slacks, a blue silk tie that cost more than my entire wardrobe. He removed the Clark Gable fedora, exposing a head full of light-brown curls.

He said, "Hi."

And I said, "Get lost."

"Bad time?"

"Yeah. Why don't you go play polo and come back in thirty years?"

"Did I do something to offend you?"

"I'd be offended by anybody who hasn't learned to write a lead yet and already thinks he's going to be running the paper. Maybe you want to get in on the office pool. Pick the date that Daddy steps up to chairman of the board and makes his baby boy publisher. Me? I got fifty bucks on never."

"Really?"

"Really."

"Because?"

"Because newspapers are a dying business, kid. Readers are deserting us. Craigslist and eBay have stripped us of most of our classified advertising. And none of that is ever coming back."

"We're just in a transition period," Mason said.

"Is that what they taught you at Columbia? Look around, for Chrissake. Papers everywhere are slashing expenses—closing Washington bureaus, cutting the number of pages they print, laying off journalists by the hundreds. And still they're hemorrhaging money. The Knight Ridder chain has already thrown in the towel. The Tribune Company looks like it's on its last legs. The *Rocky Mountain News,* the *Seattle Post-Intelligencer,* and the *San Francisco Chronicle* are teetering on the edge of collapse. If you think it's not going to happen here too, you're kidding yourself. The scuttlebutt around the newsroom says we lost two or three million last year."

"More," Mason said.

"Aw, shit. Really?"

"Yeah."

"How much more?"

"I'm not permitted to say."

"So I guess layoffs are coming, huh?"

"Father and I will do everything in our power to prevent that."

"Unless you can go back in time and get Al Gore to un-invent the Internet, there's not much you can do about it," I said. "Newspapers are circling the drain, kid. By the time you're ready to take over, there won't be anything left to run."

Mason was about to respond when Pemberton strolled up.

"I see you two are getting acquainted," he said, his light tone clashing with the worried look etched on his face. "Mulligan treating you right so far, Edward?"

"I was just inquiring how he got that great 'Dumb and Dumber' quote, Mr. Pemberton. And he chewed me out for even asking. Said a reporter never reveals his confidential sources. I've got a lot to learn, and Mr. Mulligan is the best mentor I could have. Next to him, the profs at Columbia are a bunch of posers. I want to thank you again for letting me work with him."

"You're very welcome, Edward. Any questions? Anything you need?"

"Not right now, Mr. Pemberton."

"Well, if there is, my door is always open."

Hasn't always been open to me, I thought, and was about to say so when Pemberton clapped Mason on the back and scurried off with that concerned look still on his face.

"Okay, kid," I said. "Let's go play reporter." A few nights cruising rat-infested streets, a meeting or two with sources in a hole like Good Time Charlie's, a couple of early mornings standing knee-deep in slush, and he'd lose his taste for the real thing soon enough.

27

A light snow was falling as we stepped out onto Fountain Street.

"So where are we going?" Mason said.

"You'll know when we get there."

"Okay if I drive?"

"Sure."

He led us a few yards down the street, pulled a remote from his pocket, and snicked open the lock to an opalescent silver-blue 1967 Jaguar E-Series coupe parked at a meter.

"Like this car?" I said.

"Sure do."

"Then we better take mine."

As we settled into the Bronco, he eyed the wires snaking from the slot where the CD player used to be.

"Leave the Jag in Newport," I said. "Get yourself a used Chevy or Ford to drive on the job. And if you ever have to park the Jag in Providence again, put it in a parking garage, lock it, remove the wheels, and take them with you."

"Got it, Mister Mulligan."

"And drop the 'Mister.'"

"I don't know your first name. Just your byline, 'L. S. A. Mulligan.'"

"Tell you what," I said. "You call me Mulligan, and I'll call you Thanks-Dad."

"I prefer Edward."

The drive to Zerilli's Market took us past two burned-out buildings. Crews from Dio Construction were busy knocking them down and loading the debris into dump trucks. I backed into a parking space right in front of the market and told the kid to stay in the car.

"How come?" he said.

"Remember that 'lesson' about confidential sources? That's why."

"Back already?" Zerilli said. "Jesus! How many Cubans can one scribbler smoke?"

"Only burned four sticks from the last box, Whoosh. Just wanted to drop by, see how you're doing."

"The Colibri working okay?"

"Hotter than Ramirez on a hitting streak, reliable as Lowell's glove at the hot corner. Which reminds me. What odds you giving on them going all the way again?"

"This week, nine to two. Gonna throw money away on 'em, oughta do it now. Word is Colón's shoulder may be okay. I hear his fastball's hitting ninety-five on the radar gun. If he's healthy, the odds will fall to four to one. Sucker bet either way, cause no way they're gonna repeat. Only two teams have done that in the last thirty years."

He tapped the ash from his Lucky and scratched his balls through his white boxers.

"Put me down for a Franklin," I said.

He threw me a disgusted look, pulled the nub of a pencil from behind his ear, and made a note, then rubbed a bruise on his right wrist.

"From the handcuffs?" I asked.

"Yeah. Put 'em on tight as a bastard, the fuckin' pricks."

"How long did they hold you?"

"Overnight. Spent half of it on a metal chair that hurt my back somethin' wicked, getting threatened by two detectives and a snot-nosed junior prosecutor who kept sayin' he'd throw the book at me on the DiMaggios' assault case 'less I rolled on Grasso. Like I'm gonna do that, the fuckin' morons. Jesus!"

"Grasso send his lawyer over to get you out?"

"Yeah. Brady Coyle showed up about eight in the mornin' looking like he just stepped out of a can of starch. Didn't need 'em, it turned out."

"How's that?"

"Just after the sun come up they led me out of the holding cell, took me up to the chief's office. Chief took the cuffs off himself, shook my hand, apologized all over the place. Set me down on one of his leather chairs, gave me coffee and a Danish. Then apologized some more. Kept callin' it a misunderstanding. Hoped I wouldn't hold it against him."

"What the hell?" I said.

And he said, "Who's the asshole in the hat?"

We were both looking at him now through the window over the grocery aisles, skinny guy in a fedora and a trench coat picking up a soft-porn mag, grimacing, and placing it back on the rack.

"He's with me," I said. "I told him to stay in the car, but he's not used to taking orders."

"Long as he doesn't try comin' up here."

"He does that," I said, "and I'll shoot him myself."

"So I was eating a Danish," he said, picking up the story, "when those two retards, Polecki and Roselli, come waltzin' in. Chief introduces them, real formal, like I don't already know the pricks."

"What did *they* want?"

"The four of 'em—the two retards, the snot-nosed prosecutor, and the chief—pull up chairs, sit in a half-circle around me. Show me a fuckin' picture—young chink in a black leather jacket watching one of the fires. The one where DePrisco got burned up, I think. Terrible thing. I put a collection can on the counter for his wife and kids."

Mason was over by the coffee stand now, pouring himself a cup of Green Mountain. He sneaked a look at Zerilli's office window, saw me staring back at him, and quickly looked away.

"Same guy that was in one of the pictures you showed me that time," Zerilli was saying. "Didn't get it from you, did they?"

"Fuck, no."

"I didn't think so."

Mason poured a second cup and grabbed some sugar packets and a couple of those little creamers.

"So then what?" I said.

"Chief said they want to talk to this guy real bad, and would I be willing to hand the picture out to the DiMaggios, ask them to be on the lookout."

"Amazing," I said.

"Yeah. One day, we're a menace to society. Next day, we're practically deputized."

"Officer Zerilli," I said.

"Fuck you, Mulligan. That ain't funny."

"So you turned him down?"

"Nah! No percentage in pissing them off. 'Sides, I want this asshole bad as they do. They give me this here stack of pictures," he said, slapping a pale, bony hand on a stack of eight-by-tens lying facedown on his keyhole desk. "Gonna hand 'em out to the boys tonight."

Mason was at the register now, paying for the coffees.

" 'Course, they asked me to make sure the boys don't rough him up, we happen to catch the asshole. I told 'em, Sure, I can do that. Then they told me to take their bats away. Citizen patrol was a great idea, they said, but arming them was askin' for trouble."

"What'd you say?"

"That I wasn't sendin' my boys out at night with nothin' to carry. Up to you, I told 'em—bats or semiautomatics."

"Good for you," I said, and got up to leave.

"Hey. Heard your CD player got ripped off the other night."

"Where'd you hear that?"

"Can't say. But if you pop over to Deegan's chop shop, he'll put one in for you free. As a favor to me. Who knows, might be the same one you lost. I told him you might be droppin' by."

I walked down the stairs, put a twenty in the collection jar, strolled over to the coffee stand, and grabbed a handful of creamers. Mason was waiting by the Bronco. He handed me a coffee, and I pried off the plastic lid, poured a quarter of it out, and dumped the creamers in.

"So what was that all about?" he said.

"It was about you not doing what you were told."

"How's the coffee? I didn't know how you take it."

"Did you hear me?"

"Yes, I did. I'm sorry, Mulligan. It won't happen again."

"And lose the stupid hat," I said.

"No, I don't think so," he said. "It's a Mallory and I rather like it. I think it makes me look older."

"Well, it doesn't."

28

The day they buried Ruggerio "the Blind Pig" Bruccola, I wore a black hoodie to the funeral. White letters splashed across the front read "Your Message in This Space."

Six hours later, I was sprawled in a fake-leather chair in some-body's idea of a classy bar on the top floor of the Biltmore. Outside the streaked plate-glass windows, the city skulked in a drizzle.

Vinnie Giordano strolled in, looked the place over, and dropped heavily into the chair across from mine. He was wearing the Provi-dence wiseguy uniform: tapered LouisBoston suit, black shirt, white silk tie, white leather belt. He flashed me his hard look, something he probably practiced in the mirror daily. It still needed work.

"Wear that to the funeral?" he asked.

I nodded.

"Lucky nobody shot you."

"I saw you there this morning, whispering in the mayor's ear," I said. "Didn't know the two of you were tight."

"We ain't. He grew up on Federal Hill, same as me and Bruc-cola and your asshole buddy Whoosh, but since he got elected he's been acting like he don't know us. I was surprised to see him there, so I was just thanking him for paying his respects."

.   .   .

The day had dawned clear and unseasonably warm. A low March sun vaporized the snow banks, conjuring a dense gray fog that drifted over the shoes of the mourners. The women's Sergio Rossi and Prada pumps, the men's Ferragamo wingtips, and my Reeboks.

To the west, the spire of Pastor's Rest Monument, the tallest in Swan Point Cemetery, floated over the fog, marking the final resting place of the city's leading nineteenth-century ministers. To the east, the gray surface of the Seekonk River crinkled like old skin. A yellow tug churned upstream with the tide.

At least one thousand mourners, a Who's Who of Rhode Island crime, politics, business, and religion, had gathered in a grassy clearing still patched with snow. All about them, an undergrowth of laurel, rhododendron, and azalea shivered in the southerly breeze. Alongside the gunmetal-steel casket with its gold-plated handles was a bonfire of funeral wreaths. Figuring an average of three hundred dollars each, it must have set the assembled back a cool hundred and fifty grand.

All the Providence city councilmen were in attendance. Enough state legislators for a quorum. Three state Supreme Court justices. And Ilario Ventola, bishop of Providence. Funny. I hadn't noticed any of them at the twins' funeral.

Brady Coyle, my teammate on the 1990 Providence College basketball team that finished 11–19, stood just behind the mayor and Giordano. At six foot six, he towered over them, bending to murmur something in Giordano's ear, the mobster another client of Coyle's thriving criminal-law practice. Whoosh was there, too, one arm draped over the widow's quaking shoulders. Near as I could tell, he was wearing pants.

Sixty yards away, a pair of state troopers steadied telephoto lenses on the roof of their black Crown Victoria. The two FBI agents and a photographer from the paper were bolder, moving in close behind the rhododendrons to snap their pictures.

I watched as Bruccola's body was lowered into the same ground that held H. P. Lovecraft, Thomas Wilson Dorr, Theodore Francis Green, and Major Sullivan Ballou. I was surprised they didn't get up and move to a better neighborhood.

But for Rhode Island's grieving criminal class, Swan Point Cemetery had been the place to be and be seen this morning. It was the social event of the season.

"We gave the old man a hell of a send-off," Giordano said.

"You did. And I won fifty bucks in the running newsroom pool on next prominent Rhode Islander to get his ticket to hell punched."

"In that case, the drinks are on you."

He flagged down a waitress and ordered Maker's Mark straight up. I ordered another club soda, and he made a face.

"Ulcer," I said.

Giordano's eyes got big as he tried to imagine life in Rhode Island without the solace of whiskey. He called the waitress back and asked her to make his a double.

"So what happens now?" I said.

"With what?"

"Succession. Arena's the obvious choice, but he's going down on that federal labor-racketeering rap. Last time there was a power vacuum in Providence, wiseguys were found stuffed in car trunks at the airport and floaters clogged the river for a year before Bruccola took over."

"Man, you're talking thirty years ago. Shit like that don't happen no more. Goombahs like Arena and Grasso and Zerilli are too old for that mess. Younger guys like me and Johnny Dio and 'Cadillac Frank,' we got business degrees from PC and Boston College. I'm a real estate developer, Johnny's in construction, Frankie sells cars. We don't shoot people no more."

"How about garroting them with piano wire or caving their heads in with lead pipes?"

"Fuck you."

"So those are the contenders, you, Dio, and Cadillac Frank?"

"Me? No way, pal. I cleared a million five from my business last year. I don't need the money, I don't need the headaches, and I don't need the heat."

A kid with a bag of newspapers shuffled in and made the rounds of the tables. Giordano tossed him some coins, glanced at the headline—POLS PAY RESPECTS TO DEAD MOB BOSS—and slapped the paper down on table.

"Jesus Christ, Mulligan. This ain't no way to make a living. How about you and me find a nice piece of land, put up some condos?"

"I promised my mother I wouldn't sell out till I'm forty," I said, "so let's talk about this again in October."

"Still not tired of life at the bottom of the heap?"

"The money sucks, but you meet a better class of people."

"Like government clerks? I hear you been at the secretary of state's office checking out the owners of the buildings that burned down in Mount Hope."

"How'd you hear about that?"

"A clerk I know. Also hear you've been snooping around the neighborhood at night."

"How'd you hear about *that*?"

"A cop I know."

He took a pull from his drink, slipped a Partagás from his jacket pocket, and snipped the end with a silver cigar cutter. The ban on smoking in public accommodations was still hung up in committee, cheating him out of an opportunity to flout it. I leaned over and gave him a light with the Colibri.

"Nice," he said. "Get that from Whoosh?"

"Could be."

He drew on the cigar and blew a cloud of fragrant blue smoke in the general direction of a frowning matron. "Tell you what, Mulligan. You did me a good turn last year, keeping my nephew's drunk-driving bust out of the paper. He's doing great, by the way, majoring in business at URI, running the campus sports book for Whoosh, clearing two grand a week. So you done a good thing there. Let me do you a favor now. Stop wasting your time in Mount Hope, and I'll toss you something better."

"Like what?"

"Manhole covers."

"Huh?"

"There's one of them big journalism prizes in it for you, Mulligan, a nice plaque you can hang on the wall of that dump on America Street. Think it over, and call me if you're interested."

Before I could ask how he knew where I lived or what the hell he was talking about, the mob lightweight hauled himself to his feet and lumbered toward the elevators. I almost felt sorry for him. It must be hard having Godfather dreams that never come true.

On the TV above the bar, Tim Wakefield chucked knuckleballs at a diluted spring-training lineup. In my mind, I could still see him trudging off the mound after giving up a walk-off home run to Aaron Fucking Boone in the 2003 ALCS. Of all the ways the Red Sox had found to lose to the Yankees over the years, that one was the most heartbreaking. Two World Series championships in the last five years had not erased the memory. All over New England, fans still grieved the loss like a death in the family.

I sipped my club soda and looked out the window. It was getting dark. The Independent Man, Rhode Island's state symbol, gleamed in his spot of golden light atop the statehouse dome. I chuckled, remembering the time they hauled the grand old statue down and lent it to the Warwick Mall to lure Christmas shoppers.

Beside the dome, the state flag, featuring an anchor and the motto Hope, drooped in the rain. If we were true to ourselves, we'd haul that sucker down and run up the Jolly Roger.

29

It was well past midnight when I heard the dead bolt snap and footfalls scrape the linoleum.

"Veronica?"

"Sorry. I was trying not to wake you."

But the grin on her face when I clicked on the bedside lamp said she wasn't all that sorry. "Had to make some last-minute adds to the latest Arena story for the city edition," she said, tossing a fresh newspaper on the bed.

I wanted to strip her naked, pull her under the covers, and cradle her in my arms. She wanted me to read what she'd written, and there would be no nude canoodling until I'd done just that.

Under her byline, another page-one exclusive, this time with verbatim grand-jury testimony from the laborers' union state president implicating Arena in an elaborate plan to embezzle three million from the union treasury. On the jump, a quote from Arena's lawyer, Brady Coyle:

Grand-jury proceedings are secret by law. Whoever is responsible for leaking this testimony to the press is in violation of federal statutes and should be prosecuted. While I can offer no proof about who is behind these leaks, they benefit the prosecution in that they tend to poison the jury pool against my innocent client. For the newspaper to print this material would be both outrageous and irresponsible.

"Guess you pissed *him* off," I said.

"Brady? Nah. He's just blowing smoke to impress his client. He's really a sweetie."

"Sweetie"? I'd heard Brady Coyle called a lot of things: Arrogant. Contemptuous. A prick. But never sweetie. I don't think I'd ever been called sweetie. I felt a twinge in my gut. Probably just the pepperoni pizza I'd recklessly wolfed at Casserta's.

"You know something, Veronica? I've been cultivating sources on both sides of the law for eighteen years, and I've never persuaded anyone to leak me grand-jury testimony. How the hell are you doing it?"

"Sorry, baby. Sharing your bed is one thing. Sharing my source is another thing altogether."

I was trying to think of a comeback when she stripped to her panties and slipped under the covers, her hip nudging my erection. Eleven more days till the test results. Sometimes eleven days is a long, long time—15,840 minutes, to be exact.

I could hear the clock ticking.

30

In the morning I found an empty space right in front of the newspaper office. A red Providence Police Department "Out of Order" hood had been tugged over the head of the meter. Free parking? Must be my lucky day.

A postal box brimming with press releases waited for me on my office chair. Apparently I'd done something to piss off Lomax again. What? No idea.

I made a show of sorting through them for a few minutes, intending to toss the whole batch, when one envelope caught my eye. It was from the Rhode Island Economic Development Council, and on it was a picture of Mr. Potato Head in his moustache-and-glasses incarnation. I couldn't resist tearing that one open. Inside was this:

MR. POTATO HEAD STATUES TO "CROP UP"
STATEWIDE TO PROMOTE TRAVEL
TO THE OCEAN STATE!

Hasbro, which makes Mr. Potato Head right here in Little Rhody, is teaming up with the Rhode Island Economic Development Council to promote the state as an ideal location for a family vacation! The promotion will include full-color ads in national magazines, a toll-free number to call for a free Family Fun Vacation Kit, and a bumper crop of six-foot-tall Mr. Potato

Head statues that will sprout up at visitor attractions all over the state. Keep your eyes peeled! We anticipate increased excitement as each new Mr. Potato Head statue is unveiled.

The promotion, the state's economic development director concluded, was "not half baked!" Oh, really? I banged out four hundred words, along with a table listing the locations where the spuds would be "sprouting up." For Little Rhody's teen vandals, it was "news you can use."

That done, I checked my computer messages and learned why I was being spanked. Coyle had called Lomax to complain about my attire at the funeral. Said it showed a lack of respect.

Damn right.

The opening lick of "Smoke on the Water" rumbled from the jean jacket draped over the back of my chair. I pulled my cell from the inside pocket and flipped it open.

"We caught the chink," a familiar voice said. "Get your butt over here fast, and maybe you can have a few words with the asshole before the cops snatch him up."

31

I rode the elevator down to the lobby and ran smack into Thanks-Dad, arriving for work fashionably late in full *It Happened One Night* regalia.

"Where we going?" he said.

"I'm going out. You're going to your desk."

I brushed by him, banged through the front door, and sprinted across the street. A red newspaper delivery truck blasted its horn at me, its brakes squealing. I snatched the "Out of Order" hood off the meter, figuring it would come in handy, and climbed in behind the wheel. Before I could snap the lock on the passenger-side door, Mason popped it open and slid in.

No time to argue. Leaning on the horn, I ran the red at the foot of Fountain Street, roared past city hall, and sped across the Providence River. Mason's manicured fingers dug into Secretariat's armrest.

"Another fire?"

"You'll find out when we get there."

Three Providence police cruisers, blue lights slashing the storefront, were parked diagonal to the curb, blocking most of the street in front of Zerilli's. Braking to a stop, I saw a uniformed patrolman slap a beefy paw on top of Mr. Rapture's head and shove it down, bulling him into the backseat of one of the cruisers. The cops took off, sirens shrieking.

"Shit!"

I grabbed the cell, caught Veronica at her desk, and told her to find a photographer and get over to the police station, which was just a block from the paper.

"If you hurry," I said, "you can be there in time for the perp walk."

Mason threw me a puzzled look.

"Don't you want the byline?"

"Fuck it. Let Veronica have it."

I'd get a description of the arrest from Zerilli and feed it to her later, but there was no need to rush now. I pulled away from the curb, cruised north on Doyle, and pulled into a space in front of the chop shop.

"Wait in the car, Thanks-Dad."

Mike Deegan was inside, watching a worker in paint-splattered overalls spray a new black identity on a burgundy Chrysler Sebring convertible.

"Been expecting you," he said. "Toss me the keys, leave your ride out front, and come back in an hour."

I collected Mason and headed back to Zerilli's, a short, sunny walk down a cracked sidewalk. The sooty mush in the gutter was all that remained of a hard Rhode Island winter.

The brass bell over the door tinkled as I pushed it open and walked into the market with Thanks-Dad.

"Where the hell you been?" Zerilli said. "You missed the whole fuckin' show."

He was standing by the register, not quite looking like himself with his suit pants on. He snatched a blue Bic disposable, lit a Lucky, and returned the lighter to the display rack.

"Should we adjourn to your office, Whoosh?"

"Nah! Just spilled the whole story to the cops, so I don't have anything to say what your lapdog can't hear."

"My name is Edward," the lapdog said, extending his hand.

Zerilli ignored it.

"'Bout eleven o'clock this mornin'," he said, "just as the

Budweiser guy finishes stocking the cooler, I glance down from my office window, and what the fuck do I see? The chink we been lookin' for all over the fuckin' neighborhood waltzing into my store big as life."

"Do something useful," I told Mason. "Pull out your notepad and take notes."

"Couple of the DiMaggios—Gunther Hawes and Whimpy Bennett—work just up the street at Deegan's, so I ring 'em up, tell 'em to haul ass over here. Then I come out, see if I can stall him. Asshole pokes around the store, then heads to the counter with a *Penthouse* and a six-pack of Michelob. Asks the girl for a deck of Marlboros, then spies the Colibri display behind the counter, says he wants to see one. You can tell by his face he likes the feel of it in his hand—probably thinkin' about using it to burn somethin' down.

"Hawes and Bennett walk in carryin' Louisville Sluggers they grabbed off the display rack out front the fuckin' store. Asshole pays for his goods, lighter included, heads for the door, sees my boys standin' in front of it. Asshole says Excuse me, tries to push past them. Hawes gives him a little tap, and he topples over into the Cheez Doodles rack. My boys stand over him with their bats, and he gets this scared-shitless look.

"That's when he yells somethin' really fuckin' funny in his dumb-ass chink accent. He says, 'Hep! Caw duh porice!' "

Mason winced and looked up from his notepad. "He wanted you to call the police?"

"So I did," Zerilli said. "Sorry I fucked it up, Mulligan. Shoulda called you first."

"Don't worry about it, Officer Whoosh."

"Fuck you. I told you before, that ain't funny."

"Call Veronica," I told Thanks-Dad, "and read her your notes."

I took a corned-beef sandwich and an ice tea from the cooler and found a seat at a little round table under the awning out front. A few minutes later, Mason sat down across from me with a bag of chips and a Coke.

"Reach Veronica?"

"I did."

"Give her all the quotes?"

"Yeah. She asked if I had one Lomax would print, one without the words *fuck, shit,* or *asshole* in it. I told her she's going to have to paraphrase."

"Give her all the details?"

"Uh-huh."

"The part about the asshole buying the lighter?"

"Uh-huh."

"The part about the Marlboros and the *Penthouse?*"

"I didn't think that was important."

"The part about Cheez Doodles spilled all over the floor by the door?"

"Didn't think that was important either."

"You can't write a good story without details, Thanks-Dad. Call her back, and this time give her all of it."

While he was making the call, I tossed my sandwich wrapper in the barrel by the door and walked back into the store. Zerilli was bent over, scooping Cheez Doodles packages from the scuffed tile floor.

"Hey, Whoosh. How'd the asshole pay for his purchases?"

"Credit card."

"Visa? Discover? MasterCard?"

"Sheila!" Whoosh shouted to the clerk. "What kinda plastic did the asshole use?"

"Visa."

"Great." I said. "Gimme the number."

Secretariat was right where I left him in front of the chop shop. As we walked up, Deegan popped out of the garage and threw me the keys.

"You're all set," he said. "Sorry for your trouble."

As I pulled away from the curb, I pushed the play button. The opening guitar lick of Tommy Castro's "Mammer-Jammer," the first cut on the CD that was in the player when it was ripped from the dash, screeched from the speakers.

Mason's hands went to his ears. "Would you mind turning that down?"

I reached over and turned it up.

A moment later, a battle of the bands ensued as Deep Purple broke in with "Smoke on the Water." I punched the CD player off and flipped the cell open.

"You!

fucking!

bastard!"

"Sorry, Dorcas, but I don't have time to chat right now."

As my favorite philosopher, Kinky Friedman, once said, "In the sky of every love affair are little tickets to hell, falling like confetti from the stars."

I found a space in front of the welfare building just down the street from the paper and yanked the "Out of Order" hood over the head of the parking meter. I didn't see the humor in it, but Mason thought it was hilarious. Princes never fully appreciate the survival tactics of their serfs. He was still giggling like a schoolgirl three minutes later as we stepped off the elevator into the newsroom.

I was reading a computer printout of Veronica's unedited copy about the arrest when Lomax walked up. "Good they finally caught the bastard," he said.

It didn't feel right, but I just nodded.

"It's a court story now, so from here on out it belongs to Veronica. Time to get cracking on that cadaver-dogs story."

"Sure thing, boss."

I decided to keep operating on the assumption he was kidding. If the Sassy/Sugar affair hadn't soured him on doggy features, nothing ever would.

I waited till he was out of earshot before placing a call to my Aunt Ruthie in the customer-service department at Fleet Bank headquarters in Boston.

"Liam! How's my favorite nephew?"

We chatted about how her son Conor was doing, his one-year parole on a Fenway ticket-scalping bust almost up, before I told her what I needed. I'd just hung up when Mason sauntered over.

"So," he said. "What do we work on next?"

"Manhole covers."

"Pardon?"

"Manhole covers."

"What about them?"

"You're supposed to be a reporter, Thanks-Dad. Got yourself a notepad, a trench coat, a fedora, a sheepskin from a fancy journalism school. Try to figure it out. Start with the city purchasing department. See if you can come up with something worth printing."

"You're giving me an assignment?" He sounded positively giddy.

"Something like that."

"Thanks, Mulligan! I was afraid you really didn't like me."

Manhole covers. I almost laughed. That should keep his inbred ass out of my business for a while.

32

Gloria leaned in close, her blond hair caressing the side of my face as we studied the perp-walk pictures on her camera's LCD screen. We were perched on adjoining bar stools. Moisture beaded the sides of our tumblers, hers filled with draft beer and mine with club soda.

We were still in a huddle when Veronica strolled into Hopes and wrapped her arms around my neck, staking her claim. She smirked at Gloria, and Gloria smirked back. Maybe later they'd mud-wrestle. The bartender brought Veronica a chardonnay without being asked, and the two of us carried our glasses to a table with a decent view of the TV over the bar. Gloria teetered in place, wondering whether to tag along. Then she caught Veronica's eye and thought better of it.

Channel 10's operatic Action News theme heralded Logan Bedford's cliché-riddled teaser for the six o'clock report: "Our long municipal nightmare is over! Our gallant men in blue have made an arrest in the Mount Hope arson case that has terrorized our fair city. Wait till you find out how they caught him. You'll be *shocked*!"

Who the hell writes that crap?

Ernie DiGregorio spun a basketball on his index finger and invited us to join the fun at Foxwoods. Cadillac Frank made a show of kicking tires with his Ferragamos and announced "an offer you can't refuse on a previously owned Seville." Then Logan was back with tape from the press conference at Providence Police Head-quarters.

It was all backslaps and congratulations, the chief, the mayor, and Polecki taking turns giving one another credit. The mayor hogged most of the camera time, attributing the break in the case to Polecki's diligent police work and doing his best to minimize the role of Zerilli and his bat-wielding vigilantes. Polecki injected a word of caution, saying "The investigation is ongoing," but the smug smiles and the celebratory mood made it clear they thought Wu Chiang was their man.

When it was over, the crowd at Hopes applauded. Three cops and a half dozen firemen, segregated at two tables in back, rose to their feet and raised their glasses in a toast. Then they crossed their invisible line of mutual hostility to share manly hugs, the black eyes and split lips from the brawl at last August's PD vs. FD softball game momentarily forgotten.

33

Seems like I'm always hustling for something—a lead, a quote, a free parking space, space above the fold. When there's time to take a breath, it usually involves sucking in a lungful of Cuban and wheezing out a cheer for the developmentally arrested millionaires with "Red Sox" stitched across their chests. Tonight I'd gotten myself into something different, and I liked the way it felt.

We strolled past Nordstrom, an anchor in the sprawling mall just downwind from the stench of the statehouse. Behind the plate-glass windows, mannequins were draped in my annual salary. I focused on my companion's hips as they drew silky circles beneath her skirt. A minute or two slipped by before I noticed she was speaking.

". . . wanted to share the byline but Lomax wouldn't go for it, so I gave you and Mason contributing lines at the end of the piece."

When I realized she was talking business, I felt oddly deflated. "We make a good team, Veronica."

"You and Mason?"

"You and I."

"I think so too," she said.

Suddenly I was hungry. I wanted food too.

Before us was one of those pretentious places with ferns, brass railings, hardwood floors, and preening waiters with names like Chad and Corey. As we settled into a corner booth, I felt Veronica shed the day. She pulled her jet-black hair out of an elastic tie and shook it loose to settle on her shoulders. Then she sighed and crossed her legs, diverting my attention from the twelve-page menu.

Veronica ordered veal. I asked for the rib eye. There are times when nothing will do but meat.

She was at it again. Talking. I caught about every third word. Arson. Deadlines. Wu Chiang. I just wanted her to tie that hair back up and pull it loose again. To uncross her legs and recross them.

"You ever get lonely, Mulligan?"

That caught me by surprise. I felt myself about to stutter, then remembered what a cool dude I'm supposed to be. "How could I get lonely with you, Gloria, and Polecki all wanting a piece of me?"

She didn't smile like I thought she would. Instead, she lowered her eyes and ran a slow finger along the rim of her wine glass.

"We kiss, we roll around in your bed, we sleep. What you want from me now is something you can get from anybody."

"No way," I said. "From Gloria, sure, but Polecki's a lousy lay."

"Is everything a joke to you?"

"Most things. Not everything."

I was quiet for a moment, not sure what to say or how to say it.

"You've figured me out," I said. "You know the shit I slog through every fucking day, how I stink of it, and you still think I'm good enough to be with you."

As she raised her eyes to stare at me, Chad or Corey materialized, working me for a tip. No, I don't want any more water. No, we haven't finished our drinks. Keep your cracked pepper to yourself. Go the fuck away.

We ate in silence. It was a cozy silence, and it scared me a little. I'd said too much. Or not enough. What exactly had I said? Ah, yes. *Shit,* and *stink,* and *fucking*—the three magic words of romance.

"Mulligan?"

Silence broken.

"You get me too. And I've been told that I'm a hard woman to love."

Love? Jesus! Who'd said anything about love?

I sawed at my rib-eye, stalling for time. Then she tossed that gorgeous mane, and my breath caught on something.

When Chad or Corey showed up with the check, Veronica snatched it, handed him her AMEX card, and headed for the ladies' room. Love? Who said anything about love? I was still pondering that when I felt her hands on my shoulders and her breath in my ear.

I followed her out of the restaurant, and we strolled arm in arm to her car. We were through the door to my place and out of our clothes before I could decide whether the rush of blood to all the right places was lust or something more.

Heavy necking, Mulligan at full mast, then a cold shower. I knew the routine. But when I stretched out on the bed, her hands were insistent. So was her mouth. Then she moved to place me inside of her.

An interesting development, to say the least. As the sportscasters say, the crowd went wild.

What had I been doing with Dorcas those two wasted years? Whatever it was, it bore no relation to this. We tangled and writhed, slipped and adjusted, bumped noses and giggled, rode and shivered. And when it was finally over we—gulp—*cuddled*. Spent and sweaty, I hoped that I had been at least mildly entertaining. This lady was a keeper.

The lady lifted her head from my chest and smiled.

"That test I asked you to get?"

"Yeah?"

"You passed."

So she *had* been just stalling for time. Be nice if she'd found a way that didn't involve me getting stabbed with a needle, but I had to admit it had worked. I suppressed a pinpoint of irritation. What exactly had been the point of waiting?

"So," she said, "are you all tuckered out, or shall we try that again?"

Love? Who said anything about love?

34

I awoke to the familiar sound of Angela Anselmo
shrieking at her kids. Something about paste, confetti, and "How
could you do that to poor little Toodles?"

I swung my feet to the floor and gazed back at Veronica in the
light filtering through the shade. Her breathing was deep and regular. Resisting the urge to bury my face in the tangle of jet hair on
the pillow, I tiptoed to the bathroom, stepped into the shower, and
lathered up. Suddenly there was a sleepy, naked court reporter beside me in the cramped stall.

"Who's Toodles?" she asked. Looking at the rivulets of hot
water streaming over her skin, I had other questions, but I answered the one she asked.

"The family cat."

I pulled her into my arms, and we kissed under the spray. She
scrubbed my back, and I took my sweet time with hers. I would
have taken all day if she hadn't reminded me that our jobs were
waiting. There's nothing better than a wet woman.

My fridge was empty, so we headed for the diner. Charlie raised
a shaggy eyebrow as Veronica and I walked in together. Aside from
Wu's arrest, it had been a slow news day in Rhode Island, the editors filling the news columns with spin from the presidential prima-
ries, lies from Washington, and gore from Iraq.

While Veronica scanned the "Lifestyle" section, I turned to the sports. Curt Schilling's shoulder had mysteriously worsened over the winter, and doctors were debating whether he needed surgery. But with Beckett, Matsuzaka, Lester, Wakefield, Buchholz, Colón, and Masterson, we had more starters than we needed anyway. Charlie scraped a layer of grease from the grill, wiped his hands on his apron, and turned to grin at us.

"Your taste in women is improving, Mulligan. Whatever happened to that skanky blonde you tripped down the aisle with, the one who thought your name was 'Bastard'?"

Whenever I ate at the diner, day or night, Charlie was there to cook for me. You've got to work a lot of hours to put a daughter through Juilliard. I grunted and dropped a twenty on the counter, grateful to be in a place where I could treat my girl to a meal without applying for a loan to cover the check.

35

"I'm about to push the send button, so go stand next to the fax machine, Liam," Aunt Ruthie said. "I don't want someone else to get his hands on this and start wondering where it came from."

It was ten pages in all, Wu Chiang's Visa charges for November, December, January, and February, and a partial bill for the first few days of March. I carried it back to my desk to check the billing dates against the dates of the fires, but a quick glance had already told me this was going to be trouble.

Wu was a copy-machine salesman, and most of the charges spoke of a mundane existence: CVS, Stop & Shop, Texaco, Target, B & D Liquors, although $249.95 spent at Victoria's Secret looked intriguing. He had a girlfriend, or maybe he was a cross-dresser. But what concerned me was a $477 November charge for a U.S. Airways flight and $2,457 for a twenty-one-day stay ending December 20 at the Hotel Whitcomb in downtown San Francisco. A business trip, maybe, or a winter vacation. Or could this have been an elaborate alibi?

I called the Whitcomb and got the concierge on the line. Yes, he remembered Wu. The guy'd been a chronic complainer. He didn't like the view from his window. He whined that his no-smoking room smelled like cigarettes. There was never enough J&B in his minifridge. And on the way out, he argued about his bill.

To be sure, I e-mailed him a photo of Wu, and the concierge called back with a positive ID.

I turned to my keyboard and started to write it up, a slam-dunk, page-one byline. Then I thought about it and realized I owed some people a heads-up.

36

"Sonovabitch!" Zerilli said.

"Technically this just clears him of the three December fires," I said. "Looks like he was in town for the others. But to suspect him now, you'd have to think more than one serial arsonist is working Mount Hope."

"Not fuckin' likely."

"No," I said. "It's not."

"Shit! Last night I asked the DiMaggios to turn in their bats. Told 'em they could keep the hats. Guess I better get 'em back on the streets."

"I think you should."

The phone jingled. He picked up, gave odds on the Celtics-Nets game, licked his pencil stub, recorded a bet on a scrap of flash paper, hung up, and absently scratched his balls through his boxers.

"Ah, fuck," he said. "Good of you to come by though, letting me know in person 'stead of havin' to read the bad news in the fuckin' paper."

We smoked silently for a moment.

"CD player workin' okay?"

"Yup."

"Out of Cubans yet?"

"Not quite yet."

"How about putting fifty down on the Yankees, hedge your sucker bet on the Sox?"

"No thanks, Whoosh," I said. "If the Yankees win, it would just feel like blood money."

The blinds were open in Jack's little apartment, and the sun slanting through the slats lifted the atmosphere from depressing to merely dreary. Jack had replaced the terry-cloth robe with pressed jeans and a blue oxford shirt. He was freshly shaven, a razor burn on his left cheek, and his thin gray hair was neatly combed. His weatherproof nylon jacket—the blue one with the letters *PFD* in white on the back—was draped over his arm. He was getting ready to go out.

"Hear the news?" he said. And then he smiled wide enough to show most of the teeth he had left.

"Jack, I . . ."

"I was just on my way over to the firehouse to hang with the guys," he said. "Wanna walk along with me?"

I grabbed his arm. "Jack, wait."

He caught my eye and saw something that stopped him.

"What's wrong, Liam? Are your brother and sister okay?"

"Jack, the police arrested the wrong guy. They probably won't want to admit it just yet, but they'll have to release him in a day or two."

"You sure? The TV said . . ."

"I'm sure."

His shoulders slumped, and I watched the air go out of him. He let the jacket drop to the floor.

"So it's not over."

"No."

"Porca vacca!"

My favorite Italian curse. Literally it means "pig cow," but it's reserved for times when most Americans would say "Oh crap!"

"This means Polecki and Roselli will start looking at you again, Jack. Remember what I told you to do if they come around again?"

"Don't say nothing. Don't go with them unless they arrest me. If they do, ask for a lawyer."

"Right. And don't tell the cops I told you not to talk."

"Yeah. I got it."

He collapsed into the armchair by the table where the Jim Beam bottle, only a couple of inches of amber left in it, still stood on the doily.

"Stay for a drink, Liam?"

Together we sat in silence and drained the bottle, not bothering with glasses.

"Come visit again when you get the chance," he said.

"Maybe next time I'll have better news."

At the door, I turned and wrapped him up in a hug. It seemed to embarrass him a little.

"Just hang in there, Jack." As I headed down the stairs, my ulcer was grumbling.

It was another thin crowd at Good Time Charlie's. Marie wasn't waiting tables this afternoon, and her body stocking was gone, replaced with nothing at all, unless you counted the garter on her right thigh. When she saw me walk in, she flowed like water to the edge of the stage and hooked a thumb in the garter so I could slip in a dollar and give her butt a pat.

"Thanks, Mulligan," she said.

"The pleasure is all mine," I said, and meant it.

I chose one of the empty booths in back, started to slide in, noticed a beer spill on the seat, and chose another with a decent view of Marie, who was hanging upside down now from the stripper pole.

A few years ago, the place would have been packed, but six new strip clubs had opened up in the last few years, most of them down in the old Allens Avenue industrial area. They'd drained a lot of the regulars from Good Time Charlie's and were pulling in customers from all over New England, some of them arriving on chartered buses from Boston, Hartford, and Worcester.

The boom had gotten underway after a bright young lawyer representing an escort service actually read the state's prostitution law and discovered it referred to the crime as "streetwalking." That, he argued, meant the law explicitly criminalized the stroll but was silent on the legality of sex for money when the transactions occurred indoors. A judge agreed, and suddenly there was no need to fly to Thailand or Costa Rica anymore. The new clubs featured strobe lights, DJs, and private booths where local girls, reinforced by silicone-enhanced talent from New York and Atlantic City, performed thirty-dollar private dances and hundred-dollar blow jobs.

So far, the only thing the state's lawmakers had done about it was make some indignant speeches. Call me a cynic, but I suspected money was changing hands. The old fart who'd operated Good Time Charlie's since the seventies limited touching to the occasional fanny pat. No wonder his business was flagging.

I was on my second club soda when Polecki showed up a half hour late and squeezed in across from me, the space between the seat and the table not quite wide enough to accommodate his Kentucky Fried girth.

"What is it now, asshole?" he said.

I didn't say anything, just slid a copy of the credit-card charges across the cigarette-scarred Formica.

"Yeah, I got that this morning from the helpful folks at Fleet Bank," he said. "All it took was the threat of a subpoena. How the hell did *you* get your hands on it?"

"I'd rather not say."

"Break a few laws in the process?"

"Not any important ones."

He tried his poor excuse for a hard look on me, saw it wasn't working, and gave it up.

"He's got alibis for four of the other fires, too," he said. "We're still checking them out, but it looks like they're gonna hold up. You sent me on a wild goose chase, shithead. Your Mr. Rapture's not our guy."

"Guess not. I wonder why he ran that time when I tried to talk to him on the street."

"Who knows? Maybe he was holding and made you for a narc. Maybe he thought you was gonna mug him. Maybe he don't like meeting new people. Maybe he just don't like assholes."

"So what happens now?"

"We got forty-eight hours to charge or release. The chief wants to lose him in the system for a while, let the twelve-year-old public defender who caught the case try to figure out where he is. Might buy a little time to find the right guy and avoid the public-relations disaster of letting Wu go when we got nothin' else."

"I see," I said, and his face scrunched up with worry.

"Christ! This is all off the record, right?"

"Come on, Polecki. You know nothing's off the record unless you say so before you start talking. Something to keep in mind if you ever find yourself with another reporter, one who's a stickler for the rules."

The skinny black girl who'd been the entertainment on our last visit sashayed up in fuck-me heels and a G-string to take Polecki's order.

"Get him a Narragansett on me," I said, and he looked at me funny.

"Figure on doing a piece about the arson chief drinking on duty?"

"Yeah, right. I buy you a beer, then do an exposé on you drinking it. Even I wouldn't stoop that low for a byline."

"You've stooped lower."

The waitress came back with his beer. I handed her five bucks, peeled off another dollar, and slipped it in her G-string, not seeing an ass worth patting.

"So we're back to square one," I said.

"There is no *we*, Mulligan. I'm an officer of the law conducting an official investigation. You're a fucking parasite."

"No other leads?"

"Just that ex-fireman."

"Jack Centofanti."

"I'm not confirming that. If you've got the name, it didn't come from me."

"Understood."

"Roselli's got a hard-on for him, but I still don't think he's good for it."

Polecki pulled a Parodi out of his shirt pocket and lit it with a paper match. The cheap black stogie smelled like shit laced with citronella.

"Don't take this wrong," I said, "but maybe you need some outside help on this."

"Look," he said, "the state fire marshal's got just three arson investigators for the whole state, and he's already assigned two of them to work with me. One of them, Leahy, he used to be the fire chief in Westerly, and he's pretty good. The other one, Petrelli, got the job because his cousin's the Democratic state party chairman. Thinks he knows it all because he took a two-week federal Fire Administration course, but he don't know shit."

"What's the federal Fire Administration?"

"Another one of them Homeland Security agencies with no idea what the fuck it's supposed to be doing."

"What about the FBI?"

"Since 9/11, if it ain't about terrorism they ain't interested."

"Still nothing to suggest it's more than a firebug?"

"Not a thing. You always think insurance scam first, but with five different companies owning the buildings . . ." He shrugged his meaty shoulders and his voice trailed off.

"The mayor is all over our ass. The city council is screaming for answers. They don't understand that arson investigations are a bitch. Any evidence the perp leaves behind usually gets burned up. Hell, if the fire's bad enough, you can't even prove how it started. Chances are this nutcase is just gonna keep setting fires till we get lucky and catch him in the act."

The stink from Polecki's stogie was strong enough to make me gag. To mask the smell, I drew a Cuban from my pocket and set fire to it with the Colibri.

"Nice lighter. Get that from your hoodlum friend Whoosh?"

"Maybe."

He smirked, finished his beer, and unwedged himself from the booth.

"Later, asshole," he said, and headed out.

As soon as I got back to the office, I was going to make a photocopy of the credit-card charges and mail it to Wu's lawyer. Public defenders rarely have time for anything besides routine court appearances, and I didn't trust Polecki to do the right thing.

Marie was shaking her stuff in the red stage lights, bopping to "Ladies' Night" by Kool & the Gang. I stood and carried my club soda up front for a closer look. Several minutes later I snapped to the fact that my face was inches from Marie's nipples, and my mind was on Veronica.

37

That evening, she cooked for me.

She arrived toting three grocery bags, prepared to whip up something elaborate, then discovered that my cookware consisted of a single scarred saucepan. Undeterred, she used it to boil penne and tossed it with olive oil on my ancient stove while grilling bell peppers, eggplant, zucchini, and mushrooms on a sheet of aluminum foil in the crusty oven.

"So that's what that thing is for," I said when she turned on the gas.

When dinner was ready, my place smelled better than it ever had. We sprawled on my bed in front of another *Law & Order* rerun, sharing Russian River straight from the bottle and eating off paper plates with plastic forks. Dorcas had all our dishes and silverware, but I didn't care. I hated doing dishes.

Later, I tossed the plates and forks in the trash, and we settled back into bed, I with the new Robert Parker novel swiped from the desk of the paper's book critic, she with a slim paperback by Patricia Smith, some lame poet she'd just discovered. The domesticity was both comfy and unsettling.

I was on chapter two when Veronica started reciting poems out loud, liking the way the words felt in her mouth. Reading poetry to me now? *Poetry?* Things *were* getting out of hand. I tried to block it out, concentrating hard now on whether the suspicious husband thought Spenser was the right man for a tail job. Veronica reached over, pulled the novel from my hands, and snapped it shut.

"You've got to hear this."

"I'm not into poetry, Veronica. It does nothing for me, unless Bob Dylan's whining it through his nose."

"Just shut up and listen."

What gave birth to jazz,
What moist, constricted passage it struggled from,
who held it aloft,
slapped that newborn ass
and sparked the glorious screaming
doesn't matter.

What matters is fluid line shredding into scat
and us owning that sweetness;
what matters is cigarette-thin men
swearing at their reflections in the bartop.
What matters is sugar browns,
hitching up homemade skirts
and pounding holes in the dance floor,
out past curfew and tired of asking the time.

"Holy shit!" And I meant it.

"Told you."

"Let me see that." She handed me the book, and I turned it over, checking out the author photo on the back cover. "Damn. She's hot too."

"Shut up!" she said, but she was smiling when she said it.

Later I turned the TV back on to watch a rerun of *The Shield*, a cop show I liked because the star, Michael Chiklis, was a rabid Red Sox fan. Veronica excused herself and scooted down the stairs to fetch something from her car. As Detective Vic Mackey and his strike team tried to figure out how the One-Niners had gotten their hands on a truckload of grenade launchers, she slipped back in carrying a duffel. She opened my closet and saw four pairs of faded jeans, three Red Sox game jerseys, a wrinkled blue blazer, and a bunch of naked wire hangers. She unzipped the duffel and hung up a few things. The domesticity was getting more comfy and more unsettling by the minute.

Veronica flopped back into bed and snaked her legs around mine. I was rolling over to grab a kiss when the police scanner broke the mood.

"Code Red on Locust Street!"

"Damn!" she said. "Is that where I think it is?"

"Yeah, it's in Mount Hope."

We pulled on sweatshirts and headed for Secretariat.

"This is more than just a story now," I said as I pulled away from the curb. "It's personal. This firebug is really pissing me off."

"How come?"

"He's messing with my sex life."

As I turned left off Camp Street onto Locust, the crew of Engine Company No. 6 was already coiling hoses and stowing equipment. Rosie was standing in the front yard of a weather-beaten bungalow, laughing.

"Liam!" she shouted. "Over here. You ought to see this."

She led us through the front door and into a parlor decorated with horror-movie posters, Heineken empties, and dirty laundry. Straight ahead was one of those collapsible staircases that pull down from a trap door in the ceiling. She snapped on her flashlight, and Veronica and I followed her up.

"Watch your head," she said, just as my skull met a rafter.

Firemen had hacked holes in the roof to vent the smoke, but the cramped attic still reeked of burned wiring and something more. Rosie swung her flashlight to the left, illuminating a crude plywood table with two-by-fours for legs. On top was a hydroponic farm, two dozen marijuana plants under a bank of charred high-intensity lights. Half of the plants were just stalks, their leaves consumed by the fire. The rest had withered in the heat.

"A house full of Brown students growing their own," Rosie said. "The lights overheated and would have burned the place to the ground, we hadn't gotten here in time."

"Mind if I inhale?"

"Be my guest," she said. "Half the crew's been up here sucking in breaths and holding them."

She laughed again, and we joined in. It wasn't that funny, but we were all giddy with relief that the serial arsonist had taken the night off. And I think Rosie was a little high.

Rosie pulled me aside and whispered in my ear. She was only two inches taller than me, so she didn't have to bend down much to do it.

"I thought you liked 'em tall."

"Short works for me, too. All the parts are still there, just closer together."

"She's beautiful, Liam."

"And she cooks."

"She got any idea how crazy you are about her?"

That stopped me. "What makes you think that?"

"Are you kidding? I can tell just by the way you look at her."

She kissed me on the cheek and said, "Buy her something nice she can wear against her skin."

On the drive home I felt jittery. Rosie knew me better than I knew myself, and what she'd said had thrown me off balance. And the adrenaline rush of a big story was still cruising my arteries with no place to go. Veronica sensed it and laid her hand on my thigh.

"Why don't we stop for a drink at Hopes?" she said.

"I got a better idea. Let's go home and get naked."

"Only if you explain something to me first."

"What's that?"

"How come Rosie gets to call you 'Liam'?"

"She's been calling me that since first grade, Veronica. I guess it's a habit she can't break."

I backed Secretariat into a parking space across from my place and was reaching for the ignition key when the police scanner crackled again.

"Code Red on Doyle!"

My adrenal glands started pumping again as I turned the Bronco around. I drove back the way we'd come, monitoring the radio chatter.

"Triple-decker fully involved. People in the windows. Engine Six needs assistance."

And then, a minute later, "Code Red on Pleasant! Single-family home fully involved. Engine Twelve needs assistance."

"You've got to be kidding me," Veronica said.

I floored the pedal as we crossed the Providence River, raced up the steep slope of Olney Street, and swung left on Camp into Mount Hope.

The radio again.

"Code Red on Larch Street. Code Red! Code Red! All hell is breaking loose out here!"

38

Veronica fished the cell from her purse.

"Which one are we heading for?" she said.

"I'll drop you at Doyle, then head for Larch."

She called the city-desk overnight supervisor, told him where we were going, and urged him to send everyone he had to Mount Hope. Then she made another call, getting Lomax out of bed.

The radio squawked again, telling us the city of Pawtucket was responding to a mutual-aid request from Providence, three pumpers and a ladder truck on the way.

From the corner of Camp and Doyle, we could see flames in the first- and second-story windows of a triple-decker fifty yards down the street. Police cruisers had Doyle blocked off, so I pulled over, told Veronica to be careful, and let her out.

I watched her charm her way through the police line; then I sped five blocks north on Camp. The cops had Larch blocked off too, so I drove half a block past the intersection and pulled the Bronco up on the sidewalk, giving fire equipment and emergency vehicles room to maneuver.

I dashed back down the sidewalk to Larch, where gawkers gathered at the police lines. They looked scared this time. Some of the women were weeping.

I shouldered my way through until a uniformed officer blocked my way. Patrolman O'Banion was not a Mulligan fan. Probably had something to do with the time I wrote about him filching joints from the evidence locker, and the chief—no doubt pissed he hadn't thought of it first—suspended him for a month without pay. I flashed my press pass at him. He glanced at it and said, "Get the fuck out of here."

I did, resisting the urge to break into a run. No point risking one of the DiMaggios mistaking me for a torch fleeing the scene. I walked a block south on Camp, turned east on Cypress, strolled up a driveway, climbed a stockade fence, found myself in another driveway, and emerged on Larch.

I heard the fire before I felt it, the flames sounding like a thousand flags snapping in the wind. I felt it before I saw it, the heat like a backhand slap from the devil.

A sheet of flame climbed the front of the duplex. Black smoke boiled from cheap asphalt siding, mixing with gray smoke that curled from the eaves. On the roof, two firemen swung axes, cutting vents to release the smoke trapped inside. The wind shot blazing tongues up the east side of the building to the peak. The two firemen gave up and scrambled down an aerial ladder on the other side as their brothers laid down a cover of spray.

The street was a snare of fire hoses. Leakage from loose couplings soaked my jeans.

Behind me, I heard a pop.

I turned and saw a flash of light in a cellar window of a two-story bungalow. Peeling yellow paint, blue Dodge ram on blocks in the front yard. The house where I'd talked to Carmella DeLucca and her Neanderthal son, Joseph. A sheet of flame shot across the basement from right to left, illuminating the three cellar windows.

"Hey!" I yelled. "Over here!"

But four firemen had already turned from the duplex and were hauling two four-inch lines across the street. Rosie and two of her men strapped on respirators, lowered their faceplates, kicked in the front door, and burst inside. Half a minute later they emerged, Rosie carrying the flailing birdlike figure of Carmella DeLucca.

"Put me down!"

So she did. The old woman appeared to be all right, but one of the firemen led her to the rescue truck. I followed, and as a medic checked her over, I tried to pump her for details.

"Mrs. DeLucca? Where were you when the fire started?"

"None of your business," she said. "And don't go putting my name in your paper."

"Want to say something about the chief? She just saved your life."

"Like hell she did. I was perfectly capable of walking out of there my own self."

Across the street, smoke from the duplex had changed from black billows to white steam, a sign that the fire was retreating, its work well done.

The bungalow took up the slack. It burped a series of dull thuds, probably old paint cans exploding in the basement. Smoke rolled from the gutters along the roofline as the fire clawed up the walls between the studs, where the streams from the hoses couldn't reach it. Thin gray smoke curled from the open front door.

That's when Joseph DeLucca lumbered down the sidewalk dragging Officer O'Banion, who was clinging to his leg. Joseph reached down with one paw, peeled the cop off, and bellowed.

"MA!"

"She's safe," I shouted, but he didn't listen.

He charged up the front walk, rushed through the door, and was swallowed by smoke. Rosie and one of the other firemen who'd just rescued "Ma" went in after him.

I stood in the street, held my breath, and counted the seconds.

Ten. The window curtains caught fire.

Twenty. A stuffed chair near the front window ignited.

Thirty. Flames chewed through the siding near the door.

Forty. A tongue of fire curled from the eaves and licked the roof.

Fifty. Joseph hurtled through the front door like he'd been thrown. Behind him, Rosie and the other fireman materialized in the smoky doorway. Joseph tried to shove past them to get back inside. They wrestled him to the ground, beating on his burning hair with their insulated gloves. Another fireman tipped his nozzle to the sky and let the spray fall on them like spring rain.

39

The next day's front page headline: HELL NIGHT IN
MOUNT HOPE. The lead photo, played four columns wide, captured
Rosie as she emerged from a smoky doorway cradling Carmella
DeLucca in her arms.

Thanks to Veronica's call, Lomax had reached the newsroom in
time to stop the city-edition press run after only twelve hundred
papers had been printed. He filed a series of updates for the online
edition and then wrote the print story himself with feeds from
reporters at the scenes. He remade the front page with dramatic
fire photos and put out a great newspaper that started flowing onto
the delivery trucks only ninety minutes past normal deadline.

"Wait till the publisher gets the overtime bill from the press-
men and truck drivers," Veronica said.

"Yeah," I said, "he'll probably dock Lomax's pay."

We were hunched over plates of scrambled eggs and bacon at
the diner, devouring the paper. Last night we'd been isolated at
separate fire scenes, and we were hungry for the whole story in one
place. There'd been five suspicious fires in all, the last one eating
through a three-story garden apartment building on Mount Hope
Avenue. I didn't even know about that one until I read what Lomax
had written.

"Bet they'll give your friend Rosie a medal," Veronica said.

"She's already got a drawer full of them."

Charlie cleared the cold, half-eaten eggs away and topped off our coffees. "Here comes that asshole I was telling you about," he said. "The one that come in here the other day asking could I whip him up a cheese soufflé."

Mason strolled in looking uncharacteristically casual in a buff cashmere sweater and knife-creased tan slacks, his left hand clutching the handle of a Dunhill briefcase worth more than my pension. He perched on the stool next to mine and asked Charlie for coffee.

"What, no café au lait this morning? No chai latte? Must be something you want that I ain't got."

"A cup of your excellent coffee would be fine."

The fry cook snorted, slammed a mug in front of Mason, and dumped in the dregs from a nearly empty pot. Mason took a sip of the sludge and pointed at the front page.

"Guess I missed a big story last night."

"Yes, you did," I said. "That's what happens when you work in Providence and live in a palace way the hell down in Newport."

"You guys did a great job."

"Why, thank you, Thanks-Dad. That means soooo much coming from you."

Veronica stretched out her right leg and gave me a kick. It hurt enough to make me wonder whose side she was on.

"Ease up on him," she said. "Not his fault his father's rich."

Mason just shrugged, snapped open the silver latch on his briefcase, and pulled out a slim file folder.

"I've been working on that manhole covers story, and I think I may have found something," he said. "I was hoping you could look it over and advise me on what to do next."

"Later. Right now, I got someplace I have to be."

Leaving the cub reporter with the hot babe, I walked out of the diner and whistled for Secretariat. When he didn't come, I fetched him from the lot across from the paper and pointed him toward Mount Hope.

40

At Prospect Terrace, a Mr. Potato Head statue stood watch over Roger Williams's grave. Sexually confused vandals had already enhanced the spud with D-cups and a big red penis.

A state fire marshal's car was parked at the curb in front of the torched triple-decker on Doyle. I pulled in behind it, got out, ducked under the yellow police tape, and skirted a sooty, soggy heap of mattresses and upholstered furniture. A uniformed cop stood with crossed arms on the concrete front stoop. He didn't tell me to get out.

"Guy from the state fire marshal's office is nosing around in the basement," he said. "Want me to see if he'll talk to you?"

"Thanks, Eddie."

While I waited, I looked over what was left of 188 Doyle Avenue, where I'd played cops and robbers with the Jenkins twins when I was a kid. Now half the roof was gone. Nothing but black behind every shattered window. A total loss. I stared at the unblinking third-story window on the southeast corner where old Mr. McCready, the teacher who'd first introduced me to Ray Bradbury and John Steinbeck, had been strangled by the smoke. The arsonist was reducing my childhood to ashes.

The crew of Engine 12, the first on the scene last night, had gotten everyone but Mr. McCready out safely, but two firemen were in

Rhode Island Hospital with smoke inhalation and another was on a slab with fried lungs. I was still looking at the window when Leahy stepped out on the stoop.

"Nothing I can say officially, Mulligan," he said.

"But?"

"But unofficially, there's heavy charring in three places on the basement walls."

"In the shape of upside-down arrowheads?" I asked.

"Yeah. I take it you know what that means."

"Signs of an accelerant," I said, my late-night reading of government arson reports beginning to pay off.

"Yeah," he said. "Signs of an accelerant. Big surprise."

"A timing device? Coffeemaker again?"

"I scraped some broken glass and melted plastic off the floor and sent it to the lab, but, yeah, that's probably what it is."

I thanked him and drove a block north to Pleasant, where a uniformed officer slumped behind the wheel of a cruiser in the driveway of a two-story bungalow. The place had been so badly burned there was no way to tell what color it had been painted.

"The people who lived here just came by," he said. "Wanted to go inside, see if they could salvage something, maybe find some family pictures. It's going to be at least a week before the arson investigators get around to this one, so I had to chase them off. Look at this place. Wouldn't you think they'd know there's nothing left that isn't drenched or burned to ash?"

On Mount Hope Avenue, the roof of the garden apartments was a skeleton of blackened rafters. Thin gray smoke wafted from the smoldering interior. A pumper crew was still on the scene, shooting a jet of water through the collapsed northwest wall. The reinforcements from Pawtucket had fought this one, arriving in time to see people leaping from second- and third-story windows. Three jumpers snapped their ankles, and two broke their legs. A fireman and six tenants, including a toddler, were hospitalized with second-degree burns and smoke inhalation.

I was looking for someone to talk to when Roselli stepped out of the wreckage and threw me the finger, his own special way of saying No comment.

At the ruined duplex on Larch, a crew from Dio Construction sprawled on the curb next to their front-end loader, popping the tabs on a mid-morning twelve-pack of 'Gansett and sharing the suds with Polecki.

"I was wondering when you were going to show up, asshole," he said.

"What are they doing here? You release this scene already?"

"Nah. The owner hired them to knock the place down and clear the rubble, which is fine with me. The roof and floors collapsed into the basement. I can't even get in there for a look until they clear some of this crap away."

Across the street, Joseph DeLucca was slumped on his front stoop, his bandaged head resting on his knees. He heard my footfalls on the flagstone walk, raised his eyes, and glared.

"Get your ass off our property, you fuckin' vulture."

He hauled himself to his feet, balled his fists, and took a step toward me. The movement made him wince in pain.

"How's your mom?"

That stopped him. He sighed and collapsed back onto the stoop.

"I don't want you writing about my ma in your fuckin' paper again," he said, but all the bully had drained from his voice.

"I won't, Joseph. I'm just wondering how she's doing."

"Pissed as hell. Got her staying with her sister, but Ma don't understand why she can't come back home."

"Why are you sitting here?" I asked, before realizing he probably had nowhere else to go.

"'Cause of that fuckin' Polack. Pozecki? Perluski? He told me I can't go in my own fuckin' house. I told him that was bullshit, so he promised to take me inside, let me look around as long as I stay out of the fuckin' basement. I gotta see if the pictures of Pa and my Nomar rookie card got burned up. If he ever stops suckin' down beers, the fuckin' prick."

"You rent this place?"

"Nah. It's Ma's. Pa left it to her after the cancer took him. It's all she's got."

"Insured?"

"Ma says we are."

"Going to rebuild?"

"I don't know, man. Ma's too old to start over. Should have sold the fuckin' place when we had the chance."

41

New volunteers swelled the DiMaggios to sixty—
two members, Zerilli cutting off enlistments when he ran out of
Louisville Sluggers. Barely trained fire academy recruits reinforced
Rosie's embattled battalion, which had now lost five men to injury
and death. Fire extinguishers and firearms flew off the shelves at
Drago Guns and Hardware on North Main. Scores of women and
children fled Mount Hope and moved in with relatives, their men
staying behind to sit up all night with revolvers or shotguns. The
paper announced a relief fund for families burned out of their homes,
the publisher chipping in the first thousand bucks. And the governor offered Rhode Island National Guardsmen to patrol Mount
Hope's streets, then recanted when he remembered they were in Iraq.

Hell Night follow-ups kept us all hopping for days. It was good
there was so much work. I didn't have time to slow down and
think about all the ways the old neighborhood was getting smaller.

It was Friday before I had time to consider what to do next. I
was still sitting at my desk thinking about it when Deep Purple interrupted with the opening licks of "Smoke on the Water." I checked
caller ID and decided to pick up anyway.

"You!
fucking!
bastard!"

"Good morning, Dorcas."

"Who's the Asian bitch you were pawing at Casserta's the other night?"

"You know, I'm glad you called. How's Rewrite doing? Are you remembering her heartworm pills? She should have one the first of every month."

"You always cared more about that fucking dog than you cared about me!"

"Well, she *was* more affectionate."

"You son of a bitch!"

"It's been nice chatting with you, Dorcas, but I have to go back to work." I clicked off before she could accuse me of screwing the dog.

As soon as I shut my loving ex off in mid-rant, Deep Purple started in again: Dah dah DAH, dah dah da-DAH, dah dah DAH, dah dah.

Note to self: Change ring tone to something without *smoke* in the title.

"We should talk."

"Got something for me?"

"Nothing hard," McCracken said, "but Hell Night doesn't make sense. A pyro sets fires so he can watch them burn. Why five fires on four streets at the same time? No way to savor them all."

I pulled a fresh bottle of Maalox from my drawer, cracked it open, and took a swig.

"Maybe it's not the fires that get him off," I said. "Maybe it's reading about them in the paper, seeing his handiwork on the TV news."

"Yeah, maybe. Or maybe it was a way of maximizing the damage. The fire department isn't equipped to handle that many fires all at once. We got too many maybes. Why don't you drop by so we can put our heads together?"

"Be there in half an hour."

I walked across town and stepped into McCracken's outer office just in time to see his secretary bend over to stuff a folder in a file cabinet.

"He's expecting you," she said, holding the pose to give me a good look at a lacy red thong under a black micro-skirt. "You can go right in."

Hell of a straight line, but I didn't touch it. I'd seen her ex-boxer boyfriend remodel too many faces.

McCracken squeezed my hand like he was trying to grind my metacarpal bones into powder.

"Heard anything from Polecki?" I said.

"Just after I called you. The triple-decker and the two single-families were definitely torched. Coffeemakers and gasoline used on all three. They're still working on the duplex and the apartment building, but we can be pretty sure what they're going to find."

"Word is the toddler they pulled out of the apartment building isn't going to make it," I said. "Another kid who won't get to grow up in Mount Hope. That makes eleven dead now, not to mention fifteen more with burns and injuries."

"Yeah," he said. "And nearly five million in fire insurance claims, three million against my company alone. Thank God I'm not in the life insurance business."

His desk was the size of a parking space. He unrolled a map that covered most of it, a topographical view of Mount Hope showing all the streets and structures. We spent the next few minutes identifying the fourteen buildings that had been torched. McCracken colored them in chronologically with a yellow marker, starting with the first fire in December and ending with Hell Night.

Initially, the fires appeared scattered: the first on Cypress, the next four blocks south on Doyle, the third over on Hope at the eastern edge of the neighborhood. But as the last half dozen boxes filled with yellow, a pattern emerged. All of the fires had been set within a misshapen rectangle bordered by Larch on the north, Hope on the east, Doyle on the south, and on the west by Camp, known in colonial times as Horse Pasture Lane. Nothing outside the southeast quadrant of the neighborhood, the part that butts up against Brown University and the pricey East Side.

"I noticed the same thing Tuesday when I drove around checking out the Hell Night damage," I said. "Could have parked the car and strolled past all fourteen torched buildings in ten minutes."

"Clear out all the old buildings between Doyle and Larch," McCracken said, "and you'd have yourself a prime piece of development property."

"You would. But that would require one hell of a conspiracy."

"Because the properties belong to five different realty companies."

"Yeah, and the DeLuccas own their place on Larch, which makes six owners."

"What about the other four Hell Night targets?"

"Don't know yet," I said. "I'll check the property records this afternoon, but that's probably going to give us still more owners."

"Probably will," he said. "Hard to see anything in it. Still, the pattern is peculiar."

"It could be random. A few years ago, I thought I'd found a cancer cluster over by McCoy Stadium. A dozen dead and dying in just four square blocks. A team from the CDC came up from Atlanta to look at it and decided there was nothing strange going on. When you've got a lot of something, like fires in Mount Hope or cancer in Pawtucket or stars in the sky, it's never spread evenly. You always get clusters."

"Still, it's something to think about," he said.

"Yeah," I said, "it is."

42

On the walk back across the Providence River, I called Veronica and suggested she join me for my usual gourmet fare at the diner. I was watching Chef Charlie burn the life out of my cheeseburger when she showed up with Mason. That irritated me a little. A squeeze and smooch from Veronica, and I almost got over it.

"I'm glad you called," she said, climbing onto the stool next to mine. "Something I meant to tell you this morning. You remember Lucy?"

"Your sister?"

"Yeah. She's driving down from Boston this afternoon to spend the weekend with me. I won't be seeing you for a couple of days, so it's good we can grab a quiet lunch together."

I looked around. Two loudmouthed women were having an expletive-laced discussion about the cheating ways of someone named Herb. Charlie hummed a little off-key ZZ Top to drown out my burger as it screamed for mercy. Some guy a couple of stools down was snoring like a champ. The diner wasn't exactly a romantic spot, and sitting between Veronica and Mason didn't feel much like quality time.

"You've got a sister?" Mason said.

"I do."

"Is she as pretty as you?"

"Younger and prettier."

"Think she'd like me?"

What was this, *High School Musical?*

Veronica tossed her mane and laughed. "She might. I'll give her your number and you can ask her yourself."

Mason grinned, then remembered he was rumored to be a reporter. He unsnapped the Dunhill and extracted a file folder.

"Got a few minutes now to consult on that manhole covers story? I think I'm on to something, and I could use your advice on how to proceed with my investigation."

Oh, great. Now he's an *investigative* reporter.

"Sorry, Thanks-Dad. No time today."

"Oh. Okay," he said, and put the file away.

He sat quietly for a moment, then said, "Mulligan?"

"Um?"

"Is this a test? Do you want to see what I am able to accomplish on my own?"

"Right. You're on to me."

"So I should use my own judgment, then?"

"Yes, that fine instrument honed in the hallowed halls of Columbia."

He nodded and smiled to himself.

Veronica and Mason were still picking at their sandwiches when Charlie cleared away my empty plate and dropped the check on the counter. I nudged it toward Thanks-Dad.

"Have fun, Veronica," I said. That sounded lame, so I pecked her cheek for emphasis.

As I headed for the door, I turned around for a last look at her bare legs curled around the stool. She had her wallet out and was showing Mason a photo of her sister. He was grinning again. I turned away and stepped out into a day that smelled like rain.

I walked to the CVS in Kennedy Plaza, bought a package of

Benadryl, dry-swallowed a couple, and made for the musty property-records room in the basement of city hall. The drug didn't help much. By the time I closed the last records book, my eyes itched and my nose dripped.

The triple-decker on Doyle, the single-family on Pleasant, and the duplex on Larch had all been bought by one or another of those five mystery realty companies in the last eighteen months. The garden-apartments complex on Mount Hope was a different story. It belonged to Vinnie Giordano's company, Rosabella Development, named after his sainted mother. Records showed the mobster had snapped it up at a tax sale three years ago. Just to be thorough, I looked up the house where the DeLuccas lived, confirming it had been in Joseph's family since the 1960s.

I wrote it all down, but it wasn't worth the time or the clogged sinuses. As far as I could see, it wasn't worth anything at all.

43

It was past nine when I finished up a few things in the newsroom and stepped out into a light rain. I didn't feel like spending the rest of Friday evening smelling traces of Veronica in an empty apartment, so I walked over to Hopes and claimed a stool at the bar. Annie, a moonlighting Johnson & Wales student, was behind the stick.

"The usual?"

My ulcer said yes, but the rest of me said Killian's.

"You sure?"

"Yeah."

Somebody fed quarters to the juke and punched up Bob Dylan's "Lonesome Day Blues." Just what I didn't need—music to fit my mood.

A cluster of firemen were laughing at the other end of the bar. I looked over and saw them shoving dollar bills at Annie. She snatched them and hiked her peasant skirt all the way up her long, long legs, giving them a good look. Then she smoothed the skirt back in place, glided back my way, saw my bottle was already empty, and brought me another.

"What was that about?"

"I got a tattoo last week," she said, "and I made the mistake of mentioning it in here. Now everybody wants a look. At first I said No way. Then guys started offering me a dollar apiece to see it.

I figured What the hell? Only way I can get some of these dead-beats to leave a tip."

I jerked my wallet out of my jeans and slid a bill on the bar.

"Give me five dollars' worth," I said.

She smirked and lifted her skirt, revealing a red-and-blue butter-fly perched just south of heaven. I thought it might take my mind off Veronica. It didn't work.

I was finishing my third beer, and my ulcer was beginning to grumble, when Annie drifted over with another bottle. "This one's on the tall, drop-dead gorgeous brunette at the table in back," she said. "She looks familiar. Haven't I seen her on TV?"

I looked where Annie was pointing and said, "Yeah. In the trailer for the new *Wonder Woman* movie."

I picked up the bottle and carried it to the table where Rosie sat alone, a shot of amber liquid in her hand and four Budweiser empties lined up in front of her. She was normally a sipper. I'd never seen her drink that much. There were frown lines around her mouth that hadn't been there before.

"Didn't see you when I came in," I said.

"I saw you. Just didn't feel like talking right away."

"How you doing?"

"Two of my men are dead, three more are in the hospital, the ones I've got left are all fucking exhausted, and I've lost count of the number of civilians killed and injured on my watch. That's how I'm doing."

I covered her left hand with mine and squeezed.

"It's not like any of this is your fault," I said.

"You sure about that?" There was that glare again, the one that took me straight back to first grade.

"Are you kidding me? You're a hero, Rosie." But the hero lowered her head and declined the honor. Her shoulders slumped, and tendrils of brown hair fell across her face. It was the first time I'd ever seen her look small.

"Know what scares me most?" she said, her voice a whisper.

"What's that?"

"Polecki and Roselli. With Dumb and Dumber on the case, we might never get out of this nightmare." She tossed down what was left of her shot and signaled Annie for another. When it arrived, she threw it back in one motion.

"You need some time off, Rosie."

"That's what the public-safety director said. I told him No way, but he ordered me to take a couple of days. I'm going to spend them getting drunk." She rummaged in her purse, pulled out an envelope, and handed it to me. "Here," she said, "you might as well have these."

I peeked inside and found two tickets to the home opener at Fenway.

"Take your girlfriend," she said. "I'm not going to be in the mood."

"She doesn't like baseball. I'd rather go with you."

"I won't be any fun."

"That's okay. We can be miserable together."

With that, she pushed back from the table, grabbed her bag, and stood to leave. I reached over and swiped her car keys from the table.

"That's sweet," she said, "but I think I'll walk."

A half hour later, I was sitting on a bar stool nursing my beer when Annie slid over with another bottle. "This one's on the blonde by the front window," she said. "Are you that hung, or is this just your lucky day?"

"Hung," I said. "Every day is lucky."

I picked up the bottle and carried it to the table where Gloria sat with a can of Bud.

"All alone on a Friday night?" she asked.

"Veronica's off playing with her sister."

"You two starting to cool off?"

"Feels more like we're heating up."

"Oh. Too bad."

I didn't know what to say to that, and I guess she didn't either. We sat quietly for a few minutes.

"Well," she finally said, "I gotta be going."

"Late date?"

She shook her head. "It's not easy finding the right guy, one who wants to spend a romantic evening driving around Mount Hope with the windows cracked, sniffing the air for the smell of smoke."

"Jesus, Gloria. Are you still doing that?"

"Most nights. Not every night. When all hell broke loose Monday, I was at the White Horse in Newport getting groped by a broker who tried to impress me with everything he knows about hedge funds. Missed the biggest story of the year, and I didn't even have a good time."

She drained her can, slid her chair back, and got to her feet.

"Stay, Gloria. Next round's on me."

"Sorry. Gotta go."

"You shouldn't be wandering around out there by yourself."

"Come with me," she said. "I got Buddy Guy on the CD player, you can smoke in my car, and this time I promise I *won't* kiss you."

I almost caved. But hell, I couldn't look after everybody. The gnawing in my stomach told me I wasn't doing much of a job of looking after myself. Besides, I wasn't sure she'd keep that promise or if I'd remember to behave if she broke it.

When I shook my head no, she turned and walked out the door. I watched her walk past the window in the rain.

I slipped a Cuban out of my jacket pocket, clipped the end, and set fire to it with the Colibri. Annie brought me another Killian's, then went back behind the bar and turned the volume up on the TV so the night shift filing in from the newspaper could catch Logan Bedford's version of the news:

"Remember Sassy, the dog that either did or didn't walk all the way across the country to find its owner? Well, the tests from the Tufts veterinary school are in, and 10 News has it exclusively. Wait till you hear what they found. You'll be *shocked*!"

No, I won't, I thought, but I carried my beer to the bar for a closer look. Bedford had a good time holding up Hardcastle's story and rubbing it in. He closed his report with two short camera shots—one of Martin Lippitt roughhousing with his dog, the other of Ralph and Gladys Fleming on their front stoop in Silver Lake, clutching each other and sobbing in the rain.

Annie wiped a tear from her cheek and brought me another beer.

"That was one of the saddest things *ever*," she said.

"Yeah. It's right up there with 'In lieu of flowers,' 'Let's just be friends,' and 'Yankees win.'"

44

That night, I couldn't sleep. I stretched out on my
bed in my undershorts, watching CNN and reading *A Pocket Guide
to Accelerant Evidence Collection* at the same time. I smelled the
gasoline before I heard the rustling at my apartment door.

I tiptoed barefoot to the kitchen, stepped in something wet,
and peered through the peephole. All I could see was the cracked
plaster wall across the hall. I flipped the dead bolt, yanked the door
open, and discovered a man squatting at my threshold, spilling a
gallon jug onto a dustpan angled to shoot the gasoline under the
door.

He set the jug down on the floor, straightened to his full height
of five foot five, and looked me up and down.

"Really?" he said. "Red Sox boxers? Isn't that taking things a bit
far?"

"You outta see my condoms."

The right corner of his mouth curled into something that could
almost be mistaken for a smile. Then he reached into his jacket
pocket and extracted a pack of Marlboros. He shook one out, stuck
it in his face, and fired it with a disposable lighter.

I didn't say anything. The little thug's lip curled again. He probably thought I was scared speechless, but that wasn't my problem. I
just couldn't find the right wisecrack. "Those things can kill you"
was too obvious. "Don't you know it's Fire Prevention Week?" wasn't

much of an improvement. "Hi—no offense" seemed beneath me. Unlike my threshold, each lacked a little something.

Finally I settled for "Sorry, but Timmy can't come out to play."

The lip curl faded.

"Pretty funny for a dead guy."

"It's only an ulcer."

"What?"

I shrugged.

"I got a message for you, Mulligan. You've been sticking your nose into places it don't belong, and that ain't healthy. Quit your snooping. This is the only warning you're gonna get. Next time I drop the cigarette."

"Mulligan?" I said. "You're looking for Mulligan? I threw that asshole out months ago. He smoked in the apartment, he never helped clean up after dinner, I caught him cheating on me, and I always welshed on his share of the rent."

The little thug wasn't buying it. He was already tromping down the stairs.

I chased after him, catching up in the narrow entry hall. I grabbed him by the shoulder and spun him. My mistake. He balled his fists, faked with his left, and shot a right uppercut to my groin. He smiled as he watched me fall, then turned and strolled out the door as if he didn't have a care in the world.

45

"Okay, asshole," Polecki said, "let's go over it again."

I repeated the description of the little thug, from his shaved head to his Air Jordans, and recited, as close as I remembered it, every word he said.

"He said he had a message for you? Did he mean it was from him, or was he delivering it for somebody else?"

"He didn't say."

"Tell me again how he managed to kick your ass, big guy like you."

"We've been over it three times already."

"Yeah, but I really like hearing that part."

It had been well past three in the morning when I got to the police station on Washington Street. The night sergeant had listened to my story, recognized its importance, and rousted Polecki out of bed. We sat across from each other now on battered metal chairs, two empty paper coffee cups on the cigarette-scarred interrogation-room table.

"This could be our break," he said. "You may have seen our guy's face."

Four hours later, I shut the last mug book, unable to find a match. I spent another hour with a sketch artist who'd found her art school

on the back of a matchbook. Based on her portrait, we were looking for Homer Simpson.

When I got home, the apartment still reeked of gasoline. Black
fingerprint dust coated the stair railing, my door frame, the door
knob, anything the little thug might have touched.

I tried to grab some sleep, but it wasn't working, so I called
McCracken to tip him off about the little thug. He promised to run
the description by insurance investigators around New England.

"He told you to stop snooping around? Those were his words?"

"Uh-huh."

"So much for your theory that he's getting his kicks from the
publicity."

"Yeah."

"Tell me again how he kicked your ass."

"We already went over that."

"Yeah, but I like hearing that part."

I hung up and fell into bed again, but I still couldn't sleep. I
decided to go for a ride.

"I see him again, and his ass is mine," I said. "Can't believe I let
him get the best of me like that."

"Hey, it fuckin' happens," Zerilli said. "Asshole hits you in the
nuts, it doesn't matter how big he is. My six-year-old grandson
Joey—you remember little Joey? He jumped on me the other day,
landed on my balls, and I dropped right to my knees."

His left hand dropped reflexively to shield the bulge in his boxers.

"The top of his head barely reached my shoulders," I said, "so
I put him at five foot five. Dark complexion, shaved head with a
couple of red scaly patches, might have been psoriasis. Shoulders
like cantaloupes stuffed in his jacket. Smokes Marlboros. Sound like
anyone you see around the neighborhood?"

"Nah. Sounds a little like a guy Arena used to bring down from
Brockton now and then for strong-arm work, but last I heard he

was doing a dime in Cedar Junction on a hijacking beef. The dumbass pistol-whips the driver, shoots the lock offa the box, and starts dreamin' about how he's gonna fence a truckload of computers. He hauls open the doors, and what do you suppose is inside? A load of folding metal chairs."

We'd already run through our ritual—he presenting me with a new box of Cubans and asking me to swear once again never to reveal what went on in this little room overlooking the grocery aisles; I swearing, opening the box, and getting one going.

"What's the line on tomorrow's opener?"

"Sox game?"

I nodded.

"One-seventy," he said.

"Seems a little steep."

"With Matsuzaka pitching? Probably should be higher."

"I'm in for a dime."

Zerilli's was a volume business. If the Sox won, he'd collect $100 from the underdog betters and pay out $100 to the favorite betters, making nothing. If the Sox lost, he'd collect $170 from the favorite betters and pay out $150 to the underdog betters, clearing $20 per bet.

Judging by the constantly ringing phone, volume wasn't a problem.

"Been getting so much action on the Sox," he said, "that I gotta lay off some of it on Grasso."

46

Baseball is a game that should be played in the summertime. This seemed especially true on this early April afternoon in Boston when the game-time temperature was in the forties and the wind swirling in from the harbor smelled of salt with a hint of sewage.

We'd caught a late-morning Amtrak train at Providence Station, Rosie in a new, hooded sweatshirt with Ramirez's name and number stitched across the back, and I in an old Red Sox warm-up jacket that had belonged to my father. We talked baseball, arson, and Veronica all the way up.

"Buy her that present yet?"

"No."

"Why not?"

"I don't know. It seems like . . ."

"Like a step."

"Yeah, I guess."

"Baby, you're way past that point already."

"I am?"

"Let me ask you a few questions, okay?"

"Sure."

"Do you think about Veronica a lot when she's not around?"

"Uh . . . yeah."

"When Annie flashed that butterfly the other night, did it take your mind off her?"

"You saw that, huh?"

"Quit stalling and answer the question."

"No. It didn't take my mind off her."

"If her fingers brush your arm, do you tingle?"

"Do I tingle?"

She just looked at me.

"Yeah, I guess I tingle. It's not always my arm, though."

"Are you up in the middle of the night, just watching her sleep?"

How in the hell did she know that? "Sometimes."

She stretched out her hand and pinched my cheek. "Aw. My little Liam is in love."

My first instinct was to argue with her, but losing would just confuse me.

We took a cab from South Station, arriving at Fenway in time for the hour-long celebration. The Boston Pops played the theme from *Jurassic Park* as a huge 2007 world-championship banner unfurled to cover the Green Monster. Tedy Bruschi, Bobby Orr, Bill Russell, and a host of other Boston sports heroes were trotted out. David Ortiz helped ancient Johnny Pesky raise the championship pennant on the center-field flagpole. Rosie and I were both hoarse from cheering by the time Bill Buckner stepped to the mound, wiped a tear from his eye, and threw the ceremonial first pitch to Dwight Evans.

Oh, yeah. They also played a baseball game. Matsuzaka toyed with the Tigers' sluggers, Kevin Youkilis slammed three hits, Ramirez tripled, and the Sox won 5–0.

Afterward I was ready for an ice-cold Killian's, but Rosie had other ideas.

"Let's go around to the players' parking lot and wave to them when they come out."

Ugh. Bad idea. I loved watching them play, but I wasn't into hero worship.

"Come on," she said. "It'll be fun."

Not as much fun as that beer. I trudged along behind her.

A manic sea of red and white pressed against the chain-link fence, going absolutely nuts every time a player came out, ignored them completely, and climbed into an obscenely expensive gas-guzzler.

"Marry me, Dustin!"

"Hey, Youk! How 'bout an autograph?"

"Josh! I wanna have your baby!"

Rosie waded into the crowed and shoved her way to the front. A couple of guys started to object, then craned their necks for a look at her and thought better of it. That's when Manny Ramirez bounded through the door like a schoolboy. He grinned and swung an imaginary bat as digital cameras clicked. Rosie let loose a shriek I'd heard only from smitten teenage girls at rock concerts.

Manny turned toward the sound and, as all men must, he noticed Rosie towering over the throng. Above the dozens of maniacs screeching his name, I clearly heard him say, "Wow."

As he approached the fence, she stuck her fingers through it. He grinned, grabbed them, and squeezed. Chief Rosella Morelli, the hero of Mount Hope, turned to mush. Then Manny turned and walked to his restored 1966 Lincoln Continental. He looked back, marveled at Rosie again, climbed in behind the wheel, and was gone.

She stared until the taillights disappeared around a corner. Then she turned toward me.

"If you ever . . .

tell anyone . . .

about this . . ."

"About what?"

We followed the crowd to the Cask'n Flagon at the corner of Lansdowne Street and Brookline Avenue for beer and pizza, then wandered down the street to shoot some pool at the Boston Billiard Club. Much later, we had last call at Bill's Bar around the corner. By then, it was too late to catch the last train to Providence, so the bartender pointed us to an after-hours joint that offered a choice of Budweiser or Miller straight from the can, Jim Beam or Rebel Yell in chipped shot glasses, and a lot of backslapping from blitzed Sox fans. We caught the first morning train, a 6:10 local, and tried to sleep it off on the way home. By the time we were deposited, happy and rumpled, at Providence Station, it was 6:55 A.M. Bedtime.

A Mr. Potato Head statue greeted us in the lobby. On its flank, someone had scrawled "Yankees Suck!" in red spray paint. I thanked Rosie again for the ticket, gave her a hug, begged her to be careful, and staggered out of the station. I walked up Atwells Avenue toward home, poured some Maalox on my screaming ulcer, and collapsed on my mattress.

It was nearly noon by the time I made it in to work. As I stepped into the city room, Lomax grabbed my arm.

"Mulligan! Hear what happened to Gloria Costa?"

47

Fifteen minutes later, I slipped into her room at Rhode Island Hospital and didn't recognize the face on the pillow. Her right eye was covered with gauze. Her nose was blue-black and hooked to the left. Her lips were split and swollen. Her right hand, encased in a cast, lay still on the crisp white sheet. Dried blood matted her blond hair. She didn't look like Sharon Stone anymore.

I reached for her left hand, then saw the IV line taped to the back of it, so I just laid my palm on her shoulder. Her left eye fluttered open, and she mumbled something that might have been my name.

I got up and removed her chart from its hook at the foot of her bed. "Severed tendon, right hand. Fractured right occipital bone. Three fractured ribs, right side. Multiple contusions to face, arms, chest, and back. Detached retina, right eye. Prognosis for regaining sight uncertain."

I couldn't remember which eye she used to look through the viewfinder.

That night Veronica cooked for me again, bringing her own wok and stir-frying a fragrant mix of shrimp, ginger, and something she called "vegetables." The rising steam misted her skin.

"How is Gloria doing?" she asked.

"She's hurting. She's not talking much. It's hard to look at her. You should go see her. I'm sure she's tired of gazing up at my face."

There was silence as Veronica turned off the burner beneath the wok. Finally she said, "I wouldn't be so sure."

The Sox game was a safer subject. As we ate, I blathered about it, stopping about ten minutes after her eyes glazed over. Then she told me about her weekend dining out and shopping at Providence Place with her sister.

"Miss me?" she said.

"Oh, yeah. I sure did."

When I got around to my encounter with the little thug, she dropped her fork and stared at me. "Jesus, Mulligan! Why didn't you tell me this first?"

"'Cause the Sox are way more important."

"What if he comes back?"

"I'm counting on it. Believe me, I can totally kick his ass, and I'm going to, first chance I get."

She picked up her fork again and stabbed at a shrimp.

"You aren't two boys on the playground, Mulligan. If this is our firebug, we already know that he kills people. What if he has a gun next time?"

"I'll just take it away from him," I said, suddenly feeling less cocksure than I sounded.

"What if he goes for this again?" she asked, her fingers brushing the front of my jeans. "With the luck you've been having lately, he might do some permanent damage next time."

I didn't like where the conversation was going, but I liked where her hand was wandering. I was a little tired, but the parts I planned on using weren't. Once we flopped into bed, I was turned down flat. For the first time since we'd first done it, we weren't doing it.

"You need to rest," she whispered. "And you need to stop acting like such a cowboy."

She pulled my head to her chest, and it felt good there. She touched her lips to my forehead, lingering on a spot I swear had never been kissed before. Suddenly, sleep became a distinct possibility. Her smell was a drug, pulling me under.

"G'night," I managed to mutter.

"Love you, baby," she said. Or maybe I dreamed it.

48

The next day, Gloria was a little better. Not much, but a little. Well, enough to try to tell me her story. She spoke in snapshots, sometimes stopping to weep, sometimes to catch her breath. Her voice was hoarse and faint. I sat at her bedside for two mornings and two afternoons before I had the story straight.

Saturday night, after I'd let her stroll out of Hopes alone, she prowled Mount Hope in her little blue Ford Focus. Just before midnight, the rain turned hard and cold. She reached for her thermos and realized she'd forgotten to fill it before starting out. Zerilli's store was still open, so she parked in the lot beside the building and dashed inside. At the coffee stand, she recharged the thermos with a quart of Green Mountain. When she stepped back outside, the rain beat down harder. Head down, she sprinted to her car and slid the key in the lock.

She had just yanked the car door open and put her right foot inside when it happened:

The heel of a hand ramming into her back. A face-first fall onto the driver's seat, the thermos slipping from her hand, clattering on the asphalt. A man's weight slamming on top of her, stealing her breath. Rain hammering the roof, drowning her screams.

Clawing out from under him. Scrambling across the console toward the passenger-side door. Fists pounding her face. Her head shoved under the dash. Her hand wrenching off a shoe, whacking it against the side window to attract someone. Anyone. The shoe torn from her hand, bashed against her skull. A knife suddenly at her throat. A voice cutting the dark:

"Gonna fuck your ass, you nosy bitch." Saying it again. And again. And again.

Lying motionless now, half on the floor, as he pulls the Nikon from her camera bag, then rummages in her purse. His voice again:

"Where's the money, bitch?"

Her voice: "In the wallet. Just a few dollars."

The fists again. The knife on the seat now as he works the clasp on her Skagen wristwatch. The knife so close. Taking a chance. Grabbing the knife, pointing it at his face. A face that is no face. Covered with a blue ski mask.

His voice: "Asking for it now, bitch."

Her small hand crushed in his, mangled, making popping sounds. The blade biting through the base of her right thumb, severing the tendon, then dropping to the seat. Her head grabbed and whacked against the dash again and again. And the mantra: "Gonna fuck your ass, you nosy bitch." A mantra just for her.

Suddenly the voice stopping, his body falling over hers, pinning her to the seat. Two of them out of sight, still as death. Was someone passing by? The DiMaggios? A police patrol?

Her car keys had gone flying when their dance began. He found them now on the passenger-side floor mat, fired the ignition, drove. She tried to peek out the window, to catch a glimpse of freedom, but he slapped her hard for it, then put his big hand on top of her head and pushed it down. She wasn't sure how long they had been driving when she felt the car slow and stop.

"It's time, nosy picture-taking bitch."

His hands at her clothes now, yanking the sweatshirt over her breasts, ripping off the bra. The fists again. An endless beating. Pointing the knife at her throat, making her tug off her jeans and panties. Thick fingers snaking clumsily between her legs.

Remembering. You don't resist a rapist. Something she read somewhere.

Her voice: "Let's get in the backseat so we can both enjoy this."

His voice: "Yeah. Go ahead, bitch."

Scrambling over the seat on all fours into the back, feeling in the dark for the lever that unlatches the hatchback. The man just behind her, his big hands groping.

Her good hand finding the latch, jerking it, flinging the hatchback open. Scrambling out. Slamming the hatch in his face. Running blindly, smack into a telephone pole. Turning and running, naked and bloody, through the cold, cold rain.

Jesus. She'd asked me to go with her.

"What did he look like?"

She mumbled something I didn't catch.

"Short? Muscular?"

Could it have been the little thug?

Another mumble.

I stopped pressing. I'd put her through enough.

49

"She never saw his face," Laura Villani, the sex—crimes sergeant, told me late that afternoon. "He kept the ski mask on the whole time. All we got is white male, smoker's voice, wedding band, green windbreaker. She never saw him standing, so she couldn't guess his height."

Did the little thug wear a wedding band? I tried picturing his hands, but I couldn't remember.

"She was prowling the neighborhood waiting for the next fire," I said.

"So she told me."

"And he called her 'nosy picture-taking bitch.'"

"Yeah," she said. "That's the angle we're working. Her description doesn't give us much to go on, but we pulled a couple of fingerprints from her vinyl camera bag. If they're his and he's in the system, we'll get him."

"If you do, I'd like to have a few minutes alone with him."

"If we do, I just might let you."

I went back to the office, pulled all my notes on the fires out of my file drawer, and stacked them on my desk. Twenty-two notepads crammed with fire scene descriptions, property ownership records, arson findings, and countless interviews with victims, firefighters, and arson investigators. Twenty-two notebooks full of nothing.

Or were they?

When a homicide detective hits a dead end, he studies the murder book, a chronological record of every detail of his investigation. I didn't have a murder book, but I did have all those notebooks. Was there something in them that I had overlooked? Was there something that should have been in them but wasn't? Could I find some sort of pattern in four months worth of scribbles? I flipped the first one open and started reading.

I'd just started the second notebook when Mason walked up.

"I'm so sorry about Gloria," he said.

"I know you are."

"I sent flowers."

"I know. I saw them in her room."

He frowned and shook his head.

"Her right eye," he said. "It's the one she uses to look through the viewfinder."

He'd noticed that? Maybe he had some reporter in him after all.

"Maybe she can learn to use her left," I said.

"Either way, she's got a job for life. I'll see to it."

He stood silently for a moment, a slim file folder clutched in his left hand.

"Whatcha got there?" I said, already knowing what it was.

"My manhole-covers file. I'd really appreciate it if you could take a few minutes and go over this with me, make sure I haven't missed anything."

"Okay. Drag that empty chair over here and let's have a look."

He sat down, pushed an empty pizza box aside, and laid the folder on my desk. He opened it carefully, as if he were handling a Gutenberg Bible, and took out three sheets of paper—photocopies of city purchasing records showing transactions with a local manufacturer called West Bay Iron.

"How many does it add up to?" I asked.

"Nine hundred and ten."

"Quit whispering, Thanks-Dad. Nobody's going to steal your story."

"The orders are spread over a year," he said, "each one kept under fifteen hundred dollars to evade the city's competitive-bidding requirement. All together, nine hundred and ten cast-iron manhole covers at fifty-five dollars each comes to just over fifty thousand."

"What does the city highway department need with nine hundred and ten new manhole covers?"

"That's what I wondered. I went over there to ask Gennaro Baldelli, but he threw me out."

"'Blackjack' Baldelli."

"Excuse me?"

"That's what our highway superintendent likes to be called."

"So I went to see his deputy, Louis Grieco. He have a nickname, too?"

"'Knuckles.'"

"Yeah, well Knuckles told me to get lost."

"Then what did you do?"

"I went over to city hall and checked campaign contribution records," he said, extracting another sheet of paper from the file folder. "Turns out that Peter Abrams, the owner of West Bay Iron, gave the legal limit to the mayor's last reelection campaign."

"Pretty good work, Thanks-Dad."

"I've been working on my lead. Can you take a look at it?"

"No."

"Why not?"

"Because you aren't ready to write."

"I'm not?"

"You don't have enough. All you've got is the city throwing a little business to a big campaign contributor. That might be a story in Iowa or Connecticut, but in Rhode Island it's not news. It's business as usual."

"I wasted my time, then?"

"Not necessarily."

"So what's my next step?"

"Find out what they're doing with all those manhole covers."

"But I already asked. They won't tell me."

"That's because you asked the wrong people. You've got to cultivate some sources, Thanks-Dad. Seduce a secretary. Find out where the snowplow drivers drink and buy them a few rounds. Chat up the men who work with shovels and don't have titles after their names."

Mason smiled, walked back to his desk, slipped the manhole-covers file in his top drawer, and reached for the phone. Maybe I'd been wrong about him. That got me to wondering what else I'd been wrong about.

I picked up the first notebook and started in again, wanting to read them all straight through without interruption. Over the next hour, six reporters and five copy editors stopped by my desk to ask how Gloria was doing. McCracken and Rosie called for the same reason, and Dorcas rang me up to offer her customary salutation.

Clearly, this wasn't going to work.

I turned off the cell phone, stuffed the notebooks in a beat-up vinyl briefcase, and headed for Secretariat.

The "Out of Order" hood I'd tugged over the parking meter was gone, and something was scrawled on the ticket tucked under my wiper blade: "Nice try." I hated losing that hood, but I still had my backup plan. I walked down the block, put the ticket on the publisher's windshield, got in the Bronco, and drove home.

I stretched out on my mattress and started in again with the first notebook, reading slowly and jotting an occasional note on a fresh yellow legal pad. It took me two hours to go through all the notebooks, the one I'd spilled beer on still mostly legible. Then I started over and read them all again. When I was done, all I had on the legal pad was a half page of scribbled questions.

Who owned the five mystery companies that had bought up a quarter of Mount Hope? Chances were it wasn't really the long-dead roster of the Providence Grays. Was there any way to find out? Were they still in the market for property in the fire-prone neighborhood? If so, why? What was it Joseph DeLucca had told me? That they should have sold their place when they had the chance. Had someone made Ma an offer?

On my second reading, I noticed that my notes on the incorporation papers included everything but the names of the lawyers who'd filed them. At the time, it hadn't seemed important. It probably still wasn't. Lawyers for clients who wanted to remain anonymous weren't likely to give me the time of day. Still, it *was* a loose end.

Why had Giordano tipped me about the manhole covers? It certainly wasn't out of concern for the civic good. What had he said when he gave me the tip? That I should stop wasting my time with Mount Hope. Was he trying to distract me from the arson story? What reason would he have for doing that? More likely he was nursing a grudge against Blackjack and Knuckles for the time they refused to give one of their no-show jobs to his brother Frank.

On one of the beer-stained notebook pages, I'd recorded seeing a Dio Construction crew knocking down a burned-out triple-decker. I'd underlined *Dio* three times. Why had I thought that might be important? I thought about it. I got up, swigged some Maalox, came back, and thought about it some more. But I didn't have a clue.

And who was the little thug? Was he the pyromaniac, or was he hired muscle delivering a message for someone else?

Either way, he was the key. If I didn't stop snooping around, he'd be back. That's what he'd promised. All I had to do to lay my hands on him was provoke him into coming for me again.

50

That evening, Veronica and I shared a pepperoni pizza at Casserta's, and I told her my plan. She didn't think it was as brilliant as I did.

"That's crazy," she said. "No story's worth getting beaten up."

"Some stories are."

"I'll bet Gloria doesn't think so."

I didn't have a response to that.

"Please, baby," she said, her voice thick with worry. "He might really hurt you this time."

"He's the one who's going to get hurt."

"Well, count me out," she said. "I don't plan on being there when he shows up. Sorry, cowboy, but you'll be sleeping alone until this blows over."

"I could come over to your place for a few hours, then go back to mine," I said.

"I'd like that, but not tonight. I'm busy."

Busy? I didn't like the sound of that, but I decided not to make an issue of it. I paid the tab, leaned across the table for a kiss, and slid out of the booth.

"Be careful, baby," she said. "Providence would be a lonely place without you."

When I got home, I snapped on the TV to catch the Red Sox' third game against the Tigers. Wakefield pitched Boston to a 4–2 lead after six, and Sox hitters mauled a trio of Tigers relief pitchers. Final score, 12–6. I grinned and shut the TV off.

I fidgeted with my cell, changing the ring tone to "Am I Losing You?" by the Cate Brothers, my favorite tune by that great Arkansas blues band. Then I took the shadow box down from the wall, pried the back open, and removed my grandfather's Colt .45. I sat cross-legged on the floor and spent a half hour cleaning it and thinking about him.

"Bust 'em or dust 'em." That's what Grandpa used to say.

Wiping away the excess gun oil, I idly thought about buying some bullets. But the little thug was, well, little. What did I need with bullets?

51

Next morning I visited Gloria in the hospital. Her voice was stronger, but she still seemed defeated somehow. She kept whispering, "Thank you, Mulligan," as if I'd done something besides let her wander Mount Hope's streets alone.

An hour later I was wheeling Secretariat through the old neighborhood, with Jimmy Thackery's "Blue Dog Prowl" growling from my CD player. It made me feel like prowling. I found Joseph DeLucca in front of his place, loading cardboard boxes onto the bed of a Bondo-patched Ford pickup.

"Hey," he said.

"Hey, Joseph. Can I give you a hand?"

"Nah. I'm about done. I borrowed the truck 'cause I thought there'd be more, but all that's left is what's in them fuckin' boxes."

It wasn't much—silverware, a few pots and pans, some mismatched dishes, a few hand tools, a couple of framed photos, a dozen water-stained books in matching leather bindings that smelled of smoke.

Out of curiosity, I reached in and pulled out a volume. *Bleak House* by Charles Dickens.

"You oughta read that, you get a chance," Joseph said. "This guy can fuckin' write!"

Joseph reads Dickens? Joseph can read? Mark Twain and I had been wrong about him. It was his bright side that he never showed to anybody.

"When I talked to you last week, you said something about wishing you'd sold the place when you had the chance. Did you have it on the market?"

"Nah. But there was this girl who come knocking on our door, asking about buyin' it."

"Just knocked on the door and made an offer out of the blue?"

"Right out of the fuckin' blue."

"When was this?"

"January. No, February, 'cause all them Nigger History Month specials was screwing with my TV shows."

I winced at his choice of words and asked, "Who was this girl?"

"Don't remember her name, but she gave me her fuckin' card."

He pulled a warped leather wallet out of his hip pocket, extracted a dog-eared business card, and shoved it at me. Raised navy blue letters printed on good stock read "Cheryl Scibelli, Registered Agent, Little Rhody Realty Co." Below it, a phone number but no address.

Little Rhody. One of the mystery real estate companies.

"Mind if I keep this?

"Knock yourself out."

I stabled Secretariat in front of Joseph's house and walked around the neighborhood knocking on the doors of single-family homes, the buildings most likely to be owner-occupied. That got me three slammed doors, four nobody-homes, two renters, and six homeowners. Turned out I knew them all—a former gym teacher, three old classmates from Hope High, Annie's mom, and Jack Hart, the guy who took over Dad's milk route when his eyesight failed. Five of the six said they'd been approached about selling. Two already had and were about to move out. Four of them still had business cards from Cheryl Scibelli of Little Rhody Realty.

I crossed Camp Street, leaving the fire-plagued southeast quadrant of the neighborhood behind, and knocked on more doors. That turned up five more home owners, none of whom had ever heard of Cheryl Scibelli or Little Rhody Realty.

On my way back to the Bronco, I cut up Catalpa Street and

passed a crew from Dio Construction loading what was left of the rooming house into a dump truck. That's when it hit me. Why was Johnny Dio's company the only one I'd seen knocking down torched buildings in Mount Hope?

52

"Little Rhody Realty!" The voice was perky and eager to be helpful.

"May I speak with Mr. Dio, please?"

"I'm sorry, sir, but there is no one here by that name."

"Well, may I speak to Mr. Giordano then?"

"I'm sorry"—the voice colder now—"but there is no one here by that name, either."

"How about Charlie Radbourn or Barney Gilligan? Actually, any dead member of the Providence Grays will do."

"I have no idea what you are talking about."

"Is Cheryl Scibelli available?"

"I'm afraid she's gone for the day, sir."

"Do me a favor, then. Next time Johnny Dio or Vinnie Giordano come in, tell them Mulligan called looking for them."

She told me again that she'd never heard of them, and maybe she hadn't. I said good-bye and hung up.

If Little Rhody had anything to do with the fires . . .

And if Dio or Giordano had anything to do with Little Rhody . . .

And if the receptionist gave one of them my message . . .

And if the little thug worked for one of them . . .

Well, then maybe I'd be getting another visit from him soon.

53

That night I picked up Chinese takeout and drove to Veronica's place in Fox Point. We ate chicken with garlic sauce and shrimp lo mein straight from the cartons as she talked about her day. The evening was a blur of food and chat until we got naked and tumbled into bed.

Again, Veronica guided my head to her chest, but not so I could relax. I took my time exploring, and by the time our bodies locked in rhythm, the woman had become a full-blown addiction.

When my breathing returned to normal I twisted away from her, snatched my jeans off the carpet, and fumbled for something in the side pocket.

"Here. I want you to have this."

She sat up in bed, opened the little blue box, and lifted the necklace out on a finger. It wasn't much, but it managed to glisten a little. A tiny sterling Underwood typewriter on a silver chain.

"It's beautiful. L. S. A. Mulligan showing his sweet side?"

I shrugged and lifted her hair as she fastened the clasp behind her neck. And then she kissed me.

Later, there was a new kind of pillow talk. Veronica wanted to discuss the future.

"What's next for you, Mulligan?"

"I've got some incorporation papers to recheck."

"No, no, not that. What do you want to do with the rest of your life?"

"Oh. First off, I want to get my divorce finalized."

"That would be good place to start."

"Then I want to sit in the center-field bleachers at Fenway Park with my best girl and watch the Red Sox win the World Series again."

"Your best girl? Would that be me?"

"It would."

"Then what?"

"Then I can die happy."

"Hey, be serious for a minute, okay?"

I thought I *was* being serious, but what I said was, "Okay."

"You've been in Rhode Island for a long time, Mulligan."

"All my life."

"Isn't it time you moved on to something better?"

"Like what?"

"*The Washington Post? The New York Times? The Wall Street Journal*, maybe?"

"Move someplace where I can't get the Red Sox on free TV? Besides, you know what the newspaper job market is like. Those rags aren't hiring; they're laying off."

"Yeah, but they always have room for an investigative reporter with a drawer full of awards."

"Nobody wants to hear about a ten-year-old Pulitzer, Veronica."

"Yes, they do," she said. "And your Polk was just two years ago."

"Um."

"What about television news? CNN, maybe."

"With *my* face?"

I waited for her to protest, but she didn't. Instead she said, "Wolf Blitzer is no prize either."

I didn't say anything.

"Think about it, baby? What would you be doing with your life if you could do anything you wanted?"

"I'm doing it," I said.

"You actually *like* it here?"

"Naked next to you? Are you kidding?"

"Be serious!"

I grinned. "Do you know how Rhode Island got its name, Veronica?"

"No, but I bet you're going to tell me."

"Actually, I'm not. Fact is, nobody knows for sure. Historians have poked into it for years, but all they've come up with are a few half-baked theories."

"So?"

"So one of them goes like this: *Rhode Island* is a bastardization of *Rogue Island*, a name the sturdy farmers of colonial Massachusetts bestowed upon the swarm of heretics, smugglers, and cutthroats who first settled the shores of Narragansett Bay."

Veronica snickered and tossed her hair. I liked it when she did that.

"They ought to change the name back," she said. "*Rhode Island* is boring. *Rogue Island* has pizzazz."

It's also apt. For more than a hundred years, pirates slipped from Narragansett Bay's hidden coves to prey on merchant shipping. In the late 1700s and early 1800s, Rhode Island shipmasters dominated the American slave trade. During the French and Indian War and again during the Revolution, heavily armed privateers skulked out of Providence and Newport to seize prizes with little regard for the flags they flew. After the Civil War, Boss Anthony, a co-owner of *The Providence Journal*, kept his Republican machine in power for decades by buying votes at the going rate of two bucks apiece. Around the turn of the century, Nelson Aldrich, a former Providence grocery clerk immortalized in David Graham Phillips's "The Treason of the Senate," helped robber barons plunder the country. In the 1950s and 1960s, a Providence mobster named Raymond L. S. Patriarca was the most powerful man in New England, deciding everything from what records got played on the radio to who lived and who died. And Mayor Carroza's predecessor, the honorable Vincent A. "Buddy" Cianci Jr., recently did federal time for conspiring to run a criminal enterprise, also known as the city of Providence.

"Of course, we do know how Providence got its name," I said. "Roger Williams christened his city in thanksgiving for God's divine guidance. Cotton Mather's suggestions, 'the fag end of creation' and 'the sewer of New England,' mercifully didn't stick."

"And this is why you like it here?"

"I grew up here. I know the cops and the robbers, the barbers and the bartenders, the judges and the hit men, the whores and the priests. I know the state legislature and the Mafia inside out, and they're pretty much the same thing. When I write about a politician buying votes or a cop on the pad, the jaded citizenry just chuckles and shrugs its shoulders. That used to bother me. It doesn't anymore. Rogue Island is a theme park for investigative reporters. It never closes, and I can ride the roller coaster free all day.

"Besides, if I tried to write about some place I don't know, I could never do it as well."

"Sure you could," she said. "Think of how much fun you'd have going after all the crooks in Washington."

Washington? That was the second time she mentioned Washington.

"You've applied to *The Post*, haven't you?"

"Let me tell you something about my family, Mulligan. My sister Lucy? She starts Harvard Medical School in the fall. My brother Charles? At thirty he's already a VP at Price Waterhouse. Me? I bust my ass covering 'the fag end of creation' for a third-rate newspaper that pays me six hundred dollars a week. Daddy feels so sorry for me that he sends me five hundred a month, and I'd be living like you if I had the pride to send it back.

"My parents are ambitious people. When I told them I was going to be a reporter, they sat me down and told me I was making a big mistake. When I wouldn't listen, they didn't nag or threaten. After I graduated from Princeton, they paid the whole bill for Columbia J-School and never once complained. But I think they're a little ashamed of me. I want them to be as proud of me as they are of Charles and Lucy. I want to be proud of myself. I'm my parents' daughter, Mulligan. I'm ambitious, too."

The speech was nice, but I was more concerned about when I'd be sleeping alone again.

"So what did *The Post* say?"

"I sent them my résumé and clips a month ago. Last week, Bob Woodward called me. *Bob Fucking Woodward!* I flew down yesterday for an interview. Bob says he loves my instincts, loves my writing, loves my reporting, especially the Arena stories. And with the pressure he's under to hire minorities, you know damned well he loves it that I'm Asian. From the way he stared at me, I could tell he also likes the way I look."

This was all happening too fast. I tried to keep the desperation out of my voice. "So when do you start?"

"He said he'll have an opening for a federal-courts reporter in a month or two. I'd write daily news briefs for the Web site and news analysis pieces for the paper. It's a great job, and it's mine if I want it."

"Now you're going to say you told him about me."

"Better than that. I wrote a kick-ass résumé for you and gave it to him with a package of your best clips."

"Did you also tell him that I'm Chinese?"

"Mulligan!"

"Would it help if we got married and I took your name?"

"Please stop with the jokes. He wants you to call him. Will you at least think about it? I love you, baby. I don't want to lose you."

I pulled her into my arms and nuzzled her hair. "I don't want to lose you either," I said. I almost said, "I love you, too," but the last time I'd said that was during the last month of my marriage, and it had been a lie. The words didn't feel right in my mouth anymore.

"Have you thought about *The Globe*?" I asked. "If they hear *The Post* wants you, they'll grab you in a second. Boston's just fifty miles up the interstate. I could drive up every weekend. Maybe we could pool our money and get a box at Fenway."

"Tell you what," she said. "If you promise to think about *The Post*, I'll promise to think about *The Globe*. Deal?"

"Yeah, okay." I felt myself about to say something that wasn't very romantic. "But if it ends up that you leave town and I stay, how about giving me your source as a going-away present?"

She sighed. "The one leaking me those grand-jury transcripts?"

"Yeah, that one."

"He'll never talk to you. He hates your guts."

Aha! Her source was a he who hated my guts. On the other hand, that didn't exactly narrow it down.

When I got back to my apartment, it was nearly midnight. I tried to read a Dennis Lehane novel, but the words kept blurring on the page. I couldn't stop thinking about Veronica. Was there anything I could say to make her stay? I sat up wondering about that until four in the morning, but the little thug didn't show. He didn't come the next night either.

54

An attendant helped Gloria out of the wheelchair, wished her good luck, and wheeled it back through the electric doors. I took her good arm as she tottered a few feet to Secretariat. Off to our left, a man with his right arm in a cast raised his left to hail a cab. Gloria saw the arm come up and cowered, burying her face in my chest. Her physical wounds were healing, but the damage cut much deeper.

I held her for a moment, my hand cradling the back of her head. Then I helped her into the front passenger seat. She yelped as I drew the seat belt across her broken ribs. I walked around the front of the Bronco, got in the other side, and cranked the starter.

"You're looking better."

"No, I'm not."

"It must feel good to get out of the hospital."

"I have to go back."

"I know."

There would be another operation to repair the tendon and two plastic surgeries on her nose and right cheek. There was nothing more they could do for her right eye.

I pulled onto I-95 heading south, and we drove silently for a few miles, Gloria squinting through the windshield at an overcast Rhode Island morning.

"Mulligan?"

"Um?"

"It wasn't your fault."

"Yes, it was."

"Did you get it?"

"I did. It's in the glove box."

She leaned forward, and the pressure from the seat belt made her yelp again. She opened the box and pulled out a canister of pepper spray.

"Thanks. What do I owe you?"

What does *she* owe *me*?

"Nothing, Gloria. Whoosh had a carton of them lying around, and he wanted you to have it. He would have given you a revolver, but I didn't think that was a good idea."

She raised her good hand, her thumb a cocked hammer and her index finger a gun barrel, mulling it over.

"You survived, Gloria. You beat him."

"What if he comes back?"

"He won't. He's running for his life now."

"Are they going to catch him?"

"They will." The police hadn't found a match for the fingerprints, but Gloria didn't need to hear that. She needed to think justice was coming.

It started to rain as I cruised through Cranston on the interstate. When I flipped on the wipers, Gloria tensed. Then she began to moan.

"Oh, no. Oh, no. Oh, no."

"What's wrong, Gloria?"

"The rain!" Screaming now. "MAKE IT STOP!" She beat her good hand on the dash.

There was no place to pull over and nothing I could do to comfort her.

"Make it stop!"

As I turned onto the East Avenue exit in Warwick, it did. Gloria's scream turned to a whimper as I drove a few miles to Vera Street and parked at the curb in front of the little yellow ranch house where she grew up. Her mother was waiting on the sidewalk to help me take her daughter into the house.

55

The lawyers who'd filed the incorporation papers
had each signed their names with a self-important flourish of swirls
and curlicues. It was easier to read the type below the signatures:
Beth J. Harpaz, Irwin M. Fletcher, Patrick R. Connelly III, Yolanda
Mosley-Jones, and Daniel Q. Haney.

I'd hoped to find that the same lawyer had filed for all five companies. That would have tied them together, given me something
to go on. Instead, all my return trip to the secretary of state's office
had gotten me was five more names I'd never heard of. But I knew
somebody who might recognize them.

I got to the newsroom shortly after noon and found Veronica
sitting in her cubicle nibbling something green and leafy. I flipped
my notebook open to the right page and dropped it on her desk.

"Take a look at these names and tell me if you know any of them."

She stared at the page for a moment. "Sorry," she said. "I don't
have the time for this. I've got to get to the courthouse. Word is the
Arena indictment could be handed up today."

She pushed herself up from her ergonomically correct desk chair,
gave me a peck on the cheek, and headed for the elevators.

An investigative reporter must be resourceful. When the first
source fails, he must find another. I opened my desk drawer and
pulled out my secret file. Beth J. Harpaz, attorney at law, was listed
in the Providence telephone directory.

"McDougall, Young, Coyle, and Limone. How may I direct your call?"

"Beth Harpaz, please,"

"May I ask your name and what this is regarding?"

"My name is Jeb Stuart Magruder. My wife of twenty-two years has taken a lesbian lover, and I wish to initiate divorce proceedings immediately."

"I am sorry, sir, but Ms. Harpaz doesn't handle divorce work. I suggest you try a smaller firm."

I thanked her, hung up, opened the phone book, and started to look up the number for Daniel Q. Haney. Then I thought better of it and hit the redial button.

"McDougall, Young, Coyle, and Limone. How may I direct your call?"

"How ya doin', sweetheart. I'm wondering if my good buddy Dan Haney is in this afternoon."

"May I ask your name and what this is regarding?"

"Tell Danny that Chuck Colson is calling to make sure he's not thinking of chickening out of our Saturday-morning golf date. He bet a grand that he can beat me, and I've already spent the money."

"I see," she said. "Hold a moment, please, and let me see if he'll take your call."

She put me on hold, and I hung up. I spent a couple of minutes practicing another telephone voice and hit redial.

"McDougall, Young, Coyle, and Limone. How may I direct your call?"

"Irwin M. Fletcher, please."

"May I ask your name and what this is regarding?"

"This is James W. McCord. I need to speak with Mr. Fletcher immediately on a matter of some urgency."

"I'm sorry, sir, but Mr. Fletcher is out of town on business. Perhaps someone else can assist you."

"The prick's never around when I need him," I said, and hung up.

Ten minutes later, the redial button again.

"McDougall, Young, Coyle, and Limone. How may I direct your call?"

"Patrick Connelly, please."

"Would that be Patrick R. Connelly Junior or Patrick R. Connelly the Third?"

"Damn! I didn't know the old man was still alive."

"The elder Mr. Connelly is only fifty-five, sir."

"So the antibiotics have his syphilis under control, then?"

"Excuse me, sir?" she said, and I hung up.

I was fresh out of telephone voices, and I figured the disembodied voice on the other end would be checking caller ID now. I got up and wandered over to Mason's desk.

"I need a favor."

"So do I."

"Me first," I said, and told him what I needed him to do.

"Yolanda Mosley-Jones, please."

Pause.

"My name is Gordon Liddy, and I am calling in regard to a criminal case she is handling for me."

Pause.

"But it's urgent I speak with her this afternoon."

Pause.

"I see. No, no. I'm on the road. I'll call back later this afternoon." he said, and hung up.

"So?"

"So Ms. Mosley-Jones is currently assisting Brady Coyle in a criminal matter at the federal courthouse and won't be available till this afternoon."

"You did good, Thanks-Dad."

"Who the hell is Gordon Liddy?"

"Never mind that. What is it I can do for you?"

"I found out what they're doing with the manhole covers."

"Tell me about it."

"I asked around and found out that a lot of the guys from the highway department like to hang out after work at a strip joint called Good Time Charlie's on Broad Street."

"I've heard of it."

"So I started hanging out there, too, wearing jeans and a sweat-shirt so I wouldn't look out of place. At first, my plan was to try to talk to them, but they're probably not going to tell me anything, right? So I just sat at the bar and eavesdropped, which wasn't all that easy because of the loud music. The first two nights, it was just a bunch of guys pawing the dancers and crowing about the Celtics and Red Sox. But on the third night, three men in work clothes came in, sat at the bar, and started complaining about this job they were supposed to do the next morning. I didn't catch it all, but it had something to do with loading a truck, and I caught the words *manhole covers*. They were pretty worked up about it. One of them wanted to file a grievance."

"Those things are heavy," I said.

"A hundred and fifty pounds each. I looked it up."

"So then what?"

"So early the next morning, I drove over to the highway depart-ment, parked on the street, and found a spot over by the railroad tracks where I could stay out of sight and watch the loading dock. About ten o'clock a truck pulled up and three guys, who looked like the same ones I'd seen at the bar, started loading it with manhole covers."

"You followed the truck?"

"I did. They turned right on Ernest and right again on Eddy Street, then jumped on I-95 going north. At the Lonsdale Ave-nue exit in Pawtucket, they got off, drove east for a mile or so, and stopped in front of a chain-link gate. They honked the horn, the gate rolled open, and they pulled in and backed up to a loading dock."

He grinned, wanting me to beg for the rest.

"What was this place?"

"The sign on the gate said Weeden Scrap Metal Company."
We both laughed.

"How much is Weeden paying for manhole covers these days?"

"Sixteen dollars apiece," he said. "I checked."

"Let me get this straight. The highway department is buying manhole covers for fifty-five dollars each from one of the mayor's biggest campaign contributors, and Baldelli and Grieco are turning around and scrapping them for sixteen dollars each."

"That's what they're doing. So far, they've pocketed fourteen thousand five hundred and sixty dollars. I did the math."

"Have you written your lead yet?"

"I've got one more interview first. I'm seeing the mayor this afternoon. I thought I should tell him what's been going on and give him a chance to comment."

"Be sure to ask him what he *thought* was going to happen when he appointed guys named Knuckles and Blackjack to run the highway department."

"Lomax said I can break the story in the online edition," he said, "and then write a longer version for the paper."

"Sounds like you've got yourself your first page-one byline, Thanks-Dad."

I went back to my desk, found the business card Joseph had given me, and dialed Little Rhody Realty. Cheryl Scibelli still wasn't in, so I left my name and number. I opened my secret file and found that her home number was listed.

No answer.

The directory gave her address as 22 Nelson Street, over by Providence College. I drove there and knocked on the door of an immaculate white cottage.

Nobody home.

56

By five o'clock McCracken's secretary was gone for the day, so I let myself in. After I told him what I'd learned about the lawyers, we sat quietly for a while and thought about it.

"You realize it doesn't prove anything," he said.

"I know."

"A big law firm like that handles a lot of incorporation papers."

"It does."

"But it's a hell of a coincidence.

"It is."

We sat and thought about it some more.

"Be good if we could find out who owns the five companies," he said.

"It would."

"But there's no way to find that out."

"None that I know of, unless one of the lawyers decides to risk disbarment and betray a confidence."

"Which isn't goddamned likely."

"No, it isn't."

He opened the inlaid cherrywood humidor on his desk, took out two maduro torpedoes, clipped the ends, and offered me one. He lit his with a wooden match, and I torched mine with the Colibri. We sat and smoked for a while.

"Did you remember to broadcast the description of the little thug?" I asked.

"To every insurance investigator I know," he said. "Didn't ring any bells."

"He said he'd come back for me if I didn't stop poking around."

"And you haven't."

"Of course not."

"What are you going to do when he comes?"

"Interview him."

"Would that be before or after you kick his ass?"

"That'll be up to him."

The Cate Brothers riffed from my pants pocket. I checked caller ID, saw it was Dorcas, and let it go to voice mail. I was stuffing the phone back in my pocket when the band came back for an encore.

"Hi baby. Just wanted to let you know I can't see you tonight. I'm meeting a source for dinner, and it could go late."

"Tomorrow, then?"

"Definitely tomorrow. Miss you like crazy. Gotta run. Bye."

Note to self: Change the ring tone to a song that doesn't have the words *losing you* in the title.

"So," I said. "Want to catch the Sox-Yankees game tonight?"

"You have tickets?" McCracken said.

"Yeah. Box seats at Hopes. I'll call Rosie, see if she wants to join us."

"Chief Lesbo?"

"Hey, I warned you about that."

"But she *is* a lesbian, Mulligan. I know for sure now."

"How's that?"

"I asked her out, and she turned me down flat."

"That's how you can tell?"

"Of course."

"You must meet a lot of lesbians."

.   .   .

Rosie settled onto a bar stool between me and McCracken just as Derek Jeter dug in against our ace, Josh Beckett. Mike Mussina matched him pitch for pitch until Ramirez homered in the bottom of the fifth. A long rain delay provided plenty of time for beer and for McCracken to give it another try with Rosie.

"Sorry," she said, "but you're not my type."

"What is your type?"

"That's my type right there," she said, pointing to the TV over the bar. The rain had finally stopped, and Manny Ramirez was running through the wet grass to take his position in front of the Green Monster. "Oh, my God, he's so hot."

Papelbon slammed the door on the Pinstripes in the ninth, Hopes erupted in the traditional "Yankees Suck" chant, somebody dumped a beer on an asshole in a Jeter jersey, and Annie grabbed the remote, switching the TV to the Channel 10 News. Then she made the rounds of the tables, snatching dollar bills and hiking her skirt up those long legs. A good time was had by all. Except the guy in the Jeter jersey.

That night, I stayed up late with a Tim Dorsey novel, hoping the little thug would finally make an appearance. About three in the morning, he did.

57

He announced his presence with the sound of splintering wood.

I rushed my shattered front door, looked down at the top of the little thug's head, and threw a left. He blocked it effortlessly with his right and kicked me square in the groin, an area he seemed to favor. Then he slammed into me, bulled me across the room into the kitchen wall, and went to work on my ribs.

My counter-punches bounced harmlessly off the top of his skull. I tried to shove him off to get punching room, but it was like trying to move a boxcar. His arms were jackhammers, pounding lefts and rights to my body. Why didn't he go for my jaw? Maybe it was too high for him to reach. When his fists finally tired of me, he took a step back, and I discovered he'd been the only thing holding me up.

I slid down the wall to the floor. He swung his short right arm and backhanded me across the face.

"Asshole," he said. "I warned you to stop snooping around the manhole covers."

Manhole covers? I felt like I'd been hit with one. That's what this was about?

I tried to form the question, but the little thug was gone, taking my dignity with him.

58

In the morning, there wasn't much blood in my urine, but my ribs hurt when I moved and even when I didn't. I walked stiffly into the newsroom and went straight to Mason's desk.

"What happened to you?" he said. "You look terrible."

"Never mind that, Thanks-Dad. Just tell me this. Is there any reason someone might think I was working on the manhole-covers story?"

"Heck, Mulligan. I've been telling everybody I've been working with you."

Great.

"Mulligan!" Lomax beckoned me over to the city desk. "Some squawk on the police scanner about a body at a construction site near Rhode Island Hospital."

Then he raised his eyes from his computer and looked me up and down. "Looks like somebody had a rough night. Are you up to this?"

"Sure," I said, but I really wasn't. Still, the assignment *was* convenient. I could stop by the emergency room and see about my ribs.

The corpse was sprawled on its belly near an idle Dio Construction front-end loader. Judging by the mess she'd left in the dirt, the victim had crawled five yards toward the hospital before her pump quit. The three big holes in her back looked like exit wounds.

A detective rolled the body over. A yellow logo was sewn over the breast pocket of her dark green blazer. "Little Rhody Realty." A few feet away, a uniformed cop rummaged in her purse and pulled out a driver's license.

"Hey, Eddie. Got an ID?"

"Come on, Mulligan. You know we can't release that till we notify next of kin."

"Suppose I tell you?"

He just looked at me.

"Cheryl Scibelli of 22 Nelson Street."

"You recognize her?"

"Something like that."

I spent two hours in the emergency room waiting my turn behind five traffic-accident victims, a dozen squalling kids with high fevers, three middle-aged men with chest pains, and a couple of elderly slip-and-falls.

My best lead, the little thug, had nothing to do with the fires. My second best lead was dead, and the message I'd left her might have been the reason why. I didn't have a clue what to do next.

The X-ray showed four broken ribs, one on the left, three on the right.

The intern who turned me into an Egyptian mummy put it all in perspective: "A couple more punches and one of these ribs would have punctured a lung."

"I guess it's my lucky day."

When I got back, Lomax watched me shuffle across the newsroom and settle gingerly into my desk chair. I was pounding out a lead on the shooting for our online edition when he walked up and sat on the corner of my desk.

"What the hell happened to you?"

I didn't want to talk about it. "I ran into a couple of New York fans who didn't appreciate my 'Yankees Suck' T-shirt."

"Ribs?"

"Yeah."

"Broken?"

"Four of them."

"After you write this up, why don't you go home?"

I didn't argue. Tonight, the Sox were starting a two-game series against the Indians, the team we beat in last year's league-championship series, and I was going to need more time than usual to suit up.

59

Getting out of my T-shirt was agony. Once I got it off, it took me five minutes to ease into my team jersey and button it up the front. By the time Veronica called, the Sox were up 1–0 in the third.

"Hey, baby. What's the plan for tonight?"

"I think we'll be staying in."

"You're kidding, right?"

"'Fraid not."

Even talking hurt.

"I need you to do me a favor." I said. "Could you get us some takeout and stop off at the Walgreens on Atwells Ave. to pick up a prescription for me?"

"Are you all right?"

"Yeah, I'm okay. I'll fill you in when you get here."

Forty minutes later, she walked in carrying a sack of deli sandwiches and a little white pharmacy bag.

"What happened to your door?"

"Nothing to worry about. The landlord says it'll be fixed in a couple of days."

"What's wrong with you? What do you need this for?" she said, dropping the pharmacy sack beside me on the bed.

I still didn't want to talk about it. I tore open the bag, wrestled the childproof cap off the vial, swallowed two Oxycodone tablets, and washed them down with Killian's.

"You're not supposed to take those with alcohol, baby."

"So they say, but in my experience they work better this way."

"Are you going to tell me what's going on?"

"The Sox just fell behind four to one, and we're coming to bat in the top of the sixth."

"Mulligan!"

She snatched the remote and turned the TV off.

"I'll tell you everything after the game," I said.

"Tell me now." She held the remote tantalizingly out of reach.

"Later. I can't miss this."

She pouted, surrendered the remote, and plopped down beside me as I switched the TV back on. She rolled over to hug me, and I yelped.

"Mulligan?"

"Soon as the game ends. Eat your sandwich."

The Sox tied the score in the eighth, Ramirez hit a three-run shot in the top of the ninth, Papelbon did his thing, and it was over.

"I don't suppose I'll be enjoying the postgame show," I said.

She answered by punching a button on the remote, and the screen went dark.

"Well?"

"Lester didn't have his best stuff tonight, but the bullpen was great."

"Enough already! Tell me what happened to you."

So I did. I tried to put a good face on it, but it was no use. I'd been beaten up by a pygmy.

When I finished my sad tale, Veronica struggled to suppress a giggle.

"I thought you were going to kick his ass."

"I was mistaken."

Then she glanced at the broken door and furrowed her brow.

"Think he'll come back again?"

"He won't. He's made his point. Besides, the manhole-covers

story is running tomorrow, so he's got nothing to gain by a return visit."

Veronica cradled my face in her hands and touched her lips to my forehead, each cheek, my chin. I reached to pull her to me and yelped again.

"Maybe you could get on top," I said. I'm nothing if not resourceful.

"Maybe we should give it a rest for a few days."

A few days?

I swallowed another Oxycodone-Killian's cocktail and chased it with Maalox. I looked at Veronica and wondered how I'd ever ended up with a woman that beautiful. I was still thinking about that when the drug kicked in and I nodded off.

In the morning, I woke to the sound of Veronica banging around in the kitchen. When she heard me turn on CNN, she came in with the paper and a tray laden with scrambled eggs, bacon, orange juice, and coffee. I used the juice to wash down a couple of painkillers, but they didn't work as well without the beer chaser.

Mason's story about the manhole covers was splashed across page one. There was no fire news. There hadn't been any fires since Hell Night.

"Why do you think that is?" Veronica said.

"There are sixty-two pissed-off DiMaggios patrolling the streets now, looking to crack a head or two. Half the population of Mount Hope is popping NoDoz and lying in wait with firearms and nervous trigger fingers. Maybe our arsonist likes living even more than he likes burning things down."

"Why doesn't he just move on to another neighborhood?"

"He seems to have a special interest in Mount Hope."

"Those lawyers you asked me about the other day? What was that all about?"

"Just some names I happened to run across."

"They lead you anywhere?"

"A dead end," I lied. Given what had happened to Gloria and to Cheryl Scibelli, the less Veronica knew, the better.

That afternoon, Veronica curled up beside me with another book by that sexy poet she'd discovered. I opened a *New Yorker* magazine she'd brought for me to pass the time. Seymour Hersh was at it again, exposing more details about the mishandling of the war in Iraq.

I'd spent the last eighteen years writing about the small-time thugs and liars who ran Rogue Island. Hersh had spent the last thirty-five writing about the big-time thugs and liars who ran the country. Maybe Veronica was right. Maybe it *was* time for me to move on, see if I could write something that would matter.

I thought about that. Then I thought about it some more. My marriage was over. My parents were dead. My sister was in New Hampshire. My brother was in California, and we weren't talking anyway. Veronica was heading for Washington, and I couldn't bear losing her. What was holding me here?

That evening, Veronica brought up that thing called the future again.

"Mulligan?"

"Um?"

"Have you called Woodward yet?"

"This week. I promise."

"You really will?"

"I really will," I said. And this time, I meant it.

Wednesday morning Veronica tried to talk me into calling in sick again, then gave it up and helped me sponge off and get into my shirt. My ribs didn't seem to hurt quite as much as they did yesterday, the Red Sox were on a winning streak, and I was on the verge of a decision about my future. If it weren't for Gloria's eye, Scibelli's corpse, the cloud of suspicion over Jack, the humiliating beating I'd taken, and five consecutive nights without sex, I might have been in a good mood.

I couldn't find a space on the street, so I paid ten bucks to park in a mob-owned lot and walked two blocks to the paper. A couple of prowl cars were double-parked out front. As I walked up the sidewalk, their doors flew open and four uniforms climbed out.

Two got behind me, the other two in front, blocking my way. One grabbed my arms, yanked them behind my back, and snapped handcuffs on tight. Then he shoved me against a prowl car, kicked my legs apart, patted me down, and turned my pockets inside out. My vial of painkillers clattered on the curb. The pain in my ribs felt like I'd been shotgunned.

"You're under arrest."

Yeah. I'd figured that part out.

The only words spoken on the short drive to police headquarters were: "What's this all about?" "Can you guys tell me what's going on?" "What the hell am I charged with?" Maybe the authorities had found out about my parking-ticket scam and didn't think it was funny.

60

Three TV news vans were double-parked in front of the station, and a welcoming committee of cameras and microphones waited on the front steps. Reporters started shouting questions the moment I was yanked from the prowl car. Logan Bedford pushed his way to the front of the pack and hollered:

"Why did you do it?"

Do what?

The uniforms pulled me by the arms into the station, bulled me into an elevator, and dragged me to a second-floor interrogation room. I was in too much pain to tell them how much pain I was in. A cop put his hands on my shoulders and shoved me down onto a straight metal chair. Then they left, slamming the door on the way out. Through a little window in the door, I could see that one of them had stayed behind to stand guard. Apparently I was an escape risk.

By the pattern of cigarette burns on the table, I could tell this was the same room where I had told Polecki about the little thug. I'd been sitting there in handcuffs for nearly an hour, savoring the aroma of old sweat and stale cigarettes, when Polecki and Roselli walked in grinning like idiots. My ribs ached and my arms were numb from elbows to fingertips.

"How about taking these things off?"

"Nah," Polecki said. "You ought to wear steel more often. Looks good on you."

"Yeah," Roselli said, "and you're gonna look even better in stripes."

"They don't wear stripes at the state prison no more," Polecki said.

"Maybe Mulligan could be a trendsetter and bring them back," Roselli said.

"Are you done," I said, "or have you got some fresh material about bending over for the soap?"

"I'm done," Polecki said. He turned to his dumber half. "You?"

"I got nothin'."

"So, Mulligan," Polecki said, "You doing drugs now?"

He reached into his jacket pocket, pulled out a plastic evidence bag, and tossed it on the table. My vial of pills was inside.

"Read the label, asshole. It's a prescription."

"Yeah?" Polecki said. "Then you won't mind if we call this Doctor Brian Israel, make sure it's all on the up-and-up."

"This is why you dragged me in here?"

"Oh, no," Polecki said. "There's more."

"Let me tell him," Roselli said.

"We'll take turns," Polecki said. "Why don't you start by reading him his rights?"

Roselli pulled a well-thumbed card from his pocket and started the spiel. Watch a few TV police dramas and you can recite Miranda backwards, but Roselli still needed that card.

"Now, then," Polecki said, "I'm so glad you could come in for this little chat."

"Yeah," Roselli said. "Good of you to drop by."

"Anything you want to confess before we get started?" Polecki said.

"Save us all a lot of time," Roselli said.

"Forgive me, Father, for I have sinned. I have fornicated a thousand times since my last confession."

"In the old days," Polecki said, "this would be the part where I slug you with a phone book."

"But we don't do that so much anymore," Roselli said.

Both took a moment now to sip coffee from paper cups. They didn't offer me any.

"You know what a criminal profile is, Mulligan?" Polecki said.

I didn't say anything.

"The FBI's real good at them," Roselli said. "You give them the details of a crime, and they come back with a description of the perp, right down to the size of his dick."

"So last week," Polecki said, "the boys and girls at Quantico took a few hours off from chasing ragheads to work up a profile of our serial arsonist."

He pulled something out of his jacket pocket and slapped it on the table—a few typewritten sheets of paper stapled together. It had to be notes he'd taken talking to an agent on the phone. The bureau never puts its profiles in writing. They don't want defense lawyers using them as exculpatory evidence if they turn out to be wrong.

"Perhaps you'd like to look it over," Polecki said. "Oh, wait. With your hands cuffed behind your back, how are you going to turn the pages?"

"That *is* a problem," Roselli said.

"We could uncuff him," Polecki said.

"Let's not," Roselli said.

"I know," Polecki said. "Why don't we summarize it for him?"

"I'll start," Roselli said. "According to the FBI, our arsonist is in his late twenties to late thirties."

"You're thirty-nine, right, Mulligan?" Polecki said.

"He lives alone," Roselli said.

"Like Mulligan," Polecki said.

"He drives an old, beat up SUV," Roselli said, "probably a Chevy Blazer or a Ford Bronco."

"Mulligan's Bronco is a piece of shit," Polecki said.

"He's in pretty good physical condition," Roselli said.

"Sort of like Mulligan," Polecki said.

"Otherwise," Roselli said, "he wouldn't be able to lug five-gallon gasoline cans around and slip in and out of cellar windows."

"But he's got some kind of nagging illness," Polecki said. "Didn't we hear that Mulligan has an ulcer?"

"The fires are meticulously planned, with little evidence left behind," Roselli said, "so we're looking for an organized killer with a high IQ."

"You're a smart guy, right, Mulligan?" Polecki said.

"He has an unhealthy attitude toward authority figures," Roselli said.

"Might even stoop to calling them names, like 'Dumb and Dumber,'" Polecki said.

"He likes to cruise around at night in his Blazer or Bronco scouting for opportunities to set more fires," Roselli said.

"Hey," Polecki said. "Didn't we hear something about Eddie pulling Mulligan over in Mount Hope late one night?"

"After he sets the fires, he likes to stand around and watch them burn," Roselli said. "But he's smart, so he'll have a plausible excuse for why he's there."

"Like, say, reporting for the newspaper," Polecki said.

"He'll find a way to insinuate himself into the police investigation," Roselli said.

"Maybe even implicate an innocent person like Wu Chiang or invent a phony suspect like a little thug to throw us off the track," Polecki said.

"He has difficulty maintaining relationships with the opposite sex," Roselli said.

"Say, how is Dorcas, anyway?" Polecki said.

And he's fascinated by fire, I thought, remembering a snippet from my nighttime reading. But there was no way Polecki and Roselli could know that about me.

"And he's fascinated by fire," Roselli said.

"Yeah," Polecki said. "What was it that Dorcas told us this morning?"

"That Mulligan is a fucking bastard."

"I meant the other thing."

"That he's been mesmerized by fire ever since he watched the Capron Knitting Mill burn down fifteen years ago," Roselli said.

Thank you, Dorcas, for finding another way to punish me.

Polecki lit a stogie with a paper match, held the flame in front of my face a moment, and then flicked it at me.

"So, Mulligan," he said, "does this profile sound like anyone you know?"

"Sounds a little like you," I said, "except for the high IQ and the part about being in shape."

"Maybe we'll be needing that phone book after all," Roselli said.

"Come on," I said. "You both know I didn't do this."

"Mulligan," Polecki said, "you have now idea how much I'd love to see you go down for it."

Dumb and Dumber made a few more empty threats, then got up and left the room. Fifteen minutes later they came back trailed by two more friendly faces. Jay Wargart, a big lug with a five o'clock shadow and fists like hams, and Sandra Freitas, a bottle blonde with rumble hips and a predatory Cameron Diaz smile. They worked homicide. What the hell did *they* want?

61

Freitas settled into the chair across from me and dropped a large manila envelope on the desk. Wargart walked around the table and stood behind me. Polecki and Roselli held up the wall near the door, the little room crowded now.

Freitas opened the envelope and extracted three crime-scene photos.

"She had your name and number on a phone-message slip in her pocketbook," she said.

I didn't say anything.

"Witnesses saw you knocking on her door a couple of days before she was shot."

I kept my mouth zipped.

"She'd been spending a lot of time looking at property in Mount Hope lately. Did she see something she shouldn't have? Is that why you killed her?"

I just looked at her. I should have asked for a lawyer an hour ago, but I wanted to see if I could learn something from the questions.

"She was shot three times with a forty-five, but of course you know that, don't you? I'm betting ballistics will show it's the same gun we found when we executed a search warrant on your shit hole of an apartment this morning."

"How much?" I said.

"Excuse me?"

"How much do you want to bet?"

Wargart kicked my chair, slamming my chest into the table. I'd seen the routine before—bad cop, worse cop. The vial of pills was still on the tabletop. My ribs were pleading for them now, but I didn't figure Dumb and Dumber and the homicide twins were going let me have any.

They grilled me about the murder for an hour before they unhooked the cuffs and gave me my one phone call. I used it to call Jack to tell him what was going on and let him know he was off the hook, at least for now.

"Jesus, Liam," he said. "Is there anything I can do?" I gave him Veronica's number and asked him to let her know why I wouldn't be home for a day or two. There wouldn't be enough to hold me once the ballistics report came back. At least that's what I told myself.

When I was done, they tossed me into a holding cell. I chatted up a couple of meth dealers and then made a study of the folk-art mural scratched into the concrete blocks. Its visceral intensity, raw energy, and undiluted emotion stood in sharp contrast to its cool interplay of realism and impressionism. Think Grandma Moses meets Ron Jeremy.

I was dead tired. I stretched out on a hard, dirty cot, but my ribs wouldn't let me sleep. It seemed like hours before I finally drifted off.

Rain pelted the courtroom windows. Gloria writhed and moaned from the witness stand: "Make it stop! Make it stop!"

Dorcas peered down at her from the bench. "I know this is difficult for you," she said, "but just answer the fucking questions." Then she reached inside her black robe and pulled out a coffeemaker and a five-gallon gas can.

The little thug rose from the prosecution table.

"Is the man who did this to you in this courtroom?" he asked.

Gloria nodded and pointed her finger.

"The record will show," Dorcas said, "that the witness has identified Fucking Bastard."

In the jury box, Hardcastle, Veronica, and Brady Coyle laughed and slapped high fives.

Dorcas was fiddling with the coffeemaker, trying to set the timer. The witness was still pointing at me, but now she had Cheryl Scibelli's face. Then the coffeemaker exploded in a ball of flame, and I woke up. My ribs felt like they were on fire.

62

After forty—eight hours, I was kicked.

They returned my pills, belt, shoelaces, Mickey Mouse watch, lighter, and wallet, but the three twenties that had been in it were gone. My Visa card was still where it belonged, but I assumed they had taken down the number to check recent purchases. Fortunately I hadn't bought any coffeemakers lately. I didn't get my grandfather's gun back.

Secretariat had been impounded and was no doubt being torn apart at the state police crime lab. I dry-swallowed a couple of painkillers and walked the half mile home from the station. The apartment had been tossed, the kitchen drawers pulled out and emptied on the floor. I was beyond caring. I stripped, stepped gingerly into the shower, and let the hot water stream over my ribs for a long, long time.

Late Friday morning, I stepped off the elevator and walked stiffly into the newsroom. Keyboard clacking dribbled into silence as two dozen reporters and copy editors stopped what they were doing to stare. At first, no one said anything. Then a drawl broke the silence.

"Burn down a neighborhood so you can write about it? Hot diggity! Why didn't I think of that?"

"Shut it, Hardcastle," Lomax said.

He rose from his throne behind the city desk, gestured that I should follow, and stepped into Pemberton's glass-walled office. I was halfway there when Veronica intercepted me.

"Are you all right?"

"As good as can be expected."

"Anything I can do?"

"Yeah," I said. I took her hand and squeezed it. "Keep me company after I have this friendly little chat."

Then I turned away, entered the managing editor's office, and sank into one of the maroon leather visitor's chairs.

Pemberton took off his glasses, wiped them with a Kleenex, and put them back on. Then he unbuttoned the cuffs of his starched white shirt and rolled up the sleeves.

"Can I get you anything, Mulligan? Bottled water? A cup of coffee, perhaps?"

"I could use some Percocet."

"Excuse me?"

"Never mind. I'm good."

"Yes, well. So let's get right to it, then. We seem to have something of a situation here."

"A situation?" Lomax said. "Feels more like a goddamned train wreck."

I didn't say anything.

"Have you observed how this unfortunate affair is playing on the TV news?" Pemberton said.

"Sorry, but the seventy-two-inch, high-def, flat-screen entertainment center in the holding cell was on the fritz."

"Yes, of course. You were being detained. It must have been quite unpleasant for you."

"Quite unpleasant indeed," I said.

Lomax glared at me and said, "Cut it out."

"Unfortunately," Pemberton said, "all the local channels have blown the matter entirely out of proportion. To hear them tell it, you'd think the newspaper itself is the serial arsonist."

"You mean, as opposed to just one wayward employee?"

"I didn't intend to imply that."

"And how is the paper handling the story?"

"Oh, that's right. You haven't seen the newspaper either. Perhaps you should read this before we continue."

He pulled a paper from a stack on his desk and passed it to me. I folded it open to the sports page. The Sox bats had pounded the Yankees 7–5 the night before. Yippie.

The name *L. S. A. Mulligan* was on page one again, but this time it wasn't a byline. The story of my arrest had been written by Lomax, the circumstances too sensitive to be entrusted to a mere reporter. I scanned it and learned that Polecki had identified me as "a person of interest" in the arson investigation. At least the cops hadn't publicly connected me to the Scibelli murder. Pemberton was quoted as saying he would have no comment until he had time to "review the situation."

I tossed the paper on the desk and looked at Pemberton.

"Funny," I said. "I didn't see anything in there about how you are standing by your reporter."

"Yes, well . . ." He looked at Lomax for help, didn't get any, and pressed on. "I do hope you understand why I have to ask you this, Mulligan. Are you in any way culpable in this dreadful affair?"

"Of course he isn't," Lomax said.

"I believe Mulligan is capable of answering for himself."

"Fuck you," I said.

"May I take that as a no, then?"

"You may."

"Good. That's settled. Now we have to decide what we are going to do with you."

63

At two in the afternoon Hopes was mostly empty, just a couple of alkies slouched at the bar sipping something bitter. I led Veronica and Mason to a table by the beer cooler in back.

"Indefinite suspension without pay," I said.

"You're kidding," Veronica said.

"At first, it was gonna be *with* pay, but only if I promised to keep my nose out of the arson investigation. I told them I couldn't do that. Especially not now."

"Baby, that's so unfair."

"Try to see it from their point of view," I said. "For the good of the newspaper, they've got to distance themselves from me. If I were in their position, I'd do the same thing."

"But without pay?"

"How's it going to look if I keep digging into the story and some asshole like Logan Bedford finds out I'm still on the payroll?"

"Back up a minute," Mason said. "Do the cops really think you set the fires, or is Polecki just trying to get even for that 'Dumb and Dumber' story?"

"Both."

"Why would they think you're involved?"

"The FBI profile *does* fit me to a T."

"Yeah, but it could fit a lot of people."

"True. And there's a flaw in it, too."

246 | Bruce DeSilva

"Which is?"

"The profile assumes the perp is a pyromaniac."

"He isn't?"

"No. This isn't pyromania. It's arson for profit."

"What makes you think that?" Mason asked.

"All in good time, Thanks-Dad."

"What are you going to do now?" Veronica said.

"I've got twelve hundred in my checking account. That gives me about a month to crack this thing. If it takes longer than that . . ."

"You haven't taken any vacation this year, right?" Mason said.

I nodded.

"And you get—what?—three weeks a year?"

"Yeah."

"So you've got some vacation pay coming. At your salary it should come to . . . ?"

"Just under twenty-six hundred," I said.

"I'll talk to Dad and get him to cut the check."

Diego, the daytime waiter, was busy with something behind the stick, so Mason got up and fetched our drinks. Campari and soda for him, chardonnay for Veronica, Killian's for me. I swallowed a couple of painkillers, washed them down with beer, and chased it with Maalox.

"Woodward called today," Veronica said.

"Oh?"

"He said he should have an opening for me soon, but he advised me to keep my distance from you until this thing blows over."

"So I guess this isn't the best time for me to call him about a job."

"Probably not."

"You taking his advice?"

"I don't know. I don't want to."

"But you're ambitious," I said. "You're your father's girl."

She pressed her lips together and stared into her wine glass.

Hardcastle came through the door with a couple of copy editors and grabbed a stool at the bar. A clerk from the courthouse wandered in. The place was filling. Hardcastle glanced over, spotted me, removed his cell phone from his jacket pocket, and placed a call.

"You need a lawyer," Veronica said.

"Can't afford one."

"If you cannot afford a lawyer, one will be provided for you," Mason said.

"Shut up, Thanks-Dad."

"Sorry. I've been hanging around with a smart-ass, and some of it is rubbing off."

In spite of myself, I was starting to like this kid.

"So what are you going to do?" Veronica asked.

"Maybe I'll ask your mystery source to represent me pro bono. After all, Brady Coyle and I were teammates at PC, and teammates are supposed to stick together."

It was an educated guess. Coyle was one of a handful of people who could have gotten access to the secret grand-jury testimony. As Arena's lawyer, he wasn't legally entitled to it until the discovery phase of the trial, but for someone with his pull, the courthouse was a sieve. And he fit that description Veronica had let slip—a he who hated my guts. When her eyes got wide, I knew I'd guessed right.

"It's hard to keep a secret in this town, Veronica. Only thing I can't figure is why Coyle's feeding you stuff that makes his client look guilty."

I was still waiting for her to say something when the cell started singing the blues in my hip pocket.

"I just heard on the radio that you were released," Rosie said. "Are you okay?

"I've had better days."

"Anything I can do? Do you need money for a lawyer?"

"I've got that covered," I lied.

"Where are you? I want to see you."

"Not until I get this cleared up. You can't be consorting with a serial arson suspect. How could you explain it to your men?"

We argued about it for a few more minutes, saying good-bye just as Logan Bedford strutted into the place with a cameraman. He surveyed the room, then headed straight for me. The little red light on the camera told me it was already on. Veronica saw them coming and bolted for the ladies' room.

Note to self: Change the cell ring tone to "Stand by Your Man."

Logan checked his hair in the mirror behind the bar and sidled up next to me so his cameraman could get us both in the shot.

"Channel 10 News has learned exclusively that you fit the FBI profile of the Mount Hope arsonist. Would you care to comment?"

"How exclusive can it be," I said, "when it's already been in the paper?"

"The public wants to know. L. S. A. Mulligan, are you the Mount Hope arsonist?"

"Logan, if you'd come in here like a professional journalist, which you aren't, instead of barging in like an asshole, which you are, I might have actually talked to you. Why don't you put *that* comment on the air?"

"What about you, sir?" he said, turning his attention to Mason. "Would you care to explain your choice of company this evening?"

Mason picked up my bottle of Maalox and offered it to Logan. "Here," he said. "You're going to need this after I shove that camera down your throat."

Yes. I was definitely starting to like this kid.

With that, Logan turned to leave.

"Hey," I said.

He turned back to look at me.

"On your way out, tell Hardcastle I said he should go fuck himself."

64

As evening fell, a thick fog rolled in from the bay. I guess Veronica thought it gave her enough cover to avoid being seen with me. We strolled out of Hopes hand in hand and got into her car together. As she started the engine, a couple of pedestrians strolled by, materializing out of the murk like ghosts. I could barely see two cars ahead as she groped her way toward my place.

That evening, we made love, Veronica rocking gently on top of me, doing her best not to jostle my ribs. Neither of us felt like talking. After she fell asleep in my arms, I nuzzled her hair, inhaling her familiar scent. I don't know how long I lay there, trying to figure a way to hold on to her. Trying to figure a way to get my job back. Trying to figure a way to catch the bastards who were turning both my childhood and my future into ashes. After a while, I untangled myself from Veronica without waking her, downed a cocktail of Maalox and painkillers, sat down at the kitchen table, and started reading through my stack of notebooks once again.

Shortly after 2:00 A.M., the police radio sprang to life. "Code Red, 12 Hopedale Road." The tenement house where I'd lived as a kid, where Aidan, Meg, and I had played hide-and-seek, where we'd watched helplessly as my dad withered away. Did I know anyone who lived there now? I couldn't remember.

I got up and stepped into the bedroom to fetch Veronica's car keys. She was sitting on the bed, pulling on a pair of jeans.

"No need for you to go," she said.

"Because I'm not a reporter anymore."

"Lie down and get some sleep, my love. I'll be back in a while to tell you all about it." .

She stretched out her right hand for the keys. I shook my head and slid them into my pocket.

The fog caught the beams from our headlights and flung them back at us as I felt my way along the familiar city streets. I held my speed at 15 mph as I rolled along Camp Street, missing the turn for Pleasant. I backed up, turned right, and clipped a parked car, snapping off its side mirror. About fifty yards down the street, as I turned left onto Hopedale Road, the lights from the fire and rescue vehicles turned the fog into a red mist.

As I straightened the wheel I heard a pop, and just like that I lost control. Veronica screamed as the car veered to the left and bounced off a utility pole.

"Are you all right?"

"I think so," Veronica said. "Are you hurt?"

My ribs were reintroducing me to real pain, so I lied. "I'm fine."

I got out to check the damage. A cracked headlight and a crumpled fender. If it weren't for the two flat front tires, it would have been drivable. I went around to the passenger-side door and helped Veronica out. She took a couple of steps, and I could see she was limping.

"I guess I banged my knee," she said.

I bent down to take a look. She had a bloody rip in her jeans.

"You need to get to the hospital."

"I'll drive you," someone said.

I looked up and saw Gunther Hawes, one of the DiMaggios, coming down the stairs of a weathered cottage. "My car's parked just down the way on Pleasant Street," he said. "Stay here and I'll be right back."

While we waited, I looked around to see if I could figure out what blew the tires. A pair of two-by-fours with spikes driven through them had been laid across the road. I flipped them upside down, tromped on them to bend the spikes, and dragged them onto the sidewalk. As I was finishing up, Gunther pulled up beside us, and I noticed his driver-side mirror was missing.

On the drive to the hospital, I apologized for the mirror, wrote down my insurance information for him, and told him about the booby trap.

"Somebody must have wanted to slow the fire equipment down," he said, "but they came in from the other end of the street."

"There was probably one there too," I said.

"We should tell somebody," Veronica said.

"Fire equipment's already on the street," I said, "so they must have already found out the hard way."

Gunther braked in front of the Rhode Island Hospital emergency-room entrance, and we both got out to help Veronica from the car. A rescue wagon, siren screaming, pulled in behind us, and the back doors flew open. Two attendants sprinted from the hospital to help the crew unload a stretcher from the back.

The patient was strapped to a backboard, a cervical collar stabilizing her neck. Part of her uniform had been burned off. The flesh underneath looked like grilled beef. I wouldn't have recognized her except for one thing.

The gurney was nearly half a foot shorter than she was.

65

On Monday, the federal grand jury handed up a sealed, thirty-two-count indictment charging Arena and three officials of the Laborers' International Union with wire fraud, embezzlement, money laundering, bribery, filing false income tax returns, perjury, obstruction of justice, labor racketeering, and conspiracy. The twelve stitches in her knee didn't seem to slow Veronica down any. Tipped by her source, she broke the story on page one, spoiling the U.S. attorney's plans for a showy press conference.

Coyle was so busy arranging bail, holding his client's hand, and condemning the government in a series of press interviews that it was a week before he could squeeze me in.

That gave me plenty of time to worry myself sick about Rosie.

She was in the intensive care unit. Only family was allowed to see her. All the hospital would tell me was that her condition was critical. They said it every time I called. Cops and firefighters hung up on me when I pressed for details, so all I knew about the accident was what I read in the paper.

HERO FIRE CHIEF CRITICALLY INJURED BY BOOBY TRAP, the headline said. She'd been driving her official car down Mount Hope Avenue, red lights flashing. At Hopedale, she turned left, approaching the fire from the north. The booby trap blew out both of her front tires, and the car lurched into a light pole. The driver of the pumper truck following behind her was blinded by the fog. He didn't see her until it was too late. The truck clipped the right rear of her car, flipping it over, and the gas tank exploded.

I kept digging, double-checking documents and reinterviewing sources. I needed something to distract me from the image of Rosie lying limp and helpless on a gurney. And I had even more reason to nail the bastards now. I felt darn right homicidal.

The firm of McDougall, Young, Coyle, and Limone occupied two full floors of the Textron Tower. I got off the elevator on twelve, pushed open the mahogany double doors, and stepped into a waiting room big enough for a pickup basketball game. To the left, a receptionist in a beige business suit juggled calls behind a large glass desk. To the right, five baby dog sharks with tiny, cruel eyes cruised counterclockwise in a hundred-gallon aquarium, the firm's way of telling you right off what kind of lawyer you'd be getting.

I stood in front of the desk until the receptionist hung up the phone, glanced at my David Ortiz jersey and Red Sox cap, and asked if I was there to pick up or drop off.

"I have a ten o'clock appointment with Brady Coyle."

"Do you, now?"

"I do," I said, hoping she didn't recognize my voice.

"Your name?"

"L. S. A. Mulligan."

"One moment, please."

She picked up the phone, spoke a few words, told me Mr. Coyle would be with me shortly, and asked me to take a seat. I spent nearly an hour obsessing about Rosie and studying the little sharks—the wait just the big shark's way of establishing his dominance—before his secretary appeared and led me up an interior staircase to his office.

"Mulligan!" he said, gripping my right hand in both of his and smiling big to display a picket fence of blinding teeth. "I haven't seen you since I took you to school in that pickup game at Alumni Hall."

Still trying to establish dominance, as if his panoramic view of historic Benefit Street, his three-inch height advantage, and his twelve-hundred-dollar suit weren't enough to do the job.

As he led me across a blue oriental rug toward a black leather visitor's chair, I took a moment to study the decor. Photos of Coyle posing with Buddy Cianci, George W. Bush, Alan Dershowitz, and Ernie DiGregorio. Four tastefully framed Jackson Pollocks. The room wasn't a vault, so I figured the paintings for reproductions.

"So," he said, settling into the high-backed leather chair behind his desk, "you should know right off that we require a twenty-thousand-dollar retainer in criminal cases."

"No problem," I said. "I just signed an eighty-thousand-dollar deal with Simon and Schuster for a book on the imminent demise of the newspaper business."

"Really!"

"Yeah," I lied. "After I give twenty grand to you and another twenty to the IRS, I'll still have enough left to buy a judge, twelve jurors, and a sex tour of Woonsocket."

"Jury tampering is not something you should joke about, Mulligan."

"What about judge buying?"

"Half of them have 'For Sale' embroidered on their robes, but speaking of it is considered uncouth."

"Thanks for the etiquette lesson."

"You're welcome. But enough with the banter. Let's see what we can do to get you out of this fix."

We discussed the FBI profile, Coyle already familiar with some of it from reading the paper.

"A profile is a useful investigative tool, but it's not evidence," he said. "This one could fit any number of people. Could they have something solid? An eyewitness? Physical evidence?"

"I don't see how."

"Nothing incriminating in your car or apartment?"

"Not unless they planted something."

"Can you account for your whereabouts when the fires were set?"

"Back in December, when a triple-decker on Hope Street was

torched, I was in Boston with an insurance investigator watching the Canadians slap-shot the Bruins into unconditional surrender. Couple of others, I was getting naked with that court reporter you've been leaking grand-jury testimony to."

He glared at me for a moment.

"Well I *am* surprised Veronica would break our confidentiality agreement, even under such intimate circumstances."

"She didn't. I guessed."

"I see." He forced a smile. "Perhaps this can remain between the three of us."

"Sure thing."

"Good. Well, then. We may be able to dispose of your case expeditiously. I can inform the chief of police that you have witnesses who will swear to your whereabouts when several of the fires were set. Since the police apparently believe all of them were set by the same individual, you should be in the clear once they check out your alibis. At that time, I will insist that the chief issue a public apology and rebuke the arson squad for naming you as a person of interest. We still require the retainer, of course, but if things are as you say, you'll be getting some of it back."

I pulled my checkbook out of my jeans. Coyle reached across the desk and handed me a fountain pen.

"Before I give you this," I said, "I want to be sure that representing me won't involve you in a conflict of interest."

"I don't see how it could."

"It's like this," I said. "Most of the torched buildings are owned by five real estate companies that have been busy buying up the neighborhood. The companies were all incorporated over the last eighteen months or so. Lawyers from this firm filed the papers."

"I don't see the relevance."

"The relevance is that the people behind those companies are the ones burning down the neighborhood. I intend to expose them. With this firm representing both me and them, things might get awkward."

Coyle raised his eyebrows, feigning shock.

"You have proof to support these allegations?"

"I'm working on it."

"I can't imagine there is anything to it. These are *not* the sort of people who would ever get involved in such a thing."

Interesting. The firm files a lot of incorporation papers. These particular documents were filed by five of its junior associates. Yet Coyle knew exactly which companies I was talking about.

"Johnny Dio and Vinnie Giordano are *exactly* the sort of people who would get involved in such a thing."

Another educated guess. I was hoping it would provoke a reaction, but Coyle was a cool customer. His eyes darted to a corner of the room, then landed back on me. Nothing more. It was so fast that I almost missed it. For a second, I considered turning around and grabbing whatever had drawn his eyes. Then I remembered my ribs—and the way Coyle used to manhandle me under the boards.

"I don't know how you came up with those names, Mulligan, but they do not appear anywhere on the incorporation papers."

"No, but they wrote the checks, didn't they?"

"I wouldn't know," he said. "I'd have to check with billing."

"Why don't you do that?"

"What would be the point? Ethics would prevent me from sharing that information with you without the clients' permission."

"And they aren't about to give permission?"

"I'd have to advise against it."

"Would those be the same ethics that prohibit leaking secret grand-jury testimony?"

"I don't believe this firm can represent you, Mulligan. This conversation is over."

"Hey, this has been great," I said. "Let's get together again real soon, maybe play a little one-on-one."

"Didn't you notice? We just did. You lost."

I didn't think so.

66

I grabbed a coffee to go at the diner and loitered in Burnside Park, proudly named in honor of Rhode Island's own Ambrose Everett Burnside, an incompetent Civil War general whose lone achievement was popularizing the facial hair that sort of bears his name.

In the middle of the park, Mr. Potato Head stood at attention, honoring Burnside's equestrian statue with a salute. On the spud's flank, someone had added a memorial in red spray paint: "Thanks for 8,000 Union casualties at Fredericksburg."

I was asked a dozen times for spare change, offered a variety of pharmaceuticals at competitive prices, snarled at by a pit bull, and growled at by a teenage hooker who felt rejected. The hooker didn't interest me, but with my ribs still aching, I *was* tempted by the Vicodin.

I called the hospital again. Still critical.

It was nearly one thirty in the afternoon when Coyle emerged from the Textron Tower and strode purposefully down the sidewalk in his Italian loafers. I watched him cross the park, dash across the street, and slip into the Capital Grille, the hot spot for pricey expense-account lunches. Then I walked over to the Textron Tower and rode the elevator back to the twelfth floor.

The receptionist was fussing with something on her desk. She didn't look up, but she must have caught a glimpse of my jeans.

"Picking up or dropping off?"

"Picking up," I said. I walked briskly past her and started up the stairs.

"Stop! Where do you think you're going?"

"Forgot my Red Sox cap," I shouted.

"You're wearing it!"

I could hear her clattering up the staircase behind me, but her high heels were no match for my Reeboks.

I tried Coyle's office door. Unlocked. I entered, spun toward the corner where his eyes had flickered, and saw a four-foot-long mailing tube.

"What are you doing? Put that down!"

I brushed past her, went through the door, and pushed the button for the elevator. As I waited for it, I heard her shouting into the phone, asking building security to intercept a thief in a Red Sox cap and jersey. He'd be carrying a large mailing tube, she said.

When the elevator opened on the first floor, two security guards were waiting. They glanced at a tall, bareheaded man in a black tank top, several large sheets of heavy paper, folded into quarters, tucked under his left arm. Then they turned away as another elevator door soundlessly slid open. I pushed through the revolving door, walked down the sidewalk, pulled my cap out of my back pocket, and tugged it on. The day was a bit chilly without my jersey, but it was stuffed into the mailing tube I'd left in the elevator, and I didn't suppose I'd be getting it back.

I walked to Central Lunch on Weybosset, settled into a booth, and ordered a bacon cheeseburger. While it was frying, I unfolded the sheets of paper, hastily refolded them, and asked the waitress to bag my order to go. Then I hurried over to the Peter Pan terminal and jumped on the first bus out of town.

I got off in Pawtucket, looked around to make sure I hadn't been followed, and took a room for the night at the Comfort Inn.

Sleep, when it finally came, was broken up by pieces of one long dream. Fenway. The sun was brighter than it had ever been. In a sea of red and blue, a tall, gorgeous woman spotted Manny Ramirez and broke into a girlish grin.

67

In the morning, I tried to hold on to that image of a smiling Rosie for as long as I could, but by the time I'd showered and dressed, it had evaporated. I strolled to the nearest Dunkin' Donuts, calling the hospital again on the way over. No change. I bought a cup of coffee and a breakfast sandwich, and carried them to a seat by the window. Outside, the Blackstone River churned over an ancient dam that once powered the first water-driven cotton mill in North America.

Slater Mill was a museum now, celebrated as the Birthplace of the American Industrial Revolution. I suppose that was one way to look at it. To me, it was the birthplace of American industrial espionage. It was here, in 1790, that an Englishman named Samuel Slater built spinning machines from pirated plans he had smuggled out of Britain.

Buses with the names of New England school districts on them were disgorging kids into the museum parking lot. I wondered if the docents would tell them that most of the mill's employees had been children. That they had worked twelve-hour days breathing air thick with lint. That when they paused in their work, they were beaten by overseers. That the machines sometimes grabbed them by the hair, dragged them in, and chewed them into ground beef.

I thought about that for a while, then opened my newspaper

and pulled out the sports section. I was reliving last night's 8–3 victory over the Rangers when Mason walked in. He gave me a nod, went to the counter for coffee and a corn muffin, and joined me by the window looking out on the museum.

"Rosie's still critical," he said.

"Yeah. I know."

He gestured toward Slater Mill. "Ever take the tour?"

"Not since I was a kid."

"My great-great-great-great-grandfather, Moses Brown, is the one who lured Samuel Slater here and gave him the money to build his machines."

"I was just thinking about that."

"It's something to be proud of," he said.

"If you say so, Thanks-Dad."

We raised our cups and sipped.

"Thanks for driving all the way out here this morning," I said.

"Sure," he said. "But why am I here?"

"I need you to keep something for me for a couple of days."

"Okay."

"It wouldn't be fair to ask you to do this without telling you that it's something I'm not supposed to have and that some bad people will be trying to get it back."

"What is it?"

"Better you don't know."

"Where do you want me to put it?"

"It's small. Maybe you can just tuck it under your spare tire and throw something over it."

"Okay."

"Just like that? No more questions?"

"Sure."

"If you're a real reporter, you won't be able to resist taking it out and looking it over."

"That's right."

"Better you don't."

"But you know I will."

"It's folded inside the business section," I said.

We talked about Rosie again for a couple of minutes. Then Mason drained his coffee, picked up the newspaper, tucked it under his arm, and strolled out the door.

I finished my breakfast, ambled down the street to an electronics store, and bought a wireless phone recorder for $21.99. Then I walked a few blocks to the Apex department store and bought a small duffel bag, socks, underwear, toiletries, two bottles of Maalox, a couple of black T-shirts, a pair of tan Dockers, a blue blazer, and sunglasses that could pass for Ray-Bans if you didn't look closely. I carried my purchases back to the hotel and flopped on the bed.

That night, I called the hospital again.

"Chief Rosella Morelli?"

"Still critical."

I plugged the recorder into the microphone jack on my cell phone and stretched out on the bed to watch the Sox battle the Angels. The Sox were trailing by three in the fourth when Tammy Wynette started whining about standing by her man. What had I been thinking? That song sucks. I checked caller ID and decided to answer anyway.

"You!
fucking!
bastard!"

"And a good evening to you too, Dorcas."

"Who are you shacked up with tonight, you son of a bitch?"

"Speaking of bitches, how's Rewrite doing? You're remembering her heartworm pills, right?"

"You love that dog, don't you?"

"Sure do."

"Good. I think I'll take her to the pound," she said, and slammed down the receiver. That was new. Usually I was the first one to hang up.

Rewrite hated cages. Four years ago, when we put her in a kennel for a few days and took a rare vacation together to the Monterey

Bay Blues Festival, she refused to eat until we got back. I told myself Dorcas was bluffing.

Youkilis had just tied the score with a home run when the cell rang again. This time I didn't recognize the number so I turned the recorder on.

68

"Red Sox Nation. How may I direct your call?"

"Mulligan?"

"Who should I tell him is calling?"

"Listen up, asshole. If you want to live to see next week, you'll give it back."

"Give what back?"

"Don't be cute."

"Okay, Giordano. What's it worth to you?"

"The price of three two-hundred-thirty-grain slugs from a forty-five."

"That would only come to a dollar and change. Given the stakes, I was hoping for a little more."

He was quiet for a moment.

"How much?"

"Consider it from my point of view," I said. "The cops have all but accused me of setting the fires. I've been suspended without pay. My journalism career is over. I need to find another line of work."

"Blackmailers have a short life span, Mulligan."

"Actually, I was thinking about getting into real estate."

"Keep talking."

"Remember our conversation over drinks at the Biltmore?"

"Yeah."

"I'm ready to take you up on your generous offer."

He fell silent again, thinking it over.

"Tell you what," he said. "I just bought twenty acres in Lincoln. Gonna put up some luxury condo units. I'll give you a five-percent share. You should clear at least a hundred grand in two years."

"What am I supposed to do for money in the meantime?"

"I've got an opening at Little Rhody Realty," he said. "Doesn't pay much, but it'll give us a chance to see if you've got an aptitude for the business."

He was offering me Cheryl Scibelli's old job. "Deal," I said. "I think this is the beginning of a beautiful friendship."

"So when do I get it back?"

"Can't be this week. I'm on the way to Tampa to visit a college buddy."

"Better get your ass back here."

"Look," I said. "My buddy got us tickets for the Sox–Rays series this weekend. No way I'm gonna miss that. The Rays are pretty good this year, so they should be great games. Besides, it'll take you a few days to get the papers drawn up on the Lincoln property for me, right?"

"Yeah, but I don't like you being out of reach."

"I was planning to stay down there a couple of weeks," I said, "but I'll rebook and fly back the day after the games. I'll give it to you as soon as I get back."

"You got it with you?"

"It's in a safe place."

He didn't like it, but there wasn't much he could do about it.

"Let me know when your flight is coming in," he said. "I'll pick you up at the airport."

"Vinnie," I said, "I suspect that beneath that cynical shell you are at heart a sentimentalist."

"Huh?"

Hard to believe there was someone out there who had never seen *Casablanca*.

I hung up and returned my attention to the game in time to see the Sox pull out a 7–6 win in their last at bat.

Wednesday I got up late, called the hospital, and then wandered over to Doherty's East Avenue Irish Pub for pastrami on rye and a club soda. That evening, I went back to Doherty's to watch the Angels beat our young left-hander, John Lester, 6–4. But we were still in first place, two and a half games up on the Yankees. Except for last night's threat on my life, Dorcas's threat to send Rewrite to the pound, Rosie's condition, and the fact that Veronica hadn't returned my calls, everything was just peachy.

69

Late Wednesday afternoon found me lurking in
Burnside Park again. This time I was wearing my new blazer, Dock-
ers, and bogus Ray-Bans. I looked almost fashionable. For me, it
was a disguise.

The same bums asked me for spare change. The same drug dealers
offered their wares. The same teenage hooker strolled by, this time
on a city councilman's arm. The pit bull was a no-show.

When the cell rang, I recognized the number.

"Hi, Veronica."

"Hi, baby. Sorry I didn't return your calls the last couple of days.
I was busy."

That word again.

"I gather you've decided to take Woodward's advice."

"I want to be with you, but we'll have to be discreet. Logan
Bedford bursting in on us at Hopes freaked me out. But this is all
going to blow over soon, right? I miss you, baby."

"I miss you, too."

"Any news about Rosie today?"

"I called the hospital a half hour ago. She's still critical."

"She's gonna beat this, baby. She's a fighter."

"That she is."

"Where are you, anyway?"

I almost blurted the truth before realizing she'd be safer if she didn't know.

"Tampa," I said.

"What are you doing *there*?"

"Following the Red Sox."

"I should have known. When are you getting back?"

"I'm not quite sure."

"Damn."

"What?"

"I was hoping we could have a secret rendezvous this weekend. Next week I start at *The Post*."

Shit. Could we manage a long-distance relationship? Woodward certainly wouldn't be hiring me now. I was damaged goods.

"Oh," I said. "Well, as soon as I get the mess I'm in straightened away, how about I come down there for a weekend of unbridled lust?"

"I'd really like that."

After we hung up, I strolled around the park some more. It was shortly after six when a statuesque black woman came through the Textron Tower's revolving door, cut across the park, and entered the Capital Grille. I recognized her from her photo on the law firm's Web site. I waited a few minutes, then followed her in.

Yolanda Mosley-Jones was sitting alone at the end of the bar, looking both professional and lusty in a hunter-green business suit. I chose a stool at the other end, asked the bartender for a club soda, and feigned interest in the menu. Mosley-Jones picked up what looked like a martini, took a small sip, and set it back down on a cocktail napkin.

Behind her, four suits were crammed into a booth, consuming vile, neon-colored drinks from highball glasses. From their furtive glances, it was apparent they were interested. Finally one of them got up, lurched over to the bar, and sat down beside her. I couldn't hear what he was saying, but whatever it was didn't take. He got back up, shoulders slumping a little, and rejoined his friends.

A half hour ticked by. She never checked her watch. Never looked up at the clock over the bar. She didn't seem to be waiting for anybody. I walked over, sat down next to her, and asked the bartender to bring her another on me.

"Sorry," she said, "but I don't date white guys."

"Neither do I."

She spun the bar stool to face me, looked me over, and frowned. Suddenly I didn't feel fashionable anymore.

"Oh," she said. "I know who you are. I saw you on the news. You were in handcuffs."

"Not my finest moment."

"Brady Coyle said you might try to pump me for information. I've got nothing to say to you."

"So don't say anything. Just listen."

"I don't think so."

She twisted away, stood, and gathered her purse and BlackBerry from the bar.

"You filed the incorporation papers for Little Rhody Realty."

She looked back over her shoulder.

"What if I did?"

"Little Rhody is a front for mobsters who are buying up property in Mount Hope. They're the ones behind the fires."

That got her attention. Eyes fixed on mine, she settled back onto the bar stool.

"They're burning out the families that won't sell. They're burning down the buildings they buy to collect the insurance. And they don't care who gets killed."

"I don't believe you," she said, but she kept her seat.

The bartender placed a fresh martini in front of her and cleared away her empty glass. I waited for him to wander down the bar before I gave her the rest of it.

When I was done, she shook her head slowly like maybe she still didn't believe it. Or didn't want to.

"Why tell me?" she said.

"Because I did my homework. I know your best friend Amy's place burned down on Hell Night, and I thought you might want to do something about it. I need you to get something for me."

When I told her what it was, she shook her head so hard her hair bounced.

"Not a chance. Maybe I believe you and maybe I don't, but what you're asking could get me fired. Even disbarred."

"There are worse fates," I said.

I told her how I watched Rosie carry Tony DePrisco's burned and broken body out of a smoldering triple-decker. I told her what Rosie looked like when they slid her out of the ambulance. I described what it must have been like for my favorite English teacher, old Mr. McCready, when he drew his last lungful of smoke. I told her about Efrain and Graciela Rueda's dreams for their children. I told her how Scott's body looked when the fireman carried him down the ladder. I told her how the smoke rose right through the sheet Melissa was wrapped in. I told her what it was like to watch them go into the ground.

I was starting to tell her about the bullet holes in Scibelli's corpse when she said, "Please stop." She picked up her drink and took a long swallow.

"Why me?" she said. "Why don't you talk to the lawyers who filed the papers for the other four dummy corporations?"

"I tried them already."

She didn't say anything, just fingered the stem of her martini glass. She had beautiful eyes. Her voice had smoke in it. And as best I could tell in that suit, her legs went on awhile.

"I'm not really white," I said. "I'm passing."

She laughed softly, but there was no joy in it. I took out one of my business cards, crossed out the address, wrote in another, and slid it into her purse. Then I took a twenty from my wallet and laid it on the bar.

70

McCracken's secretary celebrated an unseason—
ably warm Thursday in April by squeezing into a short, low-cut
yellow sundress. Her nipples showed dark against the thin fabric.

"She might as well have come to work naked," he said, after closing his inner door.

"Maybe she's working her way up to that."

"Something to look forward to," he said. "Listen, I've been
worried about you. Are you all right?"

"I've got four broken ribs. I've been identified as a person of
interest in a series of heinous crimes. The paper has suspended me
without pay. My best friend is in the hospital. My best girl doesn't
want to be seen with me. And I'm pretty sure Vinnie Giordano is
planning to shoot me. But the Sox are in first place, so on balance
I guess I'm doing okay."

"Why would Giordano want to shoot you?"

"Because of the documents I lifted from Brady Coyle's office."

"You stole documents from Brady Coyle's office?"

"Gee. When you put it that way, it almost sounds illegal."

McCracken sat down behind his desk, opened his humidor,
extracted two maduro torpedoes, clipped the ends, and offered me
one. I took it and collapsed into a visitor's chair.

"Tell me all about it," he said, and I was about to when Mason
came through the door with a big yellow envelope under his arm.

"Did you look at it?" I asked him after handling the introductions.

"I did."

"Then you might as well stay."

He dropped into the other visitor's chair and handed me the envelope. I opened it, pulled out the papers, and started to unfold them.

"Wait a minute," McCracken said. "Is that what I think it is?"

"Uh-huh."

"And you had him bring it *here*?"

"I figured you'd want to have a look."

"Christ! What if he was followed?"

"I wasn't," Mason said.

"No reason he would be," I said. "No one knew I was having him hold it. I'm the one they are looking for, and so far I've got them fooled into thinking I'm out of state."

"What if someone spotted you coming in here?"

"That's the reason for the disguise," I said. I stood, removed the blazer, draped it over the back of the chair, and took off the sunglasses. McCracken stared at me now like he thought I was an idiot. He might have been on to something.

"Look," I said. "Do you want to see this or not?"

He shoved some papers aside to clear desk space, and I smoothed the first document out in front of him. Anyone who'd been stuck in Providence as long as we had could recognize it as a plat map of Mount Hope's southeast quarter. The existing buildings were gone, though, replaced by a rough layout of what appeared to be a large real estate development. In the lower right hand corner, a name and address: "Dio Construction Corp., 245 Pocasset Avenue, Providence, RI."

"Holy shit!"

"Wait. There's more."

Four more documents, in fact, each an exterior architectural rendering or floor plan for what looked to be very expensive condominiums.

"I removed it from a mailing tube addressed to Brady Coyle. The return address was Rosabella Development."

"Isn't that Vinnie Giordano's company?"

"It is."

"Holy shit!"

"Speaking of Giordano, give this a listen," I said. I laid the phone recorder on the desk and pressed play.

When I clicked it off a few minutes later, McCracken said it again: "Holy shit!"

"My Latin's a little rusty," I told Mason, "but I think that's Roman Catholic for 'Wowie.' "

"I don't get it," Mason said.

"Get what?"

"How could they think they could keep this a secret? When the buildings start to go up, the developer and the builder will be a matter of public record."

"It'll go something like this," McCracken said. "The five dummy corporations will keep buying up property. When they've got everything they need, the arsons will stop. In the aftermath, there'll be a lot of public hand-wringing about how to rebuild the neighborhood. Giordano and Dio will come to the rescue, offering to build something Providence can be proud of. They'll buy the property from the five dummy companies, and no one will know they'll actually just be buying it from themselves."

"Except us," I said.

McCracken offered Mason a cigar, and he surprised me by accepting. I leaned over to give him a light, and the three of us smoked for a while. Suddenly McCracken's face changed as if he'd just remembered something. He slid open his top drawer, pulled out an envelope, and tossed it to me.

"This came by messenger this morning," he said.

It had been sent to my attention at McCracken's office. The address was printed in block letters. There was no return address.

Inside was a computer printout of billing records from McDougall, Young, Coyle, and Limone. If I was right, they were going to show that the fees for incorporating the five dummy corporations had been charged to Dio or Giordano. But I was wrong.

They had been paid for personally by Brady Coyle.

I handed it to Mason. He looked at it and then passed it to McCracken.

"Giordano to Dio to Coyle," I said.

"The three of them are in it together," McCracken said.

"So," I said. "How do we make them pay?"

McCracken got up, took three glasses down from a cabinet, filled them with ice from his minifridge, and poured us each three inches of Bushmills. We smoked, sipped our drinks, and thought about it for a while.

It was McCracken who broke the silence.

"Legally, I think we're screwed."

"I think so, too," I said.

"Why's that?" Mason said.

"The billing records were delivered anonymously," McCracken said. "No way to prove they're genuine."

"Besides," I said, "once Coyle realizes we have them, he'll delete the records from the firm's computer."

"The building plans are stolen property," McCracken said. "Might make it difficult to get them admitted as evidence. Worse, they were stolen from Dio's lawyer, which probably means they are protected by lawyer-client privilege."

"What about the recording?" Mason said.

"It's illegal," I said.

"How so?"

"Rhode Island is one of a handful of states in which it's a crime to record your own phone conversation unless you inform the other party. Besides, who does it incriminate? The way the cops will hear it, I stole some documents and used them to shake down Giordano."

"Use what we've got," McCracken said, "and Mulligan's the one who ends up doing time."

"When you add all this up," I said, passing my hand over the documents and digital recorder, "what does it really prove, anyway?

Just that Giordano, Dio, and Coyle have a secret plan to build pricey condos in Mount Hope. We don't have any hard evidence that they're behind the arsons."

"But we know they are," McCracken said.

"Yeah. We do."

"If we can't go to the authorities," Mason said, "is there any way we can get what we know into the newspaper?"

It was worth a try. The three of us worked until midnight, pouring everything we had into an exposé under Mason's byline.

71

In the morning, I bought some flowers at Downtown
Florist and caught a cab to Warwick.

"She'll be happy to see you," Gloria's mother said as she ush-
ered me into the house. "She's been following the news, and she's
been worrying about you."

She's been worrying about *me?*

Gloria rose from the couch, where she'd been watching TV,
met me in the middle of the living room, wrapped her arms around
me, and gave me a squeeze. That's when it dawned on me that my
ribs were feeling better. I guess hers were too.

We sat together on the couch and caught up. I told her there
was still no news about Rosie but that I hoped to be exonerated
and back to work soon. She told me the surgery on her hand had
gone well and that she was scheduled for her first plastic surgery
next week. Her bruises were faded now, and the fear was no longer
in her eyes. She was animated. She seemed hopeful. Her smile was
lopsided, but it was still a smile.

Before I left, I asked her if I could borrow her car.

"Keep it as long as you like," she said. "With one good eye, it'll
be a while before I get up the nerve to drive."

She took the keys from her purse and dropped them in my
palm.

72

That afternoon I hid out in McCracken's office, smoking and killing time. I fiddled with my cell, changing the ringtone to the "Peter Gunn Theme." By five, I still hadn't heard from Mason, and I was starting to get anxious.

Then the orchestra began to play: "Waaaaah, wah! Waaaaah, *wah*-wah!"

"So how'd it go?"

"Not good."

"Ah, shit."

"Yeah. After Lomax and Pemberton killed the story, I went upstairs to see Dad and got the same song and dance."

"Start from the beginning and give me all of it, Edward."

"Hey! That's the first time you called me by my real name."

"Yeah, yeah. Just tell me what happened."

"First off, Lomax kept asking if I had really come up with all this on my own. Wanted to know, did I have help from you."

"And you said?"

"That it was my work."

"He believe you?"

"I don't think so, but he let it slide."

"Then what?"

"He had a lot of questions about sourcing. Where did I get the architectural drawings? Where did the billing records come from? How did I know they were genuine?"

"And you said?"

"That I couldn't reveal my confidential sources."

"And then?"

"Lomax said there was no way the paper would put its reputation on the line based on the work of a cub reporter who couldn't disclose his sources. Not even a cub reporter whose daddy was the publisher. When I pressed the argument, he backed off and said he'd discuss it with Pemberton. He walked into the aquarium, and the two of them went into a huddle. In the middle of it, Pemberton took a call, talked for a few minutes, and hung up. After a half hour or so, they both walked over to my cubicle looking pretty mad."

"Why mad?"

"Pemberton asked, did I know that my story was based on documents you had stolen from Brady Coyle's office?"

"How the hell did he know *that*?"

"That call he took? It was Coyle threatening to sue the paper for invasion of privacy, libel, and a couple of other things Pemberton told me that I can't remember just now."

"What? How did Coyle know about the story?"

"That's what I'd like to know. At that point, I lost my temper. Said some things I shouldn't have."

"Like what?"

"That Giordano, Dio, and Coyne are scum. That they are arsonists and murderers. That the three of them were going to get away with it because we didn't have the balls to take them on."

"Oh, boy."

"Yeah. I was loud about it, too. Pemberton just shook his head and said I had some growing up to do. When I went upstairs to see Dad, he said the same thing."

"Thanks for trying, Mason."

"This isn't over, is it?"

"Maybe not," I said, "but there are two outs in the bottom of the ninth, and we're down by ten."

McCracken and I were commiserating when the cell rang again.

"Hello, asshole."

"Brady! How good of you to call."

"Glad to hear from me, are you?"

"It's always a pleasure to talk with an old teammate."

"Forgive me if I doubt your sincerity. After all, I'm scum. I'm an arsonist and a murderer. Isn't that what your lapdog says? That's malice per se, Mulligan. I almost hope the paper *does* print your lies. By the time I get done suing, I'll own everything from the delivery trucks to the printing presses."

And then he guffawed. He was still at it when I hung up. That was the first time I'd ever heard anyone guffaw. I didn't like it much.

I called Mason back.

"This is important," I said. "Who overheard your rant about Giordano, Dio, and Coyle?"

"I'm not sure."

"It was just a few minutes ago, right?"

"Yeah."

"Stand up and look around. Who's there now?"

"Uh . . . Lomax and Pemberton, of course. Abbruzzi, Sullivan, Bakst, Kukielski, Richards, Jones, Gonzales, Friedman, Kiffney, Ionata, Young, Worcester. And Veronica's here. It's her last day."

"What about Hardcastle?"

"I don't see him. Wait a minute. Yeah, there he is. He's just coming out of the men's room."

"That it?"

"There are some others, but they're too far away to have over-heard."

"Okay, thanks," I said, and hung up.

73

Ten minutes later, I was double—parked on Foun—
tain Street with the motor running. At 6:45, a gray Mitsubishi
Eclipse pulled out of the parking lot across from the newspaper. I
let a few cars go by and then followed. The Eclipse turned right on
Dyer, lurched onto I-195, and zoomed across the Providence River.

TV cop shows make a big deal over how hard it is to tail somebody. It's bull. When you're driving a nondescript subcompact in
light traffic and the person you're following has no reason to be
suspicious, it's as easy as stealing on Wakefield's knuckleball.

In East Providence, we turned south on Route 114 toward the
fashionable suburb of Barrington. Fifteen minutes later, the Eclipse
stopped in front of a big Tudor-style house with a well-manicured
lawn.

I idled half a block away as Veronica got out of her car, locked
it, and started up the front walk. As she rang the doorbell, I rolled
slowly by the house. The door swung open, revealing a man with a
wine glass in his hand. He handed it to her, and she took it. Then
she stood on her tiptoes, and he brought his face down to hers.

As I pulled away, Veronica and Brady Coyle were still in a lip-lock.

I didn't feel much like driving back to Providence. I took 114 south
to Newport, parked on Ocean Avenue, and sat there all night

listening to the breakers beat their brains out on the rocks. I thought about the dead twins. I thought about Tony. I thought about Mr. McCready. I thought about the bullet holes in Scibelli's body. I thought about Rosie. I wondered if Veronica had asked Coyle to get an AIDS test. I wondered if she'd ever talked to him about the future. I wondered if she'd told him she was her father's girl. She certainly wasn't mine.

I wondered if I'd see the bullet coming.

74

There was nothing to do but run.

In the morning, I crossed Narragansett Bay on the majestic Claiborne Pell and Jamestown bridges. When I reached the little town of West Kingston, I parked Gloria's car at the train station and bought a northbound ticket.

As the local pulled into Providence, I buried my head in a newspaper and kept it there until we arrived at Boston's South Station. Before I got off, I turned my cell phone on, muted the ringtone, and wedged it between the seat cushions. If Giordano had any cop friends who could track me through its signal, they'd go crazy chasing me up and down the Northeast Corridor until the battery ran down.

Aunt Ruthie put me up in my cousin's old room. She was glad for the company.

I bought a Nokia prepaid to keep track of things back home. McCracken said he'd locked the original documents and the Giordano recording in his safe-deposit box, and that as far as he could tell, no one but Mason and I knew he had them. Whoosh said the word on the street was that someone, he wasn't sure who, had a contract out on me, and what the hell had I gotten myself into? Mason said he didn't think they'd be coming after him, but that Daddy had hired a couple of former Treasury agents as bodyguards just in case. Jack said Polecki and Roselli hadn't hassled him lately, but that he still wasn't welcome at the firehouse. Gloria said her first plastic surgery had gone well and that her mother had found the car right where I'd left it. The hospital said Rosie was still critical.

I didn't give anyone my number. I didn't tell anyone where I was.

I grew a beard and let my hair grow. The beard surprised me by coming in gray. Weekdays, when Aunt Ruthie went to her job at Fleet Bank, I'd get into a pickup basketball game at the Y or stretch out on her floral damask couch and devour Ed McBain's 87th Precinct novels. I was used to writing every day, and I missed it. After a couple of weeks, I'd read so many crime novels that I started thinking I could write one. I banged out sixty pages on Ruthie's old Smith Corona before I realized I was wrong.

Rosie and Veronica haunted my dreams. Each morning I awoke with a strand of razor wire wrapped around my heart. First thing, before sitting down to breakfast with Aunt Ruthie, I'd punch the familiar numbers into my prepaid and always get the same news about Rosie. And the wire around my heart would tighten.

Ruthie insisted on buying the groceries and wouldn't hear of me paying rent. With Maalox and cigars my biggest expenses, the twenty-six hundred dollars in vacation pay I'd withdrawn in cash before leaving Rhode Island just might last till Christmas. I didn't dare use my credit card.

Nights and weekends, we sat together in her parlor and watched the Red Sox on TV. By the beginning of June, Ortiz was on the shelf with a torn tendon, Ramirez was day-to-day with a hamstring, and the team had slipped a game and a half behind the upstart Rays.

On rainy days, I used Ruthie's laptop to check the news from Providence. When the weather was good, I took the Red Line to Cambridge in the afternoon and bought the Providence newspaper at Out of Town News in Harvard Square. Summer headlines heralded Carozza's big lead in the polls, bid-rigging at the Providence Highway Department, kickbacks in Pawtucket, the exposure of another pedophile priest, and sixty-three parishioners getting sick on polluted shellfish at the Church of the Holy Name of Jesus's annual summer clambake. None of the stories carried my byline. I missed the rush.

I tried to distract myself on those daily subway trips by reading the graffiti or inventing lives for my fellow riders. But my mind wandered. Suddenly Veronica would be sitting beside me, reaching for my hand. I imagined whole conversations, trying out different explanations for her betrayal. Each day, she had a new reason. None of them mattered. People are what they do.

It was a summer of painful obituaries. First George Carlin. Then another of my favorites, Bernie Mac. I never believed the old saw about death coming in threes, but I found myself dreading the third one anyway. Then Carl Yastrzemski checked into a hospital for triple-bypass surgery. Yaz had been one of my father's favorites, which made him one of mine too, but given the alternative, I almost hoped the third one would be him.

The news about the newspaper business was all bad. Desperate to stem the tide of red ink, papers all over the country slashed employee pay and laid off journalists by the thousands. *The Miami Herald. The Courier-Journal* of Louisville. The *Los Angeles Times. The Kansas City Star. The Baltimore Sun.* The *San Francisco Examiner. The Detroit News. The Philadelphia Inquirer* . . . Not even *The New York Times* or *The Wall Street Journal* were immune.

By late July, I was no longer a suspect, and the paper had reinstated me. Wu Chiang's lawyer, more grateful than she needed to be for the credit-card records I'd mailed to her, had followed Brady Coyle's script exactly, providing Polecki with my alibis and pressing the chief of police for a public exoneration and apology. Polecki dragged his feet as long as he could before grudgingly issuing a statement. The cops had released my Bronco and my grandfather's gun, and the lawyer said she was holding them for me. I didn't give *her* my number, either.

I wanted to go home. I missed the scent of salt, spilled petroleum, and decaying shellfish that rose like Lazarus from the bay. I missed the bellowing of the parti-colored tugs that bulled rusting barges up the river. I missed the way the setting sun turned the marble dome of the statehouse the color of an antique gold coin. I missed Annie's tattoo, Mason's fedora, Charlie's omelets, Zerilli's

Cubans, McCracken's crushing handshakes, Jack's Italian curses, and Gloria's one good eye. I missed knowing the names of almost everyone on the streets.

But there was still a price on my head. And it was only a matter of time before Providence joined the layoff trend. Would there be a job waiting if it were ever safe for me to return?

One evening Ruthie pulled out her photo albums, and we paged through them together on the couch. Ruthie and her sister—my mother—holding tennis rackets and mugging for the camera. Their father looking sharp in his Providence PD uniform, his chest bedecked with medals. Aidan and Meg ripping open Christmas presents. Little Liam playing with a Tonka hook-and-ladder truck.

When I was six, that truck and I were inseparable. I'd even slept with it. "Wow!" I said. "I'd forgotten how much I loved that thing."

Ruthie smiled, got up, rummaged in the hall closet, and came back cradling the truck in her arms. I remembered it as a huge thing in my life, but when she handed it to me, I was surprised how small it was.

"I rescued it from the basement after your mother died," she said. "You should have it."

Maybe I'd sleep with it again. Better than sleeping alone.

In early August, the paper's owners finally tired of bleeding money and laid off 130 employees, 80 of them news staffers. I called Mason to learn the names. Abbruzzi. Sullivan. Ionata. Worcester. Richards . . . So many old friends.

"You and Gloria were on the list, too," Mason said, "but I talked to Dad."

I was touched that he'd done that for me. I wasn't surprised he'd kept his promise to her. But if readers and advertisers kept on deserting us, this wouldn't be the last of the layoffs. Mason might not be able to save us next time.

By mid-August, the Yankees were finished, their stars looking old and slow and the young pitchers they'd counted on not yet ready for the big time. But the Sox trailed the surprising Rays by seven games now, and three of our starting pitchers, our right fielder, our shortstop, and our third baseman were all on the disabled list. Ortiz had returned from his wrist injury, but he wasn't the same. And the great one, Manny Ramirez, was gone, traded to the Dodgers after throwing one tantrum too many about his pitiful twenty-million-dollar contract. I wondered what Rosie would have said about that. Me? After all that had happened, it was hard to care about baseball anymore.

On a Sunday afternoon in early September, the Providence paper's banner headline grabbed me before I grabbed it from the newsstand: ARSON RETURNS TO MOUNT HOPE.

I carried the paper to the Algiers Coffee House on Brattle Street and read it over a cup of Arabic coffee and a lamb-sausage sandwich. A duplex on Ivy Street had burned to the ground, and a fast-moving fire had gutted Zerilli's Market on Doyle Avenue. The story, under Mason's byline, quoted Polecki as saying the fires were definitely suspicious but still under investigation. When I turned to page eight for the rest of it, I was thrilled to see that the fire picture on the jump page was credited to Gloria.

Mason's story went on to speculate that the arsons had resumed because, after a quiet summer, the police and the neighborhood vigilante group known as the DiMaggios had "let their guard down." I made a mental note to talk to Mason about clichés.

I tried to call Whoosh, but his home number was unlisted and the phones in his store were melted lumps of plastic.

75

Next morning, I borrowed Aunt Ruthie's immaculate two-year-old Camry and headed south on I-95. An hour later I turned off at Branch Avenue, parked on the street by the gate to the North Burial Ground, opened the trunk, and took out my Tonka hook-and-ladder truck. A bunch of dead mums slumped against the headstone that marked the final resting place of Scott and Melissa Rueda. I placed the toy on the twins' grave and took the dead flowers away.

Then I walked to the car, cruised a few miles east, and swung into Swan Point Cemetery. Rosie was buried among the rhododendrons, about fifty yards west of where they'd planted Ruggerio "the Blind Pig" Bruccola. Her grave was smothered in a mound of dead flowers. I cleared them away, preserving the mementos her fellow firefighters had placed there—three fire hats, a brass nozzle from a fire hose, several dozen Providence FD patches, and a few score more from other fire departments around the state. I draped a signed Manny Ramirez jersey over the shoulders of her gravestone, kneeled in the grass, and talked with her for a while, just the two of us reminiscing about our Hope High days while watching a tug churn its way up the Seekonk River. I kidded her about the neon flowered monstrosity she'd worn to the prom. She made fun of my awkward, left-handed layups. We agreed we had made a mistake, that one time we slept together, but we weren't sure if the mistake was doing it at all or not giving it another try.

"I'm so sorry I missed the funeral, Rosie. I would have been there, but Aunt Ruthie talked me out of it. If she hadn't, I'd probably be lying right next to you."

When the chat between two friends turned into a conversation between the living and the dead, and I couldn't hear her voice anymore, I walked back to the car, taking the jersey along with me. She'd want to wear it again the next time I dropped by to talk, and there was no point in leaving it behind so some punk could steal it.

I took a shortcut past Brown Stadium and swung Ruthie's car onto Doyle Avenue. The store was a blackened shell, and Whoosh was standing out front supervising a sidewalk sale of smoke-damaged goods. I parked on the street, strolled over to him, and stuck out my hand.

"Do I know you?"

"You do."

"You're gonna have to remind me."

"Look harder," I said, and removed my sunglasses.

He squinted at my face, then said, "Ah, shit. I didn't figure you for a suicide."

"Hard to recognize me with the beard?"

"Yeah, but what really threw me was the Yankees cap and jersey. Fuckin' good disguise."

"Take a walk with me."

"Hang on a sec," he said.

He walked through the store's charred doorway and disappeared into the ruins. A couple of minutes later, he emerged carrying a stack of six wooden cigar boxes.

"Might as well have these," he said. "The heat dried them out, but throw some apple slices into the boxes, and some of them should come back okay."

I thanked him and locked the boxes in the trunk of Ruthie's car. Then we strolled together under the old, half-dead maples lining the sidewalk, where a few of the leaves were starting to turn.

"I'm so sorry about Rosie. I know the two of you were close."

"My best friend."

"John McCready was mine, so I know how you must feel." He threw his arms wide. "So many fucking fires. So many neighbors dead."

"Sorry about the store," I said.

"Hell, that's the least of it."

"Going to rebuild?"

"Gonna reopen next week in a storefront on Hope Street," he said. "It's a good space. Giordano gave it to me in a straight swap for the old place. Guess he's thinking of building something here. Damned good of him, though. And to think I had him pegged for an asshole."

"The DiMaggios still on patrol?"

"They disbanded back in June when it looked like the fires had stopped. Big fuckin' mistake. As of last night, they're back on the streets. They catch the prick what burned my place down and I won't be calling the cops next time. He's going right into the Field's Point sludge incinerator."

"Whoever he is, he's just a hired hand," I said. "Want the names of the bastards who sent him?"

76

"It's Mulligan. I need a favor."

"Name it."

"I need you to get the recording and documents out of your safe deposit box and bring them to me."

"What's up?"

"Better you don't know."

"Okay. When and where?"

"The Battleship Cove visitors' parking lot in Fall River at eleven A.M. Saturday."

"I'll be there."

"You still driving the black Acura?"

"Yeah."

"Just pull in, and I'll see you."

77

Saturday morning, I splurged on a couple of Tommy Castro CDs at Satellite Records in Boston. "Take the Highway Down" boomed from the speakers of Aunt Ruthie's Camry as I cruised south on Route 24 toward Newport, the documents and recording McCracken had delivered locked in the trunk. As I crawled along Ocean Avenue looking for an address, I cued the CD to "You Knew the Job Was Dangerous."

The house was a sprawling Nantucket-style cottage with weathered shingles, a broad white porch, and an expanse of chemical-green lawn. It perched on a rocky outcrop with a glorious view of the sea.

As I turned into the crushed-shell drive, two heavyset men stepped in front of the car and ordered me to get out. They were dressed in identical navy blue suits with chalk pinstripes, and from the way their jackets hung, I could tell they were carrying. They patted me down, politely asked me to unbutton my David Ortiz jersey so they could be sure I wasn't wearing a wire, and then swung the car doors open. They felt under the seats, checked the glove box, and asked me to open the trunk for inspection. When they were done, they directed me to continue up the winding drive and park under the trees. I nosed in behind five new Cadillacs, their paint shielded from the sun by sprawling oaks. All of the cars had "Cadillac Frank" emblems affixed beside their brake lights.

As I walked across the lawn to the house, Whoosh stepped down from the porch to shake my hand. Then he took me by the arm and guided me around back, where the smell of good cooking mingled with the salt air. A slight old man with a spatula in his hand was fussing over two gas grills laden with steaks, chicken breasts, and Italian sausages. Three somewhat younger men in white Bermuda shorts and Tommy Bahama shirts lounged by a glistening pool. Babes in thong bikinis passed among them with trays of tall frosty glasses decorated with little umbrellas.

"Nice," I said.

Whoosh looked at me and smirked.

"What were you expecting? Satriale's Pork Store?"

He handled the introductions, but I already knew all their names.

Giuseppe Arena, free on bail pending his labor-racketeering trial, put the spatula down, wiped his hands on his "Kiss the Cook" apron, and clasped my right hand in both of his. "Good of you to come," he said. "Grab yourself a drink. The meat will be ready in a few minutes."

We ate with Gorham sterling knives and forks, balancing Limoges plates on our laps. Music poured softly from poolside speakers. Joan Armatrading, Annie Lennox, India.Arie—voices that sparkled like the Atlantic on this cloudless late-September day.

I turned to Whoosh, who was meticulously constructing a sandwich from a heap of sausage, tomatoes, peppers, eggplant, and Italian bread.

"Great choice of music."

He smirked again.

"What were you expecting, Wayne Newton?"

The conversation veered from the Red Sox to the attributes of the waitresses and back around to the Red Sox again. The Sox had stormed back when I wasn't looking and had a headlock on a play-off spot. With Rhode Islanders going out of their minds placing bets on the looming play-offs, Whoosh was primed for a killing.

By three in the afternoon, as the plates were being cleared away, I fetched the recording and documents from my car. Then Arena led us down the sloping lawn toward a stone breakwater that thrust forty yards into the sea. Halfway down the breakwater, a long table covered with a white tablecloth had been set with wine glasses and carafes of red and white. No worries about listening devices in this unlikely meeting spot.

Arena claimed the chair at the head of the table. The rest of us seated ourselves as Whoosh filled our glasses. Arena, labor racketeer and acting boss. Carmine Grasso, Rhode Island's biggest fence. "Cadillac Frank" DeAngelo, car dealer and chief executive of the state's biggest luxury-car theft ring. Blackjack Baldelli, the no-show jobs king. And Whoosh, Rhode Island's most successful bookmaker.

Johnny Dio and Vinnie Giordano were conspicuously absent.

Two more men in chalk-striped navy suits stood at the end of the breakwater, binoculars hanging from their necks, making sure none of the sailboats tacking in the light breeze ventured too close.

Once, Raymond L. S. Patriarca had ruled the rackets from Maine to central Connecticut from his little storefront office on Atwells Avenue. But in the seventies and eighties, federal investigators used their new toys—electronic surveillance and the RICO act—to break the power of the Mafia here, just like almost everywhere else. Now the mob was small-time, scratching for a piece of the action against the big boys who ran the drug cartels, the state lotteries, the Indian casinos, and the "escort services" that let you choose your whore on their Web sites.

"Okay," Arena said. "Let's see what you've got for us."

I spread the lot plan and architectural renderings out on the table. The men stood and hunched over them. Whoosh pointed a bony finger at the "Dio Construction" label in the right-hand corner of the lot plan and muttered, "Bastard."

Once they were satisfied, I placed the billing records for the incorporation papers on the table. Arena picked them up, examined them, and passed them to his right.

When they were done, I put the recorder on the table and pressed play. It was hard to hear over the cries of the gulls and the swish of foot-high waves breaking on the rocks.

"Play it again," Arena said.

When it got to the part where Giordano mentioned the vacancy at Little Rhody Realty, Grasso picked up the recorder, pressed rewind, and played that part again.

"Cheryl Scibelli was my wife's sister's kid," he said.

The recording played to the end again, and I clicked it off. No one spoke. Arena pushed his chair back from the table, stood, turned his back on us, and stared out to sea.

It was a minute, maybe two, before he rejoined us at the table. He had questions.

Where'd I get the architectural drawings?

I'd stolen them from Brady Coyle's office.

How'd I get my hands on the billing records?

I respectfully declined to say.

"My fucking *lawyer* is part of this?" Arena said.

"He is," I said. And then I told him it was Coyle who'd been leaking grand-jury testimony to the newspaper.

"You know this for a fact?"

"I do."

"Why the hell would he do that?"

"Would you have sanctioned the arsons?" I asked.

"A warehouse fire to collect the insurance, sure. We'd be okay with something like that. But torching a whole neighborhood? Roasting babies and firemen? Burning Whoosh's store down? Involving Carmine's niece in it and then whacking her to cover it up? Fuck, no."

"Coyle knows that," I said. "He's sandbagging your case to get you out of the way."

Arena walked over to me. I stood. He grasped my hands in both of his again, then reached up and draped an arm across my shoulder.

"We are all in your debt," he said.

It was my signal to go. I gathered the documents from the table, shoved the recorder in my jeans, and walked up the sloping lawn toward the house.

78

Tuesday I slouched in front of Aunt Ruthie's TV and fell asleep watching the final game of the regular season, a meaningless tune-up against the Yankees.

That was the day it happened. The news was a gaudy headline in the next day's paper.

Shortly after noon, according to witnesses, a stranger in an ankle-length black raincoat strode briskly through the yard at Dio Construction. He entered the main building through the side entrance and stepped into Johnny Dio's outer office.

"I thought it was odd," the secretary told the homicide twins later. "It wasn't raining." But what she said to the stranger was, "May I help you?"

The man brushed past her, threw open the coat like he thought he was "Doc" Holliday, and raised an 8-shot pistol-grip Mossberg shotgun. He opened the inner door, fired three blasts, let the gun fall to the floor, told the secretary to wait ten minutes before calling the police, and walked out into a sunny afternoon.

"It happened so fast!" the secretary told the cops. No, she couldn't provide a description.

As Dio bled to death on his office floor, gunshots disturbed the perfect ambiance of the main dining room at Camille's on Bradford Street. Afterward, no one could remember how many shooters there had been, what they looked like, or what door they'd left by. All anyone could say for sure was what the police could plainly see: Vinnie Giordano had enjoyed his last plate of Chef Granata's justly famous Vongole alla Giovanni.

Brady Coyle knew none of this as he and his luncheon companion sipped from their glasses of Russian River and perused the menu at the Capital Grille. She settled on the pan-fried calamari appetizer and the Maine lobster salad. He ordered the clam chowder and the seared citrus-glazed salmon. As they waited for their food, he told lawyer jokes. She toyed with the little silver typewriter on the chain around her neck. She'd come up from Washington to see him, and he planned to make the most of it. He reached across the table and took her hand.

As they dug into their main courses, Channel 10 interrupted its regular programming with a bulletin about a shooting at Camille's. But the volume was turned low on the TV over the bar, and neither of them took notice. They decided against dessert.

He paid the tab and left a generous tip. Outside on the sidewalk, she stood on tiptoes as he leaned in for a kiss. Out of the corner of her eye, she saw a man approaching. He stood about five foot five, not much taller than she, but big in the shoulders. Red scaly patches speckled his shaved skull.

The man drew a little black pistol from his windbreaker and pressed it into Coyle's ear.

She screamed.

The gun popped.

She was surprised it wasn't louder.

Coyle toppled into the gutter.

The man stood over him and fired three more shots, making sure.

He turned then and looked at her, thinking about it. The magazine of his .25-caliber Raven Arms semiautomatic still held two rounds.

"No," she said. "Please, no."

He shrugged and let the gun slip from his hand. It landed soundlessly on Coyle's body. Then the little thug crossed the street and strolled through Burnside Park as if he didn't have a care in the world.

The woman's shoulders shook. For just a moment, she thought she was going to lose her expensive lunch. Then she regained her composure, opened her purse, took out a pen and pad, and started taking notes.

I read Mason's sketchy story about the hits in the Providence paper. A breathless, blow-by-blow, first-person account of Coyle's execution appeared in *The Washington Post*. Veronica's source had paid off for her one last time.

79

My old landlord let me move back into the America
Street apartment in return for half the back rent, which I covered
with an advance on my Visa card. He wasn't happy about the ar-
rangement, but nobody else had wanted the dump.

I wiped away the dust, hung my grandfather's forty-five back
on the cracked plaster wall, and arranged to have the utilities and
phone turned back on. Guess who called first?

"You!

fucking!

bastard!"

"Hello, Dorcas. How nice to hear your voice."

"Where the hell have you been?"

"Visiting Aunt Ruthie."

"For the whole fucking summer?"

"That's right. Hey, how's Rewrite doing? You didn't really take
her to the pound, did you?"

"What if I did?"

"Are you remembering her heartworm pills?"

"Fuck you," she said, and I hung up.

In the morning I shaved the beard, saddled up Secretariat,
rolled down Atwells Avenue past Camille's, crossed over I-95, and
parked at a fifteen-minute meter in front of the newspaper.

When I stepped off the elevator, Mason got up from his desk to greet me. I stuck out my hand. He ignored it and wrapped me up in a bear hug. Gloria dashed over from the photo desk to do the same. I liked her hug better.

"Hey, everybody!" Hardcastle shouted. "The arsonist's back from summer camp."

It was good to hear his drawl again, but it was sad to see so many of the cubicles bare and empty. I walked to my desk past the one where Dante Ionata and Wayne Worcester had spent the last ten years exposing the polluters who were poisoning the bay. The bastards would be getting away with it from now on.

I logged on to my computer and checked my messages. There were several hundred. The most recent one, from Lomax, had been sent this morning:

CADAVER DOGS FEATURE DONE YET?

His way of saying "Welcome back."

Shortly after ten, Lomax asked Mason and me to join him in Pemberton's office.

"The truth now," Pemberton said. "Which one of you really wrote that arson exposé last spring?"

"Mason did," I said.

"Mulligan did," Mason said.

"I see. Well, how about a double byline, then? If the two of you can put your heads together and update it this afternoon, we'd like to lead the paper with it tomorrow."

"Sure, we can do that," I said. Of course, there were a few details I'd have to leave out.

"How come we can run it now when we couldn't run it then?" Mason said.

"Because dead men don't sue," Lomax said.

Mid-afternoon, my desk phone rang.

"Mulligan?"

"Yeah."

"I heard you were back to work."

"You heard right."

"I'm glad."

"That why you called? To welcome me back?"

"I just wanted to say I'm sorry."

"I don't believe you."

"I don't want it to end like this."

"What sort of ending do you have in mind?"

"That lust-filled weekend you talked about? We can still have it. Why don't you come down this weekend? Or maybe I could come up there."

"I'm busy."

She was silent for a moment. I could hear her breathing.

"He didn't mean anything to me."

"That I can believe, but how does that make it better?"

She didn't have anything to say to that. I could hear her breath again. While I was away, Verizon had worked some new digital miracle with the phone. I smelled the sweet scent that collected in the curve of her neck. Her lips brushed the side of my face. It made me shiver.

"Don't you miss me?"

"Hell, yes."

"So why can't you forgive me?"

Preachers say forgiveness is good for the soul. That it does more for the person who forgives than for the one who is forgiven, cleansing the mind of anger and resentment. What a load of crap.

"Mulligan? Forgive me, please?"

"I won't because all of me wants to, regardless of the consequences, and because you've counted on that from the very beginning."

"What? I didn't quite catch that."

I didn't say anything. Doesn't anybody watch *The Maltese Falcon* anymore?

"I don't understand anything that's happening," she said, her voice small now, not quite a whimper. "Who was the man with the gun? Why did he shoot Brady?"

"Because he deserved it," I said. "Check the Providence paper's Web site tomorrow and you can read all about it."

"I could have been killed," she said. "Don't you care?"

"You're lucky I wasn't the one holding the gun," I said, and hung up.

After work, Gloria invited me to the Trinity Brewhouse for a drink.

"What about Hopes?"

"I like this new place," she said. "I don't drink at Hopes much anymore."

For a second, I flashed on an intimate evening with Gloria. Over the last few months, I'd been beaten, betrayed, and bereaved, and now I needed somebody's arms around me. But not Gloria's. At least, not right now. I still ached for Veronica, and Gloria was not a woman to be trifled with. I told her I was tired. I told her I just wanted to go home.

But that's not what I did.

I peeled the yellow parking ticket off my windshield, stuck it under the wiper of the publisher's BMW, and drove over to Camp Street to catch up with Jack Centofanti for a few minutes. Then I popped into Hopes and found McCracken drinking alone at a table in back.

"So," he whispered as I sat across from him with my club soda. "I guess I'm an accessory to murder."

"Sorry I had to involve you."

"Aw, that's okay. Only one thing I'm sorry about."

"What's that?"

"The pro who set the fires is still out there, for hire to the next asshole who wants something burned down."

"The guy who attacked Gloria and killed Rosie is still out there, too," I said.

"Probably the same guy."

After he left, I flirted with Annie and asked her when she got off. She laughed and turned me down flat, so I finished my drink and drove to Good Time Charlie's, where Marie was just finishing her shift.

I wooed her with a cheap dinner at the diner, brought her home, and took her to bed. She was athletic and enthusiastic. I told myself she could give Veronica lessons. I was so full of shit.

In the morning, I awoke to the familiar sound of Angela Anselmo screeching at her kids. I got up, stepped into the bathroom, and noticed that Veronica's yellow toothbrush was still in the porcelain holder above my sink. I plucked it out, snapped it in half, and tossed it in the garbage.

Marie and I showered together. She scrubbed my back, and I took my sweet time with hers. She was dressing when I heard rustling at the apartment door.

Peering through the peephole, I saw nothing but the cracked plaster wall across the hall. I flipped the dead bolt, yanked the door open, and discovered something black and hairy sitting at my threshold.

"Rewrite!"

She leaped at me and almost knocked me down.

Her hair was matted and she smelled bad. A note was tucked under her collar: "You take care of the bitch for a while."

I fed her some cold cuts from the fridge. Then Marie helped me give her a bath in the tub.

"What am I going to do with you?" I said out loud as I rinsed the suds from her thick, curly coat. Rewrite cocked her head and looked at me with her glistening brown eyes. The landlord would pitch a fit, and with my crazy hours, how could I take care of her anyway?

Then it dawned on me.

There was a nice couple in Silver Lake who knew how to love a dog.

ACKNOWLEDGMENTS

Patricia Smith, one of our greatest living poets, edited every line of every draft and helped this befuddled male create credible love scenes—both on the page and off. Thank you, baby, for permission to excerpt your poem "Spinning 'til You Get Dizzy."

Paul Mauro, a New York City police captain; Ted Anthony, an Associated Press assistant managing editor; and Jack Hart, the world's greatest writing coach, read the first draft with care and made many insightful suggestions. Every writer should have such friends.

Thank you, Otto Penzler, for reading the book, making useful suggestions, and recommending me to LJK Literary Management. Susanna Einstein at LJK is much more than an agent. She is the best editor I have ever worked with, and I've worked with some of the greats.

I am in Jon Land's debt for recommending my book to his publisher, Tor/Forge. My thanks to all the folks at the publishing house, especially Eric Raab, for taking a chance on a first-time novelist and doing a fine job with the final edit.

And to sixteen of my favorite crime novelists—Ace Atkins, Peter Blauner, Lawrence Block, Ken Bruen, Alafair Burke, Sean Chercover, Harlan Coben, Michael Connelly, Thomas H. Cook, Tim Dorsey, Loren D. Estleman, Joseph Finder, James W. Hall, Dennis Lehane, Bill Loehfelm, and Marcus Sakey: Thank you for your encouragement and support along the way.